SUGAR AND ICE

AVEN ELLIS

Sugar and Ice

Cover Design by Becky Monson

Formatted by AB Formatting

BOOKS BY AVEN ELLIS

Connectivity

Surviving The Rachel

Chronicles of a Lincoln Park Fashionista

Waiting For Prince Harry (Dallas Demons #1)

The Definition of Icing (Dallas Demons #2)

Breakout (Dallas Demons #3)

On Thin Ice (Dallas Demons #4)

Playing Defense (Dallas Demons #5)

The Aubrey Rules (Chicago on Ice #1)

Trivial Pursuits (Chicago on Ice #2)

Save the Date (Chicago on Ice #3)

The Bottom Line (Chicago on Ice #4)

Reality Blurred (Rinkside in the Rockies #2)

Squeeze Play (Washington DC Soaring Eagles #1)

Swing and a Miss (Washington DC Soaring Eagles #2)

A Royal Shade of Blue (Modern Royals Series #1)

CONNECT WITH AVEN

http://www.amazon.com/-/e/B00GHUYO90
http://avenellis.com
https://www.facebook.com/AvenEllis1
https://twitter.com/AvenEllis
https://www.facebook.com/groups/597292903766592/
http://eepurl.com/dvajmT

For Heidi and Angie

Heidi-Thank you for sharing your world with me. I value our friendship so much!
Angie-Thank you for being such a great friend. I'm truly blessed.

ACKNOWLEDGMENTS

Thank you to Becky Monson for believing in this journey to write a new hockey series. I'm forever grateful for your belief in me and the way I tell a story. Thank you for being such a wonderful and supportive person in my life.

CeCe Carroll, you did a brilliant job copy editing this book. Thank you for your dedication and guidance in taking my work to the next level.

Thank you to my Beta Baes. Thank you for always giving me what I need, and not just with the writing process. Thank you for reassurance, for reading, for being a part of my life every day. None of these books happen with you.

To Alexandra, my assistant. Thank you for being you on a daily basis and always being my calming center.

To all my Lovelies-thank you for your endless support and cheerleading. This journey doesn't happen without all of you.

Amanda and Claudia-Your love, friendship and support is always a given. I love you so much!

Thank you Karri Lynn and Ashley Barrett for graciously sharing your outdoor adventures with me and letting me use them for JoJo.

Valerie Smith, my partner in crime in everything, thank you for sharing your food science expertise to help me create JoJo. Your patience with questions and detailed answers brought her passion to food for life. You are the best.

Thank you Crystal Guthrie for sharing your professional baking knowledge. You were gracious with your time and answers, and I'm so grateful for your help.

Lauren Linwood, thank you for always providing your thoughts and your feedback. You are the best.

To Jaclyn Paz, thank you for reading my work, providing advice, and most of all, being my friend.

To my Twinnie, Holly Martin- Thank you for always reading my work, offering suggestions, helping me be a better author. But it is your friendship I value about all else. I love you.

Tanya Shelton, thank you for reading every word I've ever written. Your belief in me has been there from the first page you read. I'm so blessed to have you in my life!

Thank you to Jennifer and Mary, who run the Aven Ellis reader group on Facebook (Kate, Skates, and Coffee Cakes.) You both are such amazing women with a passion for books. I love you ladies so much!

And thank you to all my readers. None of this happens without your support. I'm truly blessed.

CHAPTER ONE

Today's Purpose and Passion Statement:

I, Josephine Camilla Rossi, will make the creamiest, most luxurious, cannoli cheesecake whipped up using only the finest ingredients. My work will be driven by my passion and love for baking, as well as by my nonna's guiding hand. My purpose is to wow my hard-to-impress boss. If all goes as planned, this cheesecake will be the key to new opportunities in the future.

I stare at today's statement, which I have printed out and pinned to my vision board in the kitchen.

My cheesecake will be lighter and fluffier than Nonna's original recipe, thanks to my homemade ricotta. My batter will have a hint of amaretto and Madagascar bourbon vanilla. Each bite will have the taste of Guittard semisweet chocolate and the brightness of orange peel. When your fork hits the bottom, you'll reach a pistachio crust that will bring the classic cannoli flavors together. The top will be covered with a luscious layer of piped whipped cream and adorned with three perfect mini cannoli pastries, artfully arranged in the center and sprinkled with candied orange peel.

It will be show-stopping perfection, in appearance and taste.

I'm determined that *this* cheesecake, the first cake I ever ate in my grandmother's kitchen, the cake that changed my life and fueled my passion for baking when I was five years old, will finally get the attention of Ms. Angelique Whitmire-Hox, my editor at *Bake It!* magazine. I work in recipe testing for the magazine, but I have my eye on a development project. And I'm hoping this cheesecake will prove I'm ready for that task.

Of course, I need to get to work right away if I'm going to have a cheesecake to present to her first thing on Monday morning, which happens to be, oh, tomorrow.

I take one last look at my vision board, studying the items I've carefully pinned to it. There's a photo of my nonna, who introduced me to baking when I was a child with a version of the cheesecake I'm baking tonight. There's another photo, this one of Julia Child, whose books I devoured as a teenager, trying to cram all of her culinary wisdom into my brain. And there are magazine clippings of recipe ideas and cards with positive messages and inspirational quotes. Since my career is everything to me now, I will achieve my dreams by visualizing my success.

Okay. Time to get going. I head down the hall and

enter my room. I have the apartment to myself today, as my roommate and best friend, Sierra Crawford, is away with her boyfriend Jude this weekend.

I slide open my closet door and grab my favorite thing to bake in: my white and navy striped T-shirt dress. I remove my jeans and tank top and tug the comfortable cotton dress over my body and then step into my navy, slip-on Converse sneakers.

I move to the back of my bedroom door, where my vintage 40's apron is hanging, and lift it off the hook. The worn checkered fabric has yellow pears and grape clusters with ruffle detailing. I love it. This apron was given to my nonna by the Rossi family and eventually passed down to me. It's been in the family since World War II.

I slip the fabric over my head and take a moment to let its history wash over me. All the meals lovingly prepared while wearing this apron. The good times and bad. The long forgotten fights and nights full of heart-warming laughter. The perfect pies, the second-servings, and the inevitable burnt batches. Every moment lived when a Rossi woman donned this apron, I can feel in my soul.

I never bake at home without it.

I move over to my dresser. My long hair needs to be pulled up for baking, so I work the dark brown strands into my signature braids and pile them up on top of my head. Once I have my hair up, I reach for a purple headscarf that coordinates with the grapes on my apron and twist it into a cute headband, which I secure around the front of my hair.

I consider my reflection in the mirror. I love how unique my eyes are, such a dark brown they appear almost black. They stand out against the olive tone of my skin. I hated them as a little girl, along with my above average height, but I have come to appreciate both traits.

My eyes move down the image of me appearing in the mirror, and I frown. My passion for baking combined with being dumped by the love of my life nine months ago has led to a net gain of ten pounds. The weight has settled around my hips and can no longer be denied.

But fall is here. It's a new season. And I will no longer shovel cheesecake in my mouth to try to forget Marco. I've learned you cannot eat away your feelings. Trust me, I've tried.

In fact, I'm over men. I'm so clueless at picking them that I can't be trusted. Why else would I have chosen a cheater who couldn't stay faithful the second I moved to Denver?

Ugh. Marco.

Dumb Marco.

Or is it dumb Josephine?

Whatever.

Marco IS dumb.

And a liar.

AND A BIG FAT CHEATER.

So what if I'm ten pounds heavier? The extra weight can serve as man repellent for all I care. My favorite J Brand jeans no longer fit and that might need to be addressed, but it can wait until tomorrow.

I clear my throat and head back toward the kitchen. My decision to give up men has a silver lining. I've refocused myself. Instead of thinking about stupid liars and cheats, I've shifted my attention to my baking career.

I enter the tiny galley kitchen and begin preparing. I pick up my phone and swipe to my playlist, letting Hailee Steinfeld's "Starving" fill the air around me. *Ha! Music to make a cheesecake by if I ever heard it*, I think. Except I'm not starving for a man's attention.

A slice of cannoli cheesecake, on the other hand? Yes, please.

I set the oven to the appropriate temperature and retrieve the necessary ingredients. I take the crust I prepared this morning out of the fridge and place the pans on the counter. I made enough for two cheesecakes so I can pick the perfect one for Miss "I'm Not Impressed, Josephine." Because of her, I've learned to always have a backup.

Quickly, I fall into the zone.

I make the filling, tasting as I go. I blend. I grate. I fold. I take a moment to savor the scents in the air, from the fresh orange rind to the magnificent bourbon vanilla.

Being a professional baker has given me an *acute* sense of smell, and elevated my ability to detect subtleties. I find I can no longer wear perfume or scented deodorant while I work because it interferes with my ability to smell and, therefore, properly blend. Being able to experience the full spectrum of these wonderful ingredients is pure bliss.

I dip a spoon into the bowl and sample the batter. *Success.* I nailed it!

If only Nonna were in Denver with me instead of back home in Chicago. I've taken her recipe to the next level, and I wish she could have a taste.

I pour the mixture into the pistachio crusts then begin preparing a water bath so the cheesecakes don't crack while baking. I fill a bright red, retro tea kettle, another Nonna hand-me-down, with water and place it on the range, and turn the burner on. I place each cheesecake in a pan and fill each pan up the side with hot water.

Now it's time to get these gorgeous babies into the oven.

I open the oven door, expecting to feel the usual rush of escaping heat, but the inside is ice cold.

"What?" I ask aloud to the empty kitchen in disbelief.

I'm sure I turned it on before I got started.

I check the settings. Yes. It's on, set to 350□F.

Realization sets in.

The oven is dead.

"No," I exclaim, shaking my head. "No, no, no!"

I slam the door shut and consider my options. My apartment complex is terrible at keeping up with maintenance. Knowing them, they won't send someone to fix it until Wednesday. And they definitely won't consider this an emergency.

Oh, but it is. It's is a total emergency.

This is a complicated cheesecake to make, and I used expensive ingredients. I can't let this go unbaked.

Not now. Not when I'm desperate to show Miss "I'm Not Impressed, Josephine" my work.

I must figure this out.

I begin pacing as I think. Too bad the guy next door is a complete jerk who blares death metal all day. I've already complained about his music, so he would never let me use his oven. There's a married couple across the hall, but I don't know them well enough to say, "Hey! If you let me use your oven, I'll give you a cheesecake. You like cannoli, right? Mind if I come in and hang out for an hour?"

Gah. Gah. Gah.

Then I remember something.

Jude.

He plays professional hockey for the Denver Mountain Lions and just returned from the UK for another season. He is away at the Broadmoor Resort in Colorado Springs with Sierra for a few days before training camp, but his roommate and teammate, Cade Callahan, has also just returned. And as luck has it, they live on the sixth floor.

I've been to their apartment before and met Cade twice, but both times he was watching TV with a baseball hat pulled down low over his face. So while I'm not a complete stranger to him, I wouldn't say we are friends.

Cade would probably let me borrow his oven.

Wow. I can be so resourceful when I'm faced with tossing a cheesecake.

I grab my keys and fly out the door, quickly locking it behind me before running to the elevator. I punch the button for their floor and say a prayer to Julia Child—because she would totally understand my predicament—that Cade Callahan is home.

And not using his oven.

Ding!

The doors chime and open to Jude and Cade's floor. I sprint down the long hall to their unit and punch the doorbell.

Jude's dog begins barking loudly, but I hear no sign of Cade inside.

All right, I can't expect Cade to answer in 2.5 seconds.

I try to be patient, but instead, I ring the bell a few more times like an annoying kid.

Ding! Ding! Ding!

Bark! Bark! Bark!

"Cade?" I yell over the sound of Jude's dog, Leia. "It's Sierra's roommate, Josephine! I have an emergency and I need your help!"

"Coming," Cade yells back. "Just a second."

"Thank God," I whisper. I can feel the use of his oven is within my grasp. I'll bake my beautiful cheesecakes and all will go according to today's Purpose and Passion plan.

Leia continues barking as I hear new noise on the other side of the door. Finally, the door is unlocked, and Cade pulls it open.

My mouth hits the floor.

Because Cade is standing in front of me in nothing but a white bath towel; it's tied dangerously low beneath the hot V-shape that tapers down from his waist. Water beads drip down his tanned, muscular skin and—oh, my God, what is that sexy Asian lettering tattooed up the side of his ribcage?

"Josephine?"

I tear my gaze away from his body and to his eyes.

They are a gorgeous jade color I've never seen before.

"Huh?" I say absently as I move from his eyes to the super-hot stubble shading his jawline.

Cade takes a moment to brush back his wet hair with one hand.

Is it hot in the hallway? I'm suddenly really freaking hot. I tug at the neckline of my apron for a bit of relief.

"I think you said you had an emergency," he says slowly, moving his hand to the knot of his towel and holding it in place, "so, how can I help you, Josephine?"

CHAPTER TWO

How can you help me? I THINK, STARING IN LUST AT Cade's gorgeous athletic body. *How can you help me?*

Well, you can start by taking off that towel, Mr. Callahan.

Ack! No! I give myself a mental slap—the 'snap out of it' kind of slap seen in the movie *Moonstruck*—and blink.

Rapidly.

"Um. I need heat," I blurt out.

Wait. Wrong. GAH!

Cade cocks an eyebrow at me. "How can I help you with *heat?*"

Josephine Camilla Rossi, get your lustful mind on track, I scold myself.

"Cade," I say.

Then I stop.

Oh, wow, even his name is hot.

"Josephine."

I shake my head. "I have a baking crisis. My oven is

out. And I have two cannoli cheesecakes that need to go into t—

"Cannoli? Those cream filled things?"

"Why? Do you like cannoli?"

"Heck, yes."

I cock an eyebrow at him. "That's a very *Napoleon Dynamite* answer."

Cade's eyes light up. "You got it."

"I watch way too many movies," I admit.

In fact, after Marco dumped me, I think I watched every film made while eating five hundred cheesecakes.

Okay. I might be exaggerating.

On the film bit.

"Me, too," Cade says. "I'm a film geek. But, anyway, you need an oven?"

I blink. Oh, right. Cheesecake catastrophe.

So much for being focused on my career. Apparently, if you throw a nearly naked hockey player in front of me, my focus goes out the window.

I clear my throat. "Yes. Can I possibly borrow yours for an hour?"

"Do I get cheesecake if I acquiesce?"

Did he just say acquiesce?

Impressive.

"I'm not some dumb hockey player. I did go to Cornell," Cade says, studying me as he rakes his hand again through his wet hair. "I have an extensive vocabulary."

My shocked expression clearly pleases him as his face lights up with a smile, revealing a dazzling set of perfect teeth and a dimple on his left cheek.

Holy cannoli.

Cannoli.

Must.get.cheesecakes.into.his.oven.

"Yes," I say, willing myself to stay on task. "I need to bake two. One will be for my boss tomorrow. We can eat the other."

"We?"

Shit.

"Um, well, I could leave you one, that's fine," I say, feeling my face burn in humiliation.

"I don't believe in eating cheesecake alone, do you?"

Oh, my.

"Um, no. One should *never* eat cheesecake alone."

Unless you've just been dumped by a cheating loser named Marco.

Then solitary cheesecake eating is permitted. In fact, it's required.

"Okay. You said there are two. Let me get dressed, and I'll help you carry them up here. Come on in."

"Thank you so much. You are really bailing me out here."

"No, not a problem. I'm glad I can help."

He steps aside, and I move past him. *Oh, God, he smells glorious,* I think as I pick up scents of cedar and sage lingering on his damp skin. Do I also detect notes of lime and bergamot?

I've never loved my perceptive sense of smell more than I do right now.

Cade shuts the door behind me, and Leia waits for me to pet her by moving in front of me and strategically sitting down. Her tail swishes back and forth across the hardwood floor in anticipation.

"Hi, Leia," I say, bending down to rub her massive head. "You're a sweetheart, aren't you?"

"She is. She's my running buddy when Jude is away. I took her back to New York with me this summer, too. Easier than Jude taking her to the UK. Anyway, I'll change and be right back."

I stand up, watching him move down the hallway, and Lord, his back is sculpted beyond belief.

I tug at my apron neckline again.

Wait.

Apron.

My hand flies up to my headscarf.

Oh, no.

No, no, no.

I totally forgot what I am dressed in.

GAH!

A string of choice Italian swear words runs through my head.

I look like a 1940's housewife.

My face burns at the thought. I glance down at my apron, covered with fruit and checks and ruffles, and want to die.

Cade must be back there shaking his head, wondering what the hell is up with Miss "Cheesecake-Obsessed Girl Dressed in Super Old Clothing" pounding on his door.

Why do you care?

I blink as my brain begins holding a sidebar conversation within my head.

Well, why do you? You're not interested in men right now.

I hear a door shut. I turn and see Cade coming down the hall, tugging a maroon T-shirt over his sculpted body. It says *Denver Mountain Lions Hockey #82* on it.

Oh, that's hot.

Cade pauses to slide his feet into a pair of flip-flops. "So, is your cannoli game strong?"

I snort. "Is my cannoli game strong? I'm *Italian.*"

"That doesn't mean you have a strong cannoli game," he counters, swiping his keys off the kitchen bar counter.

"Oh, it's *definitely* strong."

"We'll see."

"What, are you a cannoli expert?" I ask as he opens the door for me to step into the hallway.

"I might be. There's a Little Italy in Poughkeepsie, where I'm from. And there's this Italian bakery that has a solid cannoli game," Cade explains as he locks the door to his apartment. "They have those rainbow cookies, too. I love those."

"Don't get me started on rainbow cookies," I say, thinking of the almond paste cookies with layers colored to represent the Italian flag. Each layer is separated by jam and topped with chocolate. "I love those. Almost as much as I love cannoli. But *nothing* is better than a decadent cheesecake."

Cade hits the elevator button and looks down at me, a curious expression filtering across his handsome face.

I've pretty much just told him cheesecake is better

than sex. Oh God, where did the thought of *sex* come from?

"I'm sorry," I blurt out. "I can't believe I'm doing this to you."

"What, talking?"

"Yes, talking. Too much. Rambling about rainbow cookies and cannoli and coming up here dressed like a housewife straight out of 1942 and banging on your door and asking to use your oven when I'm su—"

"I wasn't thinking 1942 housewife," he interrupts.

"What?" I ask, surprised he cut me off.

"I was thinking of Rosie the Riveter in the 'We Can Do It!' World War II posters," Cade says as the elevator chimes. He holds up his arm in the iconic pose and flexes his bicep for me.

I can't help but laugh as the elevator doors open. I step inside and Cade follows before punching the button for my floor.

"Okay, there's a reason why I'm dressed like this," I say.

"Sounds like a story," he says, staring down at me.

"There is, but it's long. Incredibly detailed. Bordering on sappy, I dare say."

"I've got time," Cade says easily. "I dare say."

I continue to play along. "I'm not sure. It's a family secret, you know. I'm probably breaking all kinds of protocol by sharing it with you."

The elevator chimes on my floor. The doors open, but Cade immediately hits the button for the lobby.

"What are you doing?" I ask.

"Hold on."

"Cade, I have to get those cheesecakes in the oven!"

The elevator hits the lobby, where people are waiting to get in.

"Come on," Cade says, tipping his head.

I follow him out, wondering what on earth he's doing.

He stops and gazes down at me.

"You know that moment when someone walks into your apartment and asks to bake cannoli cheesecakes in your oven, wearing an apron and scarf in her hair and talking a big game about her mad cannoli skills? And in that moment you think, 'Wow, this girl is really different?'"

Butterflies appear out of nowhere in my stomach.

"I'm weird," I admit, smiling at him. "I own that, but what does that have to do with the apron story?"

"Correction. I didn't say weird. I said different. Different is good in my book. Because I'm going to let you in on something."

"What?"

"I'm different, too."

Ooooh!

"How so? Do you have an apron?" I tease.

A brilliant smile lights up his face.

"No. But why don't we walk down the street, get some coffee, and while your cheesecakes are baking, you can tell me the story. I'm kind of hoping you'd throw in the scarf thing, too, but if you only want to talk about the apron, I'll settle."

"And you'll tell me how you're different after that?" I ask.

"Oh, I'll tell you. So is your conversation game as strong as your cannoli game, Josephine?"

Swoop! The butterflies are fluttering wildly now.

"My conversation skills are *solid*," I say.

Cade grins. "Good to know. This might call for an extra large coffee. If you say yes, that is. So what do you think?"

CHAPTER THREE

"I can't believe Jude has an electric kettle," I say, pouring some freshly heated water around the cheesecakes. "They're so handy. We have them in the test kitchen at work, but it would be nice to have one at home, too."

I can feel Cade studying me from his spot at the kitchen counter. We went and got coffee, then my cheesecakes, and after preheating the oven, I'm ready to slide them in at last.

"Jupe is British," Cade explains. "He drinks tea all the time and had to have this thing. I asked why he can't just microwave water and he mumbled something under his breath about it tasting horrible."

I look up. "Jupe?"

"You know, *Jupe.* When we were in Hawaii during All-Star break and you and Sierra got drunk. She was texting him why it was over and they had that miscommunication. And Jude became Jupe in text.

Apparently, it was an overdose of red wine and cheesecakes. Hmmmm. I wonder who had the idea to bring cheesecake to the man-bashing party?"

He lifts an eyebrow at me.

Ack! I shift my attention back to the cheesecake. We did get drunk that night. And bash Marco and Jude, er Jupe.

And, apparently, Jude shared the story with Cade.

"I *might* have suggested cheesecake," I say, putting down the electric kettle. "But we were both screwed over. Well, Sierra wasn't, though we didn't know that then, but I was totally screwed over."

I open the door, pick up the first pan and slide it in. Then I retrieve cheesecake number two and place it in the oven before shutting the door.

I turn to find Cade studying me.

"Screwed over sounds like a story."

Ugh. I need to learn to shut up.

Or become a mime.

But if I were a mime, I'd just act everything out and humiliate myself that way. Because my brain apparently can't function in front of Cade.

Mute not mime. I need to become mute in Cade's presence.

"You only get one story at a time, Cade Callahan," I say.

Wow. That was smart. And on my feet, too. Whoo hoo! My brain is back!

I untie the string on my apron and carefully lift it over my head. I fold it up and place it on the countertop, then turn to find Cade's jade eyes flickering over my T-shirt dress.

"Do I need to save my 'you bake in a dress' question?"

Okay, he's not repelled by my hips and the ten extra pounds of cheesecake indulgence I'm carrying there.

Wait. Cade doesn't care about my hips.

He's intrigued by the fact that I'm not a cookie-cutter girl.

Instead, I'm the different girl who happens to own a cookie cutter collection.

Ack.

I clear my throat and unknot my scarf, removing it and placing it on top of my apron.

"This needs to be a mutual exchange of information," I say, staring at him in mock seriousness.

Cade lets out an infectious laugh that makes me smile.

"This must be what it was like in the 1980's. The last decade of the Cold War. You're a CIA agent willing to give information in exchange for intel on the KGB. I feel like we should be sitting on a bench with a briefcase in between us to exchange."

"You like history?"

Cade's eyes widen as if he's surprised by my guess. "Why do you ask?"

"That is your second historical reference since I've been around you tonight," I say.

"Is that bad?"

I almost feel like he's testing me with his question.

"Why would it be bad?"

Cade shrugs. "I'm not supposed to be smart."

I blink in surprise.

"What? Why not?"

"I think you need to answer the apron question first. Since you want an equal exchange of information, you know."

Oh, Cade is someone I could develop a serious crush on.

Wait.

Never mind.

NO.

I'm a *career* woman now.

I've given up men.

No more crushes for me.

Especially not on a man who is so dangerously delicious.

"Come on, let's have a seat," Cade says, picking up his coffee. "You said this will take an hour, right? We might as well be comfortable."

Comfortable. Ha-ha, right. How can I be comfortable sitting next to this super hot man? One who I'm detecting has so much more underneath his hockey player persona than the rest of the world sees? An exciting feeling of anticipation floats down my spine.

I nod as he motions for me to go first. I take a seat on one end of the living room sofa, and Cade sits on the other. Leia jumps up in the middle and drops her head on Cade's lap, filling the space between us.

Since I had a pedicure yesterday, I feel confident enough to slip my feet out of my Converse and tuck my legs underneath me.

"Mmmm," I say after taking a sip of my pecan pie

latte and sinking back into the sofa cushions. "This is so good. I *die* for lattes, and this one is perfect. I can taste the roasted pecans, the richness of the maple syrup, and of course, the hint of nutmeg and cinnamon that gives it a nice kick of spice."

Cade stares at me for a second. "You can taste all that in a *sip?*"

I grin. "I can. It's one of my magical powers."

"But how?" he asks, perplexed.

"I have a very sensitive palate," I explain. "I'm considered a super-taster because I have a natural ability to detect the slightest amount of something in a dish."

"That's crazy."

"Crazy awesome," I say. "But if it doesn't come naturally, you can train your palate, too."

"How?"

"Did you just place the imaginary briefcase down between us? Is this your first question, or should I answer the apron question first?"

Oh, my banter game is on point right now.

Cade's jade eyes flicker with interest.

"You are different."

"I promise I didn't oversell my oddness."

"Sorry about all the questions," Cade says, raking his hand through his rich brown locks and pushing them back off his forehead. "I'm very inquisitive by nature. As soon as a question pops into my head, I ask it. It drives some people crazy."

He pauses to take a sip of his iced latte, and I think about what he just said.

"But questions show you are listening, so how can that drive someone crazy?"

"Did you just put a briefcase down?" Cade teases, parking his coffee cup on the end table. "Because that sounds like a question."

Then he flashes me a beautiful smile.

Oh, he's sharp.

I like this.

I could like him.

I clear my throat to get those dangerous thoughts out of my head.

"Okay. The apron is very old. It dates back to World War II, and it belonged to one eighteen-year-old Camilla Napoletano, who lived in Naples. The Americans set up a base of operations in Naples after liberating the city in 1944. One day, Camilla was at home baking when there was a knock at the door. It was one Joseph Rossi from Chicago, who was looking for a different family but had the wrong address.

"It was love at first sight. They courted. They married. Then Camilla moved to Chicago and never saw Italy again. She was willing to take a leap for love. To be fearless and believe in Joseph and the life she could have if she were brave.

"This apron," I continue, "has been passed down in my family to Rossi women that showed a deep passion for cooking, as that was Camilla's passion outside of Joseph. She loved to cook for those she loved. Now the passing of the apron is a tradition. My nonna gave it to me when I was accepted into the Kendall College of Culinary Arts."

I pause for a moment to see if Cade thinks this is the most boring story he's ever been told in his life. I love this story with all my heart because it tells of great love. Of the man who loved Camilla, of her love for him, and her passion for both him and cooking for those most important in her life.

"You mean . . . that apron in there," Cade says, inclining his head toward the kitchen, "has all that *history?*"

My heart soars.

He gets it.

Marco never got it. Marco never cared about that story and glazed over when I told it to him.

"Yes," I nod. "That's why I love it so much."

"That's amazing," Cade says, his voice full of interest. "Think about it. That apron lasted through *World War II.* Through shortages and rations and then made the journey here."

"I know," I say. "My nonna—my grandmother—says it was the nicest thing Camilla owned during the war. She treasured it. And then when she came to Chicago, it was her link to her past, but also part of her future cooking in her new kitchen in America."

"Man, if that apron could talk, the stories it would have," Cade says as he winds his fingers through Leia's fur. "I would love to hear about how she survived World War II. What they thought of the Allied troops being there after liberation, too."

"I know. It's more than an apron. It's *history.* I know this sounds weird, but I can feel it when I put it on. And that's why I always bake with it on when I'm at home."

"That's an incredible story," he says, his eyes locking with mine.

"I think so, too."

"Do you have any pictures of her from that time?"

"I'm sure my nonna does. She's the keeper of all the family history stuff. Both in words and photographs. I'll have her scan one and send it to me."

"I would love to talk to your nonna. It sounds like she has done a good job keeping the stories of Camilla and Joseph alive. World War II fascinates me."

I smile at him. "I'm putting my briefcase down now, but I demand two answers from you right off the bat. Because my story was outstanding."

Cade laughs. The beautiful sound is becoming more familiar to me.

And I like it.

"I'll grant you that. It was a fantastic story. Go ahead."

"Okay. First question. Tell me about your love of history. Where did it come from?"

"Are you sure? I can go on about it too much. I've seen people nearly pass out from boredom."

"I won't pass out. Besides, if I do, my timer for the cheesecakes will wake me up."

"Oh, sassy, aren't you?"

He raises an eyebrow to show me he's teasing.

"Of course I am," I say, grinning. "But quit stalling. Tell me about your interest in history."

"I told you I was different, so just remember that up front," Cade says. "I'm a total history nerd. I've loved it since elementary school. I wanted to know how things happened. Why they happened. My head has been full of questions since kindergarten when we learned about the Niña, the Pinta, and the Santa Maria," he explains, talking about the ships Columbus used to sail west. "So, while other kids were busy pasting sails on ships, I was asking my teachers questions. I exasperated them, I think."

"You were bright very early on," I say, studying him.

Cade appears embarrassed. "Yeah. I guess so. I drove my classmates crazy because whenever the teacher asked, 'Do you have any questions?' my hand would shoot up."

"I love that you knew your passion early on. That's great."

Cade gives me the side-eye. "Oh, yes, it made me *very* popular," he says dryly. Then he shifts. "What about you? When did you learn you loved cooking?"

"It's a weird story, but you should expect that by now."

Cade props his arm up on the back of the sofa. "I would be disappointed if it wasn't. Weird is good."

Oh, I like him.

I clear my throat. "When I was five, while you were discovering Columbus' ships, I was discovering *The Golden Girls* reruns with my nonna," I explain, referring to the old sitcom.

"Hold on. *The Golden Girls* shaped your future?"

I can't help but laugh. "It did. Because Nonna always had it on, and, in one particular episode, the characters were sitting around a table eating cheesecake. I heard that and told Nonna cheese in a cake was icky.

And she said, oh no, JoJo—that's what she calls me—cheesecake is *divino.* Divine. Anyway, she whipped out that same apron, and we made one together.

"I loved being in the kitchen, standing on a chair and helping her mix the ingredients. It was magic, seeing how all these things individually could come together and make something so absolutely different and wonderful. That is when my passion for baking began."

"I can see why you were given the apron," he says.

"Thank you. I hope I can do it justice. But I want to talk more about you. Tell me more about your love for history."

Cade furrows his brow. "You don't want to know about hockey?"

I see a look of skepticism in his eyes. As if all people want to know about is the hockey career that has given him fame and money.

"Well, I do, but I'd rather hear about history first," I say honestly. "That's different. And I like different."

His jade eyes widen a bit. "You mean that, don't you?"

I simply nod in response.

His beautiful eyes linger on mine for a moment, and I'm mesmerized by the unique shade of green they are.

"Okay. But fair warning, I can talk forever about history, so you can tell me to shut up whenever."

"I won't do that."

"You say that now."

"And I won't say it later."

Another smile lights up his face.

"All right. So anyway, I've loved history for as long as

I can remember. How things in history repeat themselves. How two different countries can have two different histories of the same event. It didn't matter what the time period was, I wanted to read about it. Whenever we had library day at school, I was always buried in the historical section."

"You're a big reader, too?"

"Only historical novels or non-fiction historical books," he explains. Then a sparkle enters his eyes. "I'm very one-dimensional."

"Ha, no, I don't think so, but go on."

"I earned a scholarship to go to Cornell because of my hockey skills," Cade says. "But I was thrilled because they have one of the top history departments in the country. That's what I majored in. I have a degree in history."

"So you didn't go straight into hockey," I say.

"Nope. I could have entered the draft after high school, but I wanted to study history first," he pauses to take a sip of coffee. "I don't regret that. I learned so much at school. And there's so much more I need to know."

Cade is different from how I imagined he would be. His dream of getting a history degree took precedence over a career that would have made him millions right away if he had gone to the league. How many people would do that?

"What do you plan to do with your degree?" I ask, taking another sip of my latte.

Cade winces. "I've never told anyone this."

I can forget avoiding a crush on Cade.

Because it's already happening.

"Only share what you want," I say.

"I'll tell you," he says, his eyes holding mine. "I want to write historical novels that are set during World War II. I'm always watching documentaries and taking notes on things to further research and ideas I could shape into a story someday. But that's what I want to do. I want to write historical novels."

He's a writer, I think in amazement. *This talented hockey player is so much more than the man who wears a Denver Mountain Lions jersey.*

"You're going to be an author," I say. "That's fantastic, Cade."

"Thank you. I've been writing stories since I was ten," Cade admits. "I have some particularly shit ones that I wrote when I was seventeen that were based during the bombing of London."

I love the image of a teenage Cade writing his version of the Great American Novel.

"Oh, I'd love to read it," I say.

Cade makes a face. "Oh, hell no. It's awful."

"I bet it's not."

"Trust me, it is. But what about you? I know you work with Sierra, but I don't know what you do."

"I'm a recipe tester and developer for *Bake It!* magazine," I say. "It's why I moved out to Denver."

"You create things for the magazine?"

"Yes. My ultimate goal is to write cookbooks someday. Start off with ghostwriting first, then hopefully, print under my own name."

"What do you mean by ghostwriting?"

"I like that you ask questions," I admit.

Cade's face grows thoughtful. "You mean that."

"I do."

"Then I'll ask again. What's ghostwriting?"

I laugh, and he rewards me with that beautiful smile.

And once again, the butterflies dance in my stomach.

"A lot of cookbooks are ghostwritten. Recipes are created by a developer, then tested, and eventually approved by the celebrity or chef for their cookbook. Some chefs and celebrities have a lot of input, others provide minimal direction."

"Chefs don't write their own cookbooks?" Cade asks, surprised.

"It depends, but if you are a TV chef running an empire, for example, when would you have time to develop a cookbook?"

"Interesting. I had no idea."

"It's true. But I would love to head in that direction eventually. It would be challenging, but I would learn so much doing it, you know?"

Cade takes a moment to study me, and his eyes hold steady on mine.

"What?" I ask.

"Josephine," he says slowly, "I know I've met you twice before, but I feel as though I'm *seeing* you for the first time tonight."

My heart jumps wildly inside my chest.

"Me, too," I admit.

How I didn't see Cade before is beyond me. Maybe I was too broken up about Marco to notice him. But as I sit here with Cade now, discovering what an interesting man he is, I can't help but think I'm lucky I got another chance.

To see the man he really is, the one outside the hockey uniform.

And right now, my head and heart are in agreement.

They both like what they are discovering tonight.

CHAPTER FOUR

"JOSEPHINE," CADE SAYS, PUTTING DOWN HIS FORK after taking a bite, "this is the best cheesecake I've ever had in my life."

I beam in response. We're sitting on the sofa, having talked for hours getting to know each other while the cheesecakes baked and cooled.

"Thank you. Cheesecake is my passion," I say, pausing to take a bite to see if I did indeed master my recipe.

"Quick. What do you taste?" Cade asks, studying my face.

I put my palate to work savoring the bite before setting my fork down on the plate.

"I taste the lightness the ricotta cheese provides. Most recipes call for cream cheese, which is much heavier," I say. "I also taste the intensely flavored chocolate mini-chips, which have a hint of vanilla. The almond kiss of the amaretto. The brightness of orange zest and the sweetness of pistachios."

I glance over at Cade, who is staring at me with an expression of awe on his face.

"That's amazing," he says with a hint of wonder in his voice.

"It's one of my talents."

Cade takes another bite of his cheesecake. "What's another one?"

I think for a moment. "I can speak Italian."

"Nice," Cade says. "What else?"

"I can recite quotes from movies. And I know lyrics to a lot of stupid songs from the 80's. As you can see, my talents are very practical and inspiring."

"Can you quote something from *Shanghai Surprise?*"

"Okay, how on earth do you know that movie?" I ask. "It wasn't exactly a masterpiece, and it was made before we were born."

"Well, World War II happened before we were born, and we both know about that."

"True, but World War II is important enough to learn about. An old Madonna movie? Not so much."

Cade's eyes sparkle in response. "I watch a lot of movies. I'll give almost anything a shot."

"Apparently so," I tease. "But in answer to your question, no, I can't quote from it. And you should be proud of me for that."

We both laugh.

"My other big talent is making homemade pasta," I tell him. "It might be bold to say, but my pasta game is as strong as my cannoli game."

Cade flashes me a smile, one that makes my heart jump.

"Well, you backed up your cannoli cheesecake game, so I don't doubt your pasta skills."

"I love the process of it. I even have a pasta machine upstairs."

"If it's as good as your cheesecake, it must be stellar."

"Thank you," I say, feeling a warm flush radiating across my cheekbones. "But that's all I have. Your turn to share talents. And don't say hockey."

Cade takes a moment to study me. "You really don't care about the hockey part, do you?"

"No, that's not true. I do care about it, but you play professionally, so that's an obvious talent. I want to know about your life off the ice, too. Your hidden skills."

Cade looks surprised. As if nobody has ever wanted to know more about his life outside of the skating rink before.

"Okay," he says, pausing to take another bite of cheesecake, "I'm good at fishing. I *love* fishing. It's so peaceful when you are out on a stream, surrounded by mountains and trees. It's one of my favorite things to do."

"I've never been fishing," I say, taking another bite of cannoli cheesecake.

"What?" Cade asks, surprised. "Never?"

I swallow. "Never."

"Oh, you *have* to go. It's an amazing experience."

"But I wouldn't know what to do," I say, parking my plate on the coffee table. "I don't even own a fishing pole, let alone know how to do the bait thing or whatever you do to fish."

"I could show you."

I freeze.

Did Cade just offer to take me fishing?

"What?" I ask, my heart pounding against my ribs.

"I could take you fishing," he says. "I have access to a private pond in Boulder. With me as your guide, you'll be good to go."

My head is spinning. Less than three hours ago, I wanted no romantic interests in my life. I was all about the cheesecake.

But now I find myself interested in Cade.

And I want to see where this could go.

"I'd love that," I say.

Cade's face lights up. "Great. Are you free Saturday morning?"

I nod. "Yes," I say. "And in return for teaching me how to fish, I could teach you how to make pasta."

"Putting your briefcase down for an equal exchange of knowledge?"

I giggle. "Apparently I am."

"Then I'll accept the pasta making lesson."

My crush on this man is going to border on ridiculous by the time I leave his apartment tonight.

Cade clears his throat. "Can I ask you something personal?"

"Sure," I say, curious.

"Why don't you have a boyfriend?"

My blush comes back again.

"I'm sorry. I shouldn't have asked you that."

"No, I don't mind," I say.

And it's the truth. I don't mind talking about Marco anymore.

In fact, I'm *glad* there is no Marco in my life.

"I was in a long-term relationship that ended last January," I explain. "I haven't dated since. Marco—that was his name—was supposed to come out to Denver once he finished grad school. But instead, he fell in love with someone else."

"Shit, I'm sorry," Cade says. "That had to be horrible."

I pause before answering. When it happened, it did destroy me. I focused on my career. I wasn't going to risk my heart for a long time.

But as I sit here with Cade, I don't feel like protecting myself.

Not anymore.

"At the time it was," I say honestly. "But I think it happened for a reason. If he was the man I was meant to be with, he wouldn't have fallen in love with someone else."

"I think he's an idiot."

I burst out laughing.

"Well, thank you, but you don't know him."

"I know all I need to know."

Oh, I like him-I like him-I like him!

I decide to ask him the same question.

"What about you? How come you don't have a girlfriend?"

Cade rakes his hand through his hair. "You might need another piece of cheesecake for that."

"No, no, we aren't *The Golden Girls.* We aren't going to eat a whole cheesecake discussing your love life."

"Why do I have a feeling I'm going to get an education in that, too?" Cade asks, cocking an eyebrow at me.

"You should be educated in *The Golden Girls.* They're amazing."

"One thing at a time. I call pasta first."

Crush, crush, crush.

"Focus," I say, speaking to both Cade and myself, although Cade doesn't know it. "Your love life. Go."

"All right. I love the *idea* of love, but it's hard for me to find. One, because I meet women who think they love me when they don't even know me. That's a major downside to being a professional athlete. You're always wondering if they really like you or the lifestyle that comes with you. If a girl gets past that, she has to like the off-ice me who reads and writes and devours history books. Who watches old movies and likes to be outdoors. I thought I had found that."

My heart stills. Had his heart been broken, too?

"What happened?" I ask.

Cade sighs. "Her name was Cassidy. I fell in love immediately. Hard. Fast. Everything you're not supposed to do, I did. It was instant for me. I followed my heart. I had no idea it was so wrong. Cassidy broke up with me last winter."

I realize we had both been going through heartbreak at the same time.

"What was her reason?" I ask gently.

"We started fighting a lot. I assumed it was

relationship growing pains, but it was the beginning of the end. She eventually dumped me. Via text."

"My turn," I say.

He furrows his brow. "Your turn what?"

"She's an idiot."

Cade laughs, and I join him.

"The closest I've gotten to love since then is watching *Is It Love?* on TV. Sad times at Casa de Callahan."

I sit straight up. "You watch that reality dating show?"

Cade looks sheepish. "Um, I admit it. Yes, I watch it."

"I *love* that show."

"Yeah?"

"Yes! Last season, I felt so bad for Skye," I say.

Skye was the unfortunate runner-up who was told "It's not love" by the bachelor looking for true love.

Cade gives me the side-eye. "Please. Skye is trouble."

"What?" I cry. "She was sweet. And she wants to open her own cupcake shop!"

"Ah-ha! You have baked goods bias," he declares. "Skye was a manipulator. That sweetness was *fake.* Or should I say 'baked' in?"

"Cade, she was not! And what about the winner, Miley? She was in it to launch a TV show."

"Oh, they're all in it to launch a TV career."

"I refuse to believe that about Skye," I say, resolute.

"Sucker."

"I am not!"

"You are, too. Mark it down. I'm calling it. Skye will be on some other TV show this fall season."

"Oh, you bet I've got it down," I say. "And I'll remind you of it when we see nothing of her."

"Right."

"You're wrong."

"Nope."

"I thought you said you were a romantic."

Cade doesn't reply rapid fire this time.

"I am," he says slowly as if he's considering his words, "for the right person. I'm going to be sure next time before I leap."

I realize just how alike we are. We're both quirky and different and live life outside the box, but, in this moment, I'm discovering a new layer.

We've both been hurt.

We're both afraid to take a chance on love again.

Yet on this night we find ourselves unexpectedly drawn toward each other, testing the waters for the first time in a long time.

"Me, too," I say, reassuring him that I understand what he's saying.

We lock eyes. Silence falls between us, the first silence since I walked through his door tonight.

I know that Cade would be worth waiting for if that's what I have to do.

"I should get going," I say, picking up my plate and standing up. "Hopefully, I'll impress my boss tomorrow with this cheesecake, and she'll let me take a stab at putting together my own feature."

Cade rises, too. "You've nailed this. There's no way she can say no."

I sigh. "Oh, there are a million ways she can say no, but I'm hoping this one time I'll get a yes."

I put my plate in his sink.

"Can I see your phone?" Cade asks.

A tingle shoots down my spine.

I reach for it on the countertop, hand it to him, and watch as he keys in a number.

"Text me, and let me know what happens tomorrow," he says as he enters his information.

"Okay," I say, excitement coursing through me as he hands me back my cell.

"What's your number?"

I happily give him my cell number and he keys it into his phone. Then he sets it down on the countertop.

"Thanks," he says, smiling at me. "Here, I'll help you carry your stuff back upstairs."

"Thank you," I say.

I leave one cheesecake in Cade's refrigerator and take the other with me. Cade grabs the baking pans and his keys, and we ride the elevator back up to my floor.

When it opens, Cade walks me to my door. I put the key in the lock and open it, and he follows me to the kitchen. We set everything down, and he walks back to the door, pausing in the doorway in front of me.

"Thank you for tonight," Cade says. "I had fun."

A feeling of pure electricity surges through me.

"Me, too," I say, smiling. "And I can't thank you enough for letting me borrow your oven."

"It was nothing. Good luck tomorrow."

"I'll let you know how it goes," I say.

"I'm counting on that," he says.

Oh!

I swear my heart is about to beat out of my chest as we stand inches apart from each other. He's so close I can smell the scent of sage and citrus on his skin, and oh God, it's driving me *mad.*

"Goodnight, Josephine," he says.

"Goodnight," I say.

Then Cade turns and moves toward the elevator. I shut the door and turn around, pressing my back against it, my mind reeling.

That just happened.

Me.

Cade.

Clicked.

His number is in my cell.

We're going fishing.

Ahhhhhhhhhh!

I can't stop the smile that spreads across my face.

Tomorrow, I know I'll have more than cannoli cheesecake on my mind.

And I couldn't be happier about it.

CHAPTER FIVE

Today's Purpose and Passion Statement:

Today, I will demonstrate my passion for the culinary arts by presenting my cannoli cheesecake to my boss. I will do so with the purpose of pitching my article idea for the romantic February *Bake It!* magazine issue, in which I create cheesecakes inspired by famous Italian desserts.

I quit typing and stare at my laptop screen. After re-reading what I wrote, I hit print so I can cut it out and pin it to my vision board while I get breakfast ready.

I don't know if I can eat my usual bowl of yogurt and muesli. My stomach is a jumble of nerves. And not just because I'm scheduled to present my idea to Angelique this morning.

My printer stirs to life as I move over to my vanity, brushing my long, dark hair up into a chignon at the base of my neck, and thoughts of Cade enter my mind.

Oh, who am I kidding?

He never *left* my mind last night.

My nerves transform into butterflies as I think of Cade. Of course, I did what every modern woman does in this day and age as soon as she meets a romantic interest.

I Googled him.

I blush as I pin my hair into place. Oh, and did I find loads on him. Fan posts, game articles, interviews. Even pictures of him with Cassidy, though those didn't bother me because I know he is over her like I am over Marco.

Of course, there were some *beautiful* pictures of him. Apparently, he doesn't wear a shirt under his jersey, and he's known for pulling it up to wipe sweat off his face.

And oh, a sexy flash of his sculpted abs and a tease of his ribcage tattoo practically had me *sweating* in response.

Cade Callahan is *hot.*

Very.freaking.unbelievably.hot.

I understand why women go nuts posting pictures of his abs all over social media. I was, however, puzzled by all the videos of him fighting on the ice.

I pause for a moment. My brain has a hard time reconciling the Cade who spoke so passionately about history and writing last night with the man who throws punches, swears, and beats the crap out of his opponents during games.

I don't know much about hockey, but I do know

fighting is a part of the game. From what I've read, Cade isn't an instigator, but he's known to defend his teammates. If something goes awry on the ice, he has no problem jumping in. He's hated by other teams but loved by his own teammates. The coach of the Denver Mountain Lions said he's the hardest worker on the ice, the first one out and the last one to leave practice. And he's always asking questions about what he can do better.

I pick up my espresso-brown eyeliner and lightly smudge some across my eyelid. I can picture Cade continually asking how to improve his game. He's no different than the five-year-old boy wanting to know all about Columbus.

The coach went on to say that Cade knows how to get into other players' heads, which I can also believe because Cade is so intelligent. Cade plays on that ability, which often results in players taking swings at him.

And Cade isn't afraid to swing back.

While I'm not a fan of fighting by any means, I do have to admit he looked smoking *hot* being such a badass.

I finish one eye and move to the other. There are so many sides to Cade I have yet to discover.

And I want to know them all.

I put down my eyeliner and reach for my waterproof mascara. Yes, I'm baking in a steaming hot kitchen, but I'm a big fan of using a little makeup. It makes me feel put together. I finish my eyes and apply a little bronzer to my cheekbones. Lastly, I swipe a rose-pink Lancôme lipstick across my lips and gently blot them with a tissue.

As I study my reflection, I know one thing for sure.

All I need is mascara, lipstick, and a latte to take on the day.

And a few thoughts of Cade Callahan for an extra-rosy glow.

I retrieve my printout and take a moment to cut the paper into a circle around the words. Then I head to the kitchen and remove the passion point from yesterday, saving it to add to my inspiration notebook tonight. I pin the new one up next to the picture of Julia Child. I study Julia's photo, then my words, and nod.

I'm going to get this article today.

I force myself to eat a few bites—and quickly decide that's not a good idea, and my stomach tells me so. I wash my cereal down the drain and decide I'll stop at Starbucks and grab a pumpkin spice latte instead. It's September, and they're finally back.

All is right in my world.

I grab my cheesecake from the fridge—I've already put it inside a beautiful pink pastry box for a professional presentation. My phone buzzes on the countertop as I shut the refrigerator door with my hip. I place the cheesecake down and glance at the phone.

It's a message from Cade.

Ah! My heart pounds against my ribs. Happiness shoots through me the second I see his name.

I eagerly swipe open the message:

Good luck this morning. Make The Golden Girls proud.

Oh, my God. He remembered what I said last night!

I text him back, which is hard because my hands are shaking with excitement.

Thank you. I think Sophia Petrillo would like my cheesecake better than her double fudge amaretto ricotta cheesecake.

I smile, knowing he will be clueless to the *Golden Girls* reference.

Cade responds right away:

I think I need to try this double fudge amaretto ricotta cheesecake. Just to compare your game to this Sophia chick's.

I type back:

Well, luckily for you, Cade Callahan, you happen to know an expert in the field of cheesecake. This can be arranged if you like.

I hit send. Who knew I could be such a flirt?

Buzz!

And apparently he likes flirting, too:

I am lucky.

Ohhhh!

Another message drops in:

I'm about to go for a run with Leia. You're going to do great. Let me know how humbled that hard to impress boss of yours is after she takes a bite of your masterpiece.

I begin to type back, but he beats me to it with another message:

And if you're up for it, wanna have dinner with me tonight? My place? My pizza ordering game is STRONG. ☺

He just asked me over for dinner.

In my head I'm doing an excited Muppet arm flail in response.

I reply yes, tell him I can't wait to see his pizza ordering game in action, and I wouldn't miss it.

Then I gather up all my stuff and prepare to take on the morning.

Starting with a visit to Angelique's office as soon as I get to work.

CHAPTER SIX

After I've set my stuff down in my cubicle and logged onto my computer, I decide to approach Angelique. She has meetings starting at nine, so I want to catch her when she is in the best—and most receptive—mood possible.

Which is usually before she starts working.

I pick up my pastry box, square my shoulders, and think confident thoughts as I head through the maze of cubicles toward the editorial offices. I see her door is open and her light is on, which it always is by eight-thirty in the morning. On the dot. Never a minute earlier, never a minute later.

I stop walking. Angelique is very regimented. Militant in the way she goes about her routine. My showing up with this cheesecake will go one of two ways. One, she'll be livid I'm wasting her time with something she never asked for; or two, she'll be impressed I had the gumption to do this without asking.

Obviously, I am throwing all of my positive energy at option number two.

I resume my journey and stop at her doorway. She has her planner open and is meticulously reviewing her notes with a Tiffany blue ballpoint pen in hand.

I watch her for a moment. Angelique is an editor for *Bake It!* magazine, but I know she has her eye on moving over to *Wine and Food Romance.* She's in her late thirties, with bright red hair that is always in a perfect short bob. Angelique is thin, impossibly thin, and only likes the *finer things*. If she had her way, all the articles in *Bake It!* magazine would involve complicated pastry recipes with exotic ingredients, served in tiny portions and decorated with elegant dots of sauce around the plate.

Which is not our demographic. At all. *Bake It!* magazine is for people like my nonna, who love to bake and are looking for a fun twist on pumpkin coffee cake.

Not a dessert with twenty components that has pumpkin foam on the side.

"Are you going to stand there and study me, Josephine? Or will you come in and ask whatever you need to ask?" she asks, not even looking up from her Whitney English Day Designer.

"Yes, I'm sorry," I say, stepping into her office.

Passion and purpose, I repeat to myself. This is my moment.

"Angelique, I've worked very hard here for nine months now."

"And would you like a medal? A blue ribbon?"

Okay. She's going to be snarky.

"Of course not. But I believe if you're passionate

about what you do, and repeatedly do good work, you prove you are ready for more responsibilities. That's what I'd like to talk to you about."

Angelique finally lifts her head. She narrows her eyes.

"I think I shall decide when you've proven yourself and are ready for more opportunities."

Shit, shit, shit. We are on the road to option number one.

I step forward, determined to show her my cheesecake.

"I have developed this cannoli cheesecake to capture the Sicilian dessert in cheesecake form. It's light, it's full of flavor, and I think our readers would enjoy it in the Valentine's Day issue," I say boldly. "This recipe is from my family and has been passed down for generations. I elevated it with additions of amaretto, Madagascar bourbon vanilla, and a pistachio crust."

I open the lid of the box and present it to her.

Angelique studies it for two seconds before her green eyes meet mine.

"No."

I stay strong.

"Would you consider trying it, please?"

"I'm not impressed with what your *granny* made, Josephine."

Her words kick me in the stomach. Her bored tone—along with her sharp words—have officially slammed the door shut on my proposal.

"Now, if you'll excuse me, I need to prepare for my

nine o'clock meeting. Put your cute cheesecake in the break room for the others to pick at."

I consider reaching across the table and shoving her face first into my cheesecake, telling her she only *wishes* she could bake as good as my nonna and she should save her belittling, rude remarks, but I somehow resist the urge.

I'm *so* adding impeccable restraint to my list of special talents.

"Thank you for your consideration," I say, turning and leaving her office.

I shake as I walk down the hall, toward the break room. Why does she have to be such a bitch? Why can't she be encouraging like Sierra's editor is? Why can't she be a woman boss who lifts up other women in the workplace instead of tearing them down?

I could have handled a no. Heard constructive feedback. Received a goal to help me work toward. But, no, Angelique doesn't have time for that. She simply wants me to test, test, test recipes all day long and run like a gerbil on a wheel.

I turn into the employee break room. I'm so mad I want to take the cheesecake and hurl it in the trash. But as I enter the room, I nearly drop my pastry box in shock.

Tae Packett, executive assistant to John Flowers, our senior editor, is getting coffee with two women.

One of whom I recognize.

It's Skye Reeve, the runner-up from *Is It Love?*

Holy cannoli, I can't *believe* it. I forget my own crisis and focus on her. Cade and I were just talking about her last night. What is she doing here? Some kind of bakery feature? That must be it. I remember her saying over and over on the show how she wanted her own cupcake shop.

I can't help but stare at her. Skye's beautiful, of course. She's tall, thin, and dressed in a super chic gray and black striped shirt, which she has knotted at the waist and paired with white jeans and high-heeled, black strappy sandals. Her honey blonde hair is long, flowing, and highlighted to perfection, and a beautiful rose-gold, double-layered crystal necklace adorns her neck.

"Oh hey, Josephine," Tae says breezily. "What do you have there?"

I blink. Yes. Time to stop staring at the reality show runner-up in the break room.

"Oh, a cannoli cheesecake I made yesterday," I say as if the sole intention of my creation was to bring it in for my coworkers to enjoy. "I was inspired to bake."

I lift the lid and set the cake on the counter. I know it will be gone in a half-hour, so I don't have to worry about coming back to stick it in the refrigerator.

"Oh, look at the mini cannoli," Skye says, leaning in to peer at my cheesecake. "They're adorable! Aren't they the *cutest* thing ever, Charlotte?" she asks, turning to the woman next to her, who has been texting on her phone since I entered the room.

"Um, yes," Charlotte says, nodding and briefly glancing at my cheesecake before going right back to her cell.

"It's a beautiful cheesecake," Skye continues, smiling at me. "You're very talented."

At least Skye notices my skills, even if my boss doesn't.

"Thank you so much," I say, smiling back at Skye.

Then I turn and exit the room. I head down the hall to the dressing area where I'll slip into my chef jacket, tie on my floral headscarf, and get ready to spend the day testing stuffed French toast recipes for a celebrity chef.

No matter what Angelique throws at me, there are things I refuse to let her change.

My passion.

My purpose.

Angelique can't change my dream.

And that's all there is to it.

THIS DAY HAS BEEN NOTHING SHORT OF A DISASTER.

I leave the kitchen around noon for my lunch break. I should have known today would be shit the second Angelique offered to give me a medal.

The stuffed French toast recipe was a complete fail. I knew as soon as I read it. The egg ratio was *way* off. Regardless, we're required to go through several rounds of testing before reporting a suspected error in a recipe supplied by a chef. In this case, the chef is from Salt Lake City and is known for owning an amazing brunch restaurant. Go figure.

But with each test, the bread came out tasting like scrambled eggs. I don't think stuffed, scrambled egg toast is what she was shooting for. So, I meticulously recorded the amounts of ingredients used, down to the ounces, and logged everything in my iPad. One thing people don't know about recipe testing it that it's very intensive, detail-oriented work.

I stop in the dressing room to take off my coat, dropping it in the bin for linen cleaning. I open my locker and remove some facial blotting tissue papers and lightly dab them on my face. I glance in the mirror I have glued to the inside door. There. I'm now matte instead of shiny. Better.

I sit down on the bench in front of the lockers and check my email on my iPad before heading off to grab a bite in the corporate cafeteria.

There's an email marked URGENT from Angelique in my inbox.

I brace myself and tap on it:

From: Angelique.Whitmire-Hox@bakeit!magazine.com
To: Josephine.Rossi@bakeit!magazine.com
Date: September 4
Subject: NEW PROJECT

Josephine. You have been selected to work with reality TV star Skye Reeve for a Valentine's Day cupcake feature in the February edition. She will need your input in recipe testing/and or development. She thought your mini cannoli were, in her words, "super cute." She lives in Los Angeles but is here tomorrow and will consult as needed to fine-tune her culinary vision for *Bake It!* magazine. She will ask for you tomorrow at ten o'clock.

Don't disappoint me.
Angelique

I read the email in shock. I'm going to work with Skye Reeve? This is crazy. Usually, I'm handed recipes to test. I make notes, turn them in to Angelique, and move on to my next assignment. She only ever lets me contact a contributor if there is a question or problem.

This is the first time I'm going to take an active role in development.

And *with a celebrity.*

This day has taken a turn, despite scrambled egg, stuffed French toast and my hard to impress boss turning her nose up at my "granny's" cheesecake.

I'm developing recipes for a celebrity feature!

And best of all, I get to tell Cade all about it tonight.

CHAPTER SEVEN

THE BUTTERFLIES ARE SWOOPING WITH ELATION AS I head toward my apartment.

Today turned out to be so much better than I thought it would. I'm doing a *development project* with a celebrity. I still can't believe it. And I love the fact that I was chosen based on my mini cannoli. I can't help but grin wickedly as I know it had to kill Angelique to give me the assignment based on that detail.

Which makes it perfect.

I ended up contacting the chef in Salt Lake City and, as I suspected, she admitted she didn't portion the recipe correctly for a home cook. We batted around revisions, and tomorrow I'll test the new version. So, that project can move forward now, thank goodness.

Now I get to share everything with Cade.

I fish for my keys in my tote, and a blush warms my cheeks. We texted back and forth today, but I haven't told him about Skye yet. He'll flip when I share that story with him.

And oh, I can't wait to see him tonight.

I put the key in the lock, turn it, and hear a dog barking on the other side of the door. Sierra and Jude must be back.

I enter the apartment and am greeted by Leia. I find Sierra and Jude in the living room, watching TV. Jude is sitting up, and Sierra is lying on the couch, her head in Jude's lap as his fingers run through her hair.

I can't help but feel joyful by simply looking at them. Jude is a great guy, and I love how happy he makes my best friend. He does romantic things all the time to show Sierra how special she is, like whisking her away for a weekend at a luxurious resort.

"Hey, welcome home," I say cheerfully as I step inside. I take a moment to close the door behind me, and then I pet Leia, rubbing her huge head. "How was the Broadmoor?" I ask, dropping my tote on our tiny kitchen table.

Sierra sits up, a huge smile lighting up her face. "Amazing! We had the best time. You and I have to go sometime for a girls' weekend. The spa was gorgeous. You'd love it."

Spa. That does sound fantastic, especially because I'm on my feet all day. I'd love a foot massage and a hot stone pedicure. Maybe a nice facial.

"We did a couples massage," Sierra continues, her eyes sparkling. "Jude surprised me. It was *fantastic.*"

Jude grins. "It was brilliant."

"We also went to Seven Falls," Sierra continues, referring to the state park, "and the waterfall was stunning. I'll show you our pics later. We hiked and zip-lined there. It was so much fun."

"That's perfect for you guys," I say, nodding. Sierra and Jude are true outdoors people, and they spend a lot of their free time doing things like kayaking and hiking.

My idea of an outdoor adventure is walking the streets of Cherry Creek North and peering into the windows of boutiques hoping to see a kick-ass sale sign.

"It was," Sierra says, reaching for Jude's hand and wrapping hers around it.

"But from what I hear, you'll be discovering the great outdoors this weekend with my roommate," Jude says, grinning at me. "After pizza tonight, that is."

He winks at me.

Cade told Jude about me.

Ahhhh!

This is a very, *very* good sign.

But of course, I have to play it cool in front of Jude. I don't want him to report back to Cade that I couldn't shut up about him. For a man who made it clear he's not going to fall hard and fast ever again, Cade doesn't need my excitement to scare him off.

I should be very cautious as well. I obviously overlooked some flaws in Marco and fell in love immediately. I won't let myself be unguarded like that ever again.

"Yes, we are," I say calmly, as if pizza with Cade is no big deal.

I glance at Sierra, and I can tell she is dying to know everything but understands we'll dish this out over lunch at work tomorrow.

"Cade's a good guy," Jude says.

"He is," Sierra adds, nodding.

"He told me I needed to disappear this evening, so he obviously likes you," Jude teases. "I was banished the second I dropped my suitcase."

Heat fills my face as my blush deepens.

"Oh, stop it, Jude," Sierra says, chiding him. Then she turns to me. "Don't listen to him. He's exaggerating."

I decide to get Jude off the subject by talking about what happened at work today.

"Sierra, you won't believe what happened at work," I say excitedly. "I got my first development project."

"JoJo, that's fantastic!" Sierra says, her eyes sparkling. "Congratulations!"

"Wait, there's more," I say excitedly. "I'm doing it with a *celebrity*."

Both Sierra and Jude stare at me.

"Who?" Sierra asks. "Can you say?"

I hesitate. I haven't signed all the confidentiality papers for this project, so I don't know if I should, but I also know I can trust Sierra, Jude, and Cade.

"Skye Reeve from *Is It Love?*" I say. "But don't breathe a word about it. I don't know if it's supposed to be confidential."

"No way," Jude says, his mouth popping open. "You mean the girl who was devastated by that wanker Tom?"

I burst out laughing. Sierra and I thought Tom, her suitor on the show, was an idiot, but Sierra told me wanker is a big step up from idiot on the scale of insults.

"Yes!"

"Oh, my God, that's so cool!" Sierra says. "You have to get all the dirt on what it's like dating on a reality TV show."

"It's not reality. The end," Jude quips.

"I'd like to believe love is sometimes involved," I say, the romantic in me coming out.

"She's trying to get on TV," Jude says.

"That's what Cade said," I say.

Jude arches an eyebrow. "Oh, already at the 'that's what Cade said' stage?"

Oh Lord, I know I've turned the color of marinara sauce.

"Speaking of Cade," I say, ignoring him, "I've got to get ready."

I excuse myself, and I head to the bathroom, shutting the door behind me. I take a quick shower then slip into my favorite robe, which is hanging on the back of the door. I wrap my long, chestnut hair in a towel and head to my room.

I slide open the closet door and stare at my clothing. Hmmm. What does a girl wear for a pizza date with Cade Callahan?

No matter what I wear, I'm obviously going to start in the bonus here because the last time he saw me I had my hair piled up on my head, no makeup on, and I was wearing an ancient apron. I'm going to look better than that no matter what I choose.

I flick through my shirts. I don't want to be too dressed up, I mean, it's *pizza.* But I still want to look cute.

I stop on an orange, off the shoulder dress. Oh! I

bought this piece while in a funk over Marco last spring and forgot because I immediately threw it in the back of my closet. It's a beautiful color against my olive skin, it shows off neckline and shoulders, and it hits above the knee for a flirty look.

Perfect, I think, grabbing it.

I change into my strapless bra and panties, and then I grab my scented moisturizer. I liberally apply some Yves Saint Laurent Black Opium to my legs and arms, inhaling the gourmand scent of coffee, vanilla, and flowers. Oh, the baker in me adores this perfume.

I hope Cade notices it.

A shiver shoots down my spine at the thought. I have no idea what will happen tonight, if we'll still get along great, if the chemistry will still be there, if he'll even kiss me—but the mere idea of him nuzzling against my neck to tell me how amazing my skin smells—

Is it hot in here?

Good Lord, I sound like my mom, who is always yelling about hot flashes.

But this is no hot flash.

It's totally Cade-driven.

Focus. The quicker I get ready, the quicker I'll be with Cade.

I slip into my dress and dry my hair. I use a round brush to add body, and I'm pleased with the result. My hair is shiny and full of bounce, perfect for tonight.

Next, I apply makeup, my usual amount. I've never needed a lot, just some mascara, eyeliner, and lipstick. I slip into some black sandals that tie around my ankles, also super cute. I slide some Kendra Scott bangles on my left wrist. Lastly, I pick up my matching Yves Saint Laurent Black Opium perfume and spray my neck and wrists, letting the gorgeous scent settle on my skin.

I set down the bottle and glance at myself one more time in the mirror. Wow. I haven't dressed up like this in . . . forever. I study myself, and I see the natural flush in my cheeks, how my dark brown eyes dance with excitement, how I appear as happy as I feel.

I'm beautiful, I think.

And now I'm off to see Cade.

Anticipation whips down my spine, giving me goose bumps. I head back out, and Sierra and Jude both look up at me.

"Wow," Sierra says, "you look so pretty, JoJo. That dress is gorgeous on you."

"Thank you," I say, smiling.

"I should warn Cade," Jude says. "He has *no idea* what is about to hit him."

I blush. "Stop it."

"It's the truth," Sierra says in agreement.

I grab my tote. "I'll see you guys later."

"Have fun," Sierra says.

I leave, shutting the door behind me. Then I catch the elevator down to Cade's floor. I'm nervous. Excited. Anxious to see him. Hoping our cheesecake night wasn't a fluke.

That was no fluke, Josephine, my heart tells me. *That night was special.*

Cade is special.

Ding!

The elevator chimes open. I walk out, drawing a breath of air to try to calm my nerves.

Or to at least get the butterflies to travel in some kind of formation instead of the rapid swoop and dive thing they are doing right now.

I reach his apartment and ring the doorbell. Oh, God. I'm an eager mess.

And being a mess has never felt as wonderful as it does right now.

I hear footsteps and then the sound of the lock being turned.

The door opens, and Cade greets me on the other side.

I can't speak.

He's gorgeous.

How can he be more gorgeous than he was last night?

Okay, dumb thought, he was in a towel, but *still.*

I allow myself to drink him in, from the blue jeans to the contemporary, white linen shirt with the sleeves sexily pushed up, revealing his tanned and muscular forearms, to the huge silver watch on his left wrist.

Oh, dear God, the man is all kinds of *hot* tonight.

"Josephine," Cade says, snapping me from my thoughts, "you look gorgeous."

I gaze up and find he's staring at me, which makes my heart beat three times as fast.

"Thank you," I say, smiling at him. "You look very handsome."

"Please, come on in," Cade says, ushering me inside.

As I move past him, I once again detect that

amazing scent lingering on his bronze skin, and my pulse burns in recognition. It's a sensual blend.

Absolutely intoxicating.

And I could get drunk off it if I'm not careful.

Cade shuts the door and turns to me.

"You look so beautiful tonight, I feel bad ordering pizza. I should take you out."

"You disappoint me," I say.

"What?" Cade asks, looking confused. "You're disappointed because I want to take you out?"

"You promised to show off your mad pizza ordering skills," I tease, parking my tote on his countertop. "And now, just as I get here, you're bailing? I sense your game is *weak*, Callahan."

"Oh, you think I'd bring a weak game tonight?" Cade says, running his hand over his sexy-as-hell facial scruff.

"I'm a culinary school graduate. I know a good pizza from a bad one."

"And you're Italian. The motherland of pizza."

"You've put extreme pressure on yourself. It's risky. Dangerous, even," I tease.

"But did you expect me to play it safe?" he asks, his jade eyes focused on mine. "Or did you expect me to take a chance with you?"

Oh, shit. I'm so not thinking about pizza right now.

We're not playing it safe.

At least I'm not.

Cade is sexy, brilliant, witty, and a good conversationalist, and I'm just at the *beginning* stages of getting to know him. I like what I see already, how much further will I fall as I discover more about him?

I promised myself I'd be careful.

I wouldn't take risks.

I wouldn't fall for anyone right now.

But I as I stand mere inches from this man, a man unlike any other I've ever met, one who is drawing me in with his gorgeous mind and unusual green eyes, I know I've already moved from the sand to the edge of the shoreline.

The question is, will I swim or will I drown?

Either way, I already know I'm going in.

"You're taking a chance," I say, my heart fluttering. "And so am I."

Our eyes remain locked on each other. There's no question we're not talking about pizza anymore. And, oh God, is he feeling this sexual tension like I am?

"Chances are good," he says.

"I agree."

"So, let's start with pizza and see where it goes tonight," Cade says. "And, hopefully, I won't disappoint you."

His words cause a tingling sensation to rush over me.

I know there's no way Cade Callahan will disappoint me tonight.

CHAPTER EIGHT

CADE PUTS HIS PIZZA ORDERING SKILLS TO WORK, getting us two pizzas: a thin crust with buffalo mozzarella on marinara for me; and an Italian sausage and mushroom for himself.

"Would you like a drink while we wait?" Cade asks. "Wine? Beer? Water?"

"Beer is a necessity with pizza," I say.

"I agree," Cade says, going to the fridge and retrieving two cans of beer. "Have you ever had Pinestripe Red Ale?"

I shake my head. "No, I haven't."

"You'll love this then. It's great stuff. It's a Colorado craft brew from Ska Brewing in Durango." Cade opens a cabinet and retrieves two beer glasses. "I'm a huge fan of craft beer."

"Then you must be in heaven here in Denver," I say, watching as he pours the ale into a glass.

"Yes," Cade says, placing the beer in front of me. "The craft beer scene is fantastic in Denver. And so creative. Have you been to Crooked Stave? They're famous for their sour beers."

"Okay, your craft beer game is strong," I say. "And as a foodie, I'm embarrassed to say this. Mine is weak. I have no idea what you are talking about."

"You'd love Crooked Stave," he declares. "It's definitely in your wheelhouse. Your fine-tuned palate would go nuts there. There's a blueberry one I like. I'm sure you could break it down and figure out why I like it."

"Oh, yes, I would like to try that place," I say, pausing to pick up my ale. "But first, I need to sample this."

"I don't think you merely *sample* anything. You're in full-on break it down mode the second you sip, aren't you?"

"I can't taste anything without going through the process in my head. It's my foodie brain at work. So here it goes."

First I smell it, inhaling the toasty aroma of the brew. Then I take a sip, and my taste buds quickly go to work. First, I detect the flavor of caramel malt. Mild hops. Then a lovely fruity finish.

"Mmm," I say, putting the beer down. "That's very nice."

Cade takes a sip of his as well. "What did you taste?"

I smile flirtatiously at him. "I might tell you later. A girl's got to have some secrets, you know."

Okay, hello, where did sexy JoJo come from?

"So that one is locked in the briefcase?" Cade asks, staring at me.

Heat fills me from his quick response. What is it about bantering that is so damn sexy?

I decide to go 2 for 2 in the sexiness department and somehow formulate a quick reply.

"For now. But I do have other classified information I'd like to share with you," I say.

"Sounds serious. Let's go to the living room to break it down."

I laugh and he does, too.

We take our same seats on the sofa, the imaginary briefcase sitting between us.

I go to put my beer on the end table but don't see a coaster. "Do you have a coaster I can put this on?"

"Um, Jupe and I don't own any. You can just set it down."

I make a mental note to get these poor boys some coasters and put my drink down. Then I turn to him.

"I'm about to open the briefcase and share some classified information with you," I declare. Then I drop my voice. "It's very top secret. Can I have your word you won't relay what I'm about to share with you to another living soul?"

Cade studies me with a serious expression on his gorgeous face.

"This sounds highly confidential."

"Extremely. Secrecy is paramount to the success of this operation."

"You could be taking a risk sharing it with me. After all, you don't know if I'm a double agent."

My heart flutters in my chest. If Cade only knew the risk I was taking at this moment just by *being* here. By allowing myself to get to know him, by spending time with him, without any guarantee of what the final outcome will be.

But right now I know this man is worth the risk.

And as such, I open the imaginary briefcase and share with him.

"I have landed my first ever development assignment," I say.

"What? I thought you said your boss said no to the cheesecake feature," Cade says, wrinkling his brow.

"Oh, she stomped on that," I say. "But I landed a different one. I'm going to help develop cupcake recipes for the Valentine's Day feature. *With a celebrity.*"

"What? Josephine, that's amazing! With who?"

"You have to keep this confidential. I'd hate to have to eliminate you for a security breach."

Cade runs his hand over his face. "I see. So if I were to leak this information, you might poison my food or something to wipe me off the face of the earth?"

"Excellent call on the method of death. I know food chemistry. I'd know exactly what to put into your food to cause death. And I bet I could make it taste good at the same time."

Cade flashes me a sexy smile, one revealing the dimple in his cheek and making my pulse soar.

"You've made the consequences clear. I'll comply."

I pause for dramatic effect.

"I'm working with *Skye Reeve.*"

Cade's eyes widen in complete surprise. "No way. Skye from *Is It Love?*"

"Yes!" I cry excitedly. "The same Skye we were talking about last night. I'm going to help her develop cupcake recipes for our romance issue."

"Holy shit, no way," Cade says. Then he cocks an eyebrow at me. "I told you she was in it for the fame."

"Cade, she had her heart broken on national TV. She should get some mileage out of it for that reason alone," I say, feeling the need to defend my future client.

"She knew what she was signing up for," Cade counters.

"Please, when the heart is involved, does anyone really know what they are signing up for? No."

"If she were signing up for love in the first place, which I find highly suspect."

"Let me guess. Did you study debate at Cornell, too?"

"I might have taken argumentation and debate in a summer session."

"I knew it," I say, smiling at him.

"I can't say it comes in handy for playing hockey, but I loved the class because I'm the kind of guy who finds identifying logical fallacies fun."

He looks at me, and I can't say anything. Does he have any idea how much his intelligence turns me on?

The fact that Cade loves to debate raises him another notch on the sexy meter in my book.

As if that were possible.

No, it's not. He's so hot the whole damn meter broke.

"And if you tell anyone I like finding logical fallacies in an argument, I might have to find a way to silence you," he says, his jade eyes shining wickedly at me.

My eyes instinctively fall to his full lips.

Kissing would be a fantastic way to silence me, I think.

There's a knock at the door.

"Ah, pizza," Cade says, getting up. "I'll let you take a moment to consider my words before you proceed."

Oh, dear God, it's ninety-five degrees in here. I might have to stick my head in his freezer so I can cool off before I implode.

Cade opens the door.

"I've got two pizzas," I hear the delivery guy say. "One cheese marinara and one with mushrooms and sausage."

"Yes, thank you," Cade says, taking the boxes and setting them on the kitchen bar counter. I watch as he grabs his wallet and pulls out some money.

"Um, you're Cade Callahan, aren't you?" the delivery guy asks.

I watch with interest. Sierra said this happens with Jude sometimes when they go out. He is often recognized and asked to sign stuff or pose for pictures.

"Yeah, I am," Cade says.

"Dude, you're such a badass," the guy exclaims. "You punch the hell out of people!"

"Um, well," Cade says, and I detect he's uneasy talking about it. "Not all the time and definitely not off the ice."

"Yeah, but you seriously punched the shit out of JP

Rochat last season. He was so pissed he broke his stick afterward."

"It's part of the game," Cade says. "Keep the change, okay?"

"Dude, awesome!" the kid exclaims. "Have a great season!"

"Thank you," Cade says, shutting the door. He turns to me. "I'm sorry about that."

"About what? I know you're famous. That's going to happen. And that's okay."

Cade goes into the kitchen and retrieves two plates from a cabinet. He places them on top of the pizza boxes and brings everything into the living room, setting it down on the coffee table.

"Do you know what I like about you?" Cade asks, sitting closer to me on the couch this time. "You being here has nothing to do with the fact that I play hockey for a living."

I gaze up into his handsome face. "No, it doesn't. I mean, I want to know all about that part of your life, but I like the guy sitting next to me now. The man who knows what a fallacy is. I like getting to know this side of you first."

Something flickers in his beautiful eyes, and I feel my breath catch in my throat in response.

"I appreciate that about you," he says. "More than you know."

As my gaze drops to his sexy mouth, the desire to kiss him hits me full force. I bring my eyes up and find he's staring at me, too. Oh, God. Could he be thinking the same thing? That he wants to kiss me as badly as I want to kiss him?

Cade clears his throat and shifts his eyes to the pizza boxes in front of him. "Let's see if this pizza meets your high standards. If you don't approve of my game, it's all over for me."

Oh, I approve of your game, Cade Callahan, I think. *And the crappiest pizza in the world couldn't change what I'm starting to feel for you.*

Rather than being close to over, we're right at the beginning.

And I can't wait to see where this evening goes.

CHAPTER NINE

"Bring me the pizza," I say dramatically to tease Cade. "And I'll see if it meets with my approval."

Cade puts his hand on the box to open it but then stops.

"This is tense," he says.

"It is."

"If this doesn't meet your standards, you're out of here."

"It could happen," I say gravely.

Cade's eyes lock on mine.

"It would be tragic if you left now."

Oh, God, I can feel the sexual tension.

"Would it?"

"Yes," he says seriously.

"Then this pizza is the most important piece of pizza I'll ever try," I say softly, keeping my eyes on his.

Nothing is said for a moment. I hear my heart beating. Anticipation runs through me. I'm falling headfirst into this crush, and while my brain should be slamming on the breaks, my heart moves forward.

Cade shifts his attention back to the pizza, opening the box containing the cheese one. The heavenly scent of melted cheese and warm crust wafts through the air, but pizza isn't the thing I'm tempted by right now.

I lean forward and select a piece, moving in to examine it.

"Perfect crust," I say, glancing underneath it. "I like a nice, chewy texture. It's wood-fired, giving it a nice crust that will crunch when you bite it but give way to a wonderful, warm, soft interior that is heaven when you taste it."

I feel Cade's eyes locked on my face as I talk, and oh, how I love the way he's staring at me.

"The sauce should be simple," I continue. "San Marzano tomatoes, known for their sweetness. Fragrant fresh basil. Garlic. Salt and pepper. Then the cheese. Fresh buffalo mozzarella with its deliciously creamy texture, melted to perfection. A drizzle of olive oil over the top to finish it off. Simplicity is my key to a perfect pizza."

I pinch some of the cheese off the top of the pizza and pull it away. "Look at the glorious melt on this," I say, breaking the strands with my fingers. "This is what you want. This texture is perfection."

I place the cheese in my mouth, savoring the taste of it.

"Mmm," I moan blissfully. "This is so flavorful. Creamy. *Delicious.*"

I put my pizza down on the plate and reach for a

napkin to blot my lips, but Cade's hand covers mine, stopping me.

I quickly look at him, surprised.

"Don't," he says softly, squeezing my hand in his. "Allow me."

I can't breathe. I can't. My heart is pounding. Anticipation burns in me like never before.

He leans in toward me. I see nothing but desire burning in his beautiful eyes. Cade oh-so-slowly lifts his hand toward my face, then takes his thumb and gently traces it over the corners of my mouth.

Oh, God.

"Nothing is sexier than you talking about food," Cade says, leaning in closer to me.

"It's my passion," I say, his mouth now inches from mine.

"I know," Cade says, placing his fingertips underneath my chin and tilting my face toward his.

"I'm Italian," I say as desire builds in me. "I'm supposed to be passionate."

"You are. And all I could think about the whole time you were sharing your passion about pizza was what it would be like to kiss these beautiful lips of yours," he says, teasingly brushing his finger over my lower lip. "I want to kiss you. I want to kiss you now, if you'll let me."

I'm drunk on him, on his sexiness and sweetness, all coming together in this moment.

"Yes, you may," I say.

Cade dips his head, and his lips brush against mine. His mouth is warm and soft. He slides his hand up to the side of my face, stroking it gently as his lips part mine.

Every nerve I have burns with desire. His mouth is warm and caressing, slowly exploring me as we kiss. I taste beer on his tongue. I inhale the sage and citrus scent lingering on him. His facial hair deliciously scratches my skin, which feels amazingly sexy.

I lift my hand and touch his face, feeling his dark stubble graze my fingertips as Cade seeks more from me. I melt into him, drinking in his kiss, feeling nothing but excitement swirling in me. Cade's kiss is sensual and seeking. It's hot, just like him.

I dare to slide my hand down his neck, to the back of his head, and I touch his hair, which is luxuriously thick. I wrap the silky strands around my fingers as we continue to kiss and touch each other.

Cade's hands don't stray from my hair and face, and it has a drugging effect on me. We continue to discover each other with slow, lingering kisses, and I realize this isn't an ordinary kiss.

This is pure magic.

Finally he breaks the kiss, staring down at me with bewilderment on his face.

"I can't believe I did that," he whispers, lifting his hand to my face. "I was trying like hell to wait, but I couldn't. I couldn't sit here and not know that, what your kiss was like. But I'm glad I didn't wait. Not when it feels so right to kiss you."

Then he presses his lips to mine again, and happiness fills me. This sexy, brilliant man with so many talents wants to kiss me tonight.

As Cade's warm mouth seeks more from me, I decide that dinner is highly overrated as a date night activity.

Not when I can be kissing Cade.

And that's exactly what I intend to do.

"YOU KNOW," I SAY, PICKING UP ANOTHER SLICE, "COLD pizza is really the perfect food."

Cade grins wickedly at me. "Is that so?"

I laugh as I take a bite. Cade and I ended up making out for hours on the couch. If we both hadn't been starving, I would have kept kissing him.

"Yes. Don't you agree?"

"If it means I get to kiss you, then yes, it's a *fantastic* dinner," he teases.

I blush, and he smiles.

"I have some confidential information to share," he says.

"Oh, do tell."

Cade brushes my hair away from my face. "I want you to know I didn't invite you up here with the intention of making out with you. I don't want you to think that."

I study him, and I see concern etched on his handsome face.

"What do you mean?" I ask, confused.

"I was going to take you out on a *date* first," Cade admits. "I thought tonight would be more about getting to know you. But God, you were sitting there looking so *beautiful* in that dress, and your skin smelled like vanilla, and it was driving me *crazy*, and then you were talking about pizza with a passion I've never seen in a woman, and I couldn't do it. All thoughts of restraint went flying out the window."

Happiness runs through me as I take in his words. Cade is reassuring me I'm not a one-night mess around for him.

He respects me.

Which I realize is something I never had with Marco.

"I appreciate that," I say, staring at him. "And don't worry, you can still learn all about me. And kiss me. Because you're a really good kisser, Cade Callahan. I'd hate to let that solid skill be wasted."

A slow, sexy smile lights up his face. "You make perfect sense."

"Speaking of getting to know you," I say, pausing to eat another bite, "I want to talk about your hockey life. Why do you get into so many fights? Your personality doesn't seem to match what I've seen on YouTube. I don't think it's the sport itself because Jude doesn't seem to get into a ton of fights."

Cade flicks open his pizza box and removes a slice.

"Jupe isn't badass like me," he quips. Then he looks at me and smiles. "Kidding."

"But why do you fight?"

Cade puts his pizza down on a plate and sets it in front of him on the coffee table.

"I want you to understand that this is *hockey* and not

how I am off the ice," he says slowly. "Fighting there is part of my game, but I don't fight off it."

My heart is touched by his words. I can tell it's important to Cade that I understand this.

"Okay," I say, nodding.

"When I play hockey, I'm all out," Cade explains. "I love the game and the mental challenges of it. If you can get in someone's head, you can change the whole direction on the ice. I discovered early on I was good at it. When I watched film, I could see what frustrated other players. Weak spots. What made them tick. And I learned how to exploit it.

"I play with passion," he continues. "I'm fired up. I'll do whatever it takes to win. But if someone cheap shots one of my teammates, I have no problem engaging them on my shift. If you watch my games, you'll see that I'm aggressive in my play. I stay on people. I'm not afraid to get physical. But I'm not a *goon.* I don't hit the ice with the intention of starting a fight. And I never will. But will I play with intensity? Yes. Will I be physical? Yes. But hit someone just to hit someone? No."

Suddenly the picture makes sense. The Cade I'm getting to know isn't a bully on the ice, so to speak, but plays with an intensity and passion that might drive opposing players to take a swing at him. And if someone went after a teammate, Cade would be the one to step in and make a statement about it.

"Do you understand?" he asks, interrupting my thoughts.

"I do," I say, nodding. "It makes sense now."

"I'm glad. I want you to understand. It would be easy to get the wrong impression of me if you just went to Google." Cade gives me the side-eye. "Did you Google me?"

Shit.

"Of course I did, but I'd Google you if your name was John Smith."

"That would be a tough search. You'd come up with millions of hits."

I laugh. "I love your humor." Then I turn serious. "Does it bother you that I Googled you?"

"Nah. Because I Googled you, too."

"What?"

Cade cocks an eyebrow at me. "You're not the only agent doing recon work, Ms. Rossi."

"Oh, did you find out anything juicy about me?" I ask, taking another bite of pizza.

"Yes," he declares. "You were voted most likely to appear on *Cupcake Wars* at St. Anne's Preparatory Catholic School."

"That's on Google?" I ask, incredulous.

"You've never Googled yourself?"

"No," I cry, shaking my head. "I don't want to know what's out there."

"Ha-ha, imagine being me," Cade says, pausing to take a bite of pizza. "I never look myself up on social media. Unless I'm in the mood to hear what a jerk I am from the opposing team's fan base."

"Okay. What if we took hockey out? What would we find?"

Cade thinks for a second. "Cade Callahan, lover of

historical documentaries, books, and asking questions. The end."

"That's not all. You love the outdoors."

"Oh, right. Lover of the outdoors. The end."

"Would you stop it? There's so much more to you than that. Like craft beer aficionado," I tease.

"Yeah, that too," Cade says, smiling. "Okay, what about you? What should Google say about you?"

"Josephine Rossi," I say. "Passionate baker. Lover of Julia Child, *The Golden Girls,* vision boards, and cheesecakes. But only if they are well made. Nothing is worse than a crappy cheesecake."

"Do not give the lady a crappy cheesecake," Cade says, finishing up his beer.

"No, not unless you want to irritate me," I say, putting my plate on the table. "I hate to see good ingredients wasted in a subpar effort."

"I'll make a note of that. What else irritates you?"

"Caps off toothpaste."

"Cliché."

"Hey! You're the writer, not me. I can do clichés," I protest, giggling.

"Okay, fine. Go with your cliché. What else irritates you?"

"When my favorite product is discontinued. That is always irritating."

"Good one."

"What about you?"

"When I can't find a pen and I need one, and I know there are like twenty of them in this apartment. I think Jupe is hoarding them in his room."

I love that we are talking about stupid things like caps off toothpaste and a black hole of pens. Cade is so *easy* to talk to, and it's just another thing for me to adore about him.

The fact that he's initiating this conversation with me just makes me tumble further down the rabbit hole of falling for him.

"I have a question. If you and Jude are both professional athletes, why are you sharing this apartment? I mean, you could both have luxury homes or penthouses if you wanted them," I ask, curious.

"That's easy. We both want to be wise with our money," Cade says, finishing up his pizza and pushing the plate back. He draws me to him, and I snuggle against his broad chest as he talks. "There's plenty of time for a house in my future. Why not save money and have my best friend as a roommate?"

Responsible with money? Check.

Another roll further down the rabbit hole? Check.

Cade winds his fingers through my hair, and I close my eyes, listening to his heart beat under the linen fabric of his shirt.

"I love your hair," Cade says as he plays with it. "It's beautiful."

"Thank you," I say, loving the compliment.

"Do you want me to call you Josephine or JoJo?"

I lift my head to look up at him. "Either is fine. Why?"

Cade gazes down at me and brushes his fingertips across my cheekbone. "Because when I call you tomorrow to wish you good morning, I want to know what name you want me to call you."

"Nearly everyone calls me JoJo," I say. "But you can call me Josephine."

"I'm glad you picked Josephine for me," he says.

"Me, too."

As his lips meet mine in a sweet kiss, I can't help but think I'm *his* Josephine.

And there's no other person I'd rather be at this moment.

CHAPTER TEN

Today's Purpose and Passion Statement:

Today I will meet with Skye Reeve to collaborate on recipes that reflect her passion for baking cupcakes. My purpose is to help her look amazing in the pages of *Bake It! m*agazine and create my first piece for my ghostwriting portfolio.

I study the words on my vision board while I wait for Sierra to finish filling her tumbler with coffee. Today is going to be a great day, I can already tell. I'm excited for my new project working with Skye.

Of course, I left one very passionate detail off my vision board.

Cade.

Goose bumps appear the second I think of him. Before I left last night, he asked what time I usually set my alarm for. I told him six, and at 5:59, he called to wake me up and wish me good morning. It was beyond romantic.

By far the best wake-up call I've ever had.

"Okay," Sierra says, screwing the top on her coffee tumbler. "Let's go."

I nod and we head out the door.

"Did you sleep at all last night?" Sierra asks as we step inside the elevator.

I blush. "That would be a no."

Sierra grins. "I knew you wouldn't."

"This is crazy," I admit, adjusting the strap of my tote on my shoulder. "It was like Cade was on replay in my head all night long. I haven't felt this way since . . . I don't know if I ever have," I admit.

"Really? Not even with Marco?"

I consider her question for a moment. "You know, I fell in love with Marco, but it was different. We grew up in the neighborhood together. Our families knew each other. I always thought he was funny and charming and good-looking, and I did love him. But it wasn't like this. With Cade, there's this magnetic feeling. That's the best way to explain it. I'm drawn to him in a way I've never felt before."

The doors open at ground level, and we begin our walk to work. Our publishing company is located in a renovated warehouse a few blocks from our apartment, so it's an easy walk to work, especially when the weather is beautiful.

"It's exciting, isn't it?" Sierra asks, her eyes sparkling at me. "When you find someone and connect like that?"

"Yes," I agree.

And terrifying, I think to myself.

I already like him a lot, and I know I could fall for him. But I felt so sure about Marco too, and that turned out to be a big lie. My life was ripped out from under me when he told me he wasn't following me out to Denver like we had planned. In fact, his future didn't include me at all. It included the new girl he had fallen in love with.

At the time, I didn't understand how he could do it. We were so perfect together. We talked about a life. Marriage. Family. Starting new in Denver, outside the eyes of our Chicago neighborhood.

But maybe it happened because I was meant to find Cade, my heart whispers. *It happened because Cade is the future I'm meant to have.*

Whoa. Okay. Bad thought. No.

You kissed him, Josephine. A kiss.

Well, actually it was a lot of kisses.

Sensual, slow, seeking, hot kisses.

Whatever.

Don't go thinking anything beyond what happened last night.

"Are you having a conversation with yourself?"

I blink.

"I hate that you know what is in my head," I declare, shifting my eyes to a bar on my left.

"I'm going to give you unsolicited advice," Sierra says.

"About working with Skye Reeve?" I say, deflecting her from a comment about Cade, which I know is where she is really about to go. "That Skye is in this for the fame? Cade already told me that."

"Ha-ha, no. I do agree with him, though."

"You cynics. Can't people simply want to find love?"

"On reality TV? No."

"Not everyone can find it in an elevator," I tease, glancing knowingly at her.

Sierra's skin turns red at the reminder of how she met Jude. Stuck in an elevator.

Hmm. I guess I should thank her because if she hadn't met Jude, I'd never have met Cade.

And he could be the love of my life.

Gah. No. Shut up, heart!

"That's true," Sierra says. "But you must allow yourself to *feel.* If you follow your heart, you won't go wrong. I say this to you because I trust your instincts. You know what you need."

I snort. "Oh, yes, but nine months ago I thought I needed Marco."

"He was practice. Marco doesn't count."

We both laugh.

As we continue walking, I take in the view of the historic district we call home. It's the oldest original settlement in the city and has undergone a magnificent revitalization. It's full of bars, restaurants, art galleries, boutiques, and it's the home of the Denver Mountain Lions. The architecture is a mix of old and new, set against the backdrop of the Rocky Mountains.

It's funny. I never thought I'd leave Chicago, but now as I study the city of Denver surrounding me, I can't imagine being anywhere else. Of course, I can't get that through my mother's head. She thinks Denver is temporary and I'll come home and raise my children in the same neighborhood I grew up in.

My phone buzzes. I fish for it inside my purse and see it is my mom calling for her morning chat. She must be a mind reader.

"Mom," I say to Sierra before answering it. "Hi, Mom."

"JoJo, how are you?" Mom asks.

Oh, great, Mom, just walking through the streets of Denver thinking I'll never leave, which will break your heart. Oh, and I had the best date ever with a badass brilliant hockey player who lives here, but what's new with you?

I decide to refine my answer.

"I'm walking to work with Sierra," I say.

Talk about editing.

"Guess who Anthony saw at Jewel last night," Mom asks, referring to my older brother and the Chicagoland grocery chain. "You won't believe it."

"I don't know," I say, wondering which scandalous person it could be.

"*Marco!*" she says dramatically. "How dare he shop at my neighborhood store? I don't want to ever run into his cheating face and think of what he did to you, JoJo."

Oh, that scandalous person.

"Mom, I don't care. I'm not even thinking about him."

It's funny. Hearing his name a few months ago was like taking a knife and stabbing it in my heart. But now? I don't even flinch.

Probably because after spending time with Cade, I realize he did me a big favor by dumping me.

Hmm. If things go well with Cade, I should send his girlfriend flowers as a thank you gift.

"*What?*" Mom shrieks. "You don't care?"

"No."

She goes silent for a moment. "Oh, my God, you've met a boy. Marcella, get in here. JoJo's met a new boy!"

Shit. Now she's calling Nonna Rossi into the mix.

"No, um, not really," I say, wanting to stop this conversation before Nonna gets on the phone. "He's—"

"JoJo, you met a boy?" Nonna asks, happiness radiating from her voice.

"She can't be with a Denver boy, she'll never come back!" Mom wails in the background. "I'll never see my grandbabies, ever. They'll be Thanksgiving and Christmas babies. Oh, I can't stand it. My heart is broken, my JoJo!"

Babies? *What?*

"Donna-Marie, stop, she's allowed to leave the house," Nonna declares. "And she's not pregnant. You aren't, are you?" Nonna asks me.

"My baby girl is not having sex before marriage!" Mom yells.

"What, do you think she just played board games with Marco? Don't be ridiculous."

"I'm not pregnant!" I blurt out, which makes Sierra burst out laughing. "We've had one date!"

"One date is enough, trust me," Nonna says knowingly. "Unless his equipment was like bad yeast and didn't rise to the occasion, if you know what I mean."

"*Nonna!*" I cry.

"If she's in love, she'll never leave Denver," Mom says. "I think I'm having an anxiety attack!"

"We'll go visit," Nonna declares, ever the problem

solver. "Now Donna-Marie, go have a glass of wine and calm down."

"Wine? It's only nine in Chicago," I say.

"It's four in Rome, close enough," Nonna declares. "Tell me about this boy."

Despite the dramatics, a feeling of excitement sweeps over me when I start talking about Cade.

"His name is Cade, and he's from Poughkeepsie, New York. He plays professional hockey, and he went to Cornell. He studied history," I say.

"Ivy league," Nonna gasps.

I can't help but smile. She skipped straight over hockey to his intellect, just like I did.

"And he loves the apron," I say proudly.

Nonna is silent for a moment.

"When did he see you in the apron?"

"Um, the first time we met. Well, we met before, but that was post-Marco and I didn't appreciate what I was seeing. But when we met again, I was wearing the apron. And he liked it, Nonna. He wanted to know all about it!"

More silence from Nonna.

"Nonna?" I ask, wondering if I said something wrong.

"You're going to marry this Cade."

"What?"

"That apron has a legend. Camilla met her husband for the first time wearing it. Family history says that any woman who meets a love interest wearing that apron will marry him."

I try to process this new information. No, that is silly. A simple story that can't be proven.

"Nonna, that's a nice story, but—"

"It's not a story," Nonna says firmly. "It's Camilla's legend. She met Joseph Rossi while wearing that apron. And she told me her gut knew other Rossi women would meet their husbands wearing it."

"That's . . . coincidence," I say, my heart beating nervously.

"No. You weren't wearing it when you met Marco. One of Camilla's daughters wore it at a church holiday baking event and met her husband," she says. "Now, you know I inherited the apron by marrying your pops," she explains, referring to my grandpa, "but you are the third Rossi woman to wear this apron and *meet a man.* Two previous Rossi women did meet their *husbands* while wearing it."

"What?" I gasp. "I never knew that!"

"I didn't want to tell you because you didn't wear it when you met Marco, and I thought, eh, the legend will die here. But no! Don't you see? Marco wasn't meant to be your husband!"

Oh, my God.

This is crazy. This can't be true.

"You are going to marry this Cade, JoJo. *He* is going to be your husband."

CHAPTER ELEVEN

So now that I have my future husband all lined up, I can start picking flavors for our wedding cake.

Oy.

I'm still reeling from what Nonna told me this morning. Yes, two out of three women have met their husbands while wearing the apron. But that was just a coincidence.

Besides, I met Cade before that night, so the whole theory is invalid.

Yet in so many ways, the night I showed up at his door wearing the apron was our first real meeting. Even Cade said he felt like he was really seeing me for the first time that night.

I wonder if perhaps the legend is right. There's a reason my oven died. That Cade was home. That we felt an instant attraction.

No. This is crazy. I can't think like this. We had *one* date. If there's one thing I've learned after my relationship with Marco, it's that I need to proceed with caution. We have a second date lined up Saturday morning. There's nothing guaranteed beyond that.

I'd be wrecked if Cade said, "let's be friends" after the second date.

Gah! I can't keep having these conversations in my head.

I refocus by reviewing the online research I did yesterday for my meeting with Skye:

**Skye is 23. From Los Angeles. One of three girls. Parents still married. She worked in food hospitality prior to going on Is It Love?. She believes in true love and that marriage is forever. Loves the beach and outdoor activities. Passion is baking cupcakes. Dream is to open a cupcake shop. BA earned in broadcasting at UCLA.*

I pause. Her broadcasting background makes me wonder if Cade and Sierra are right. It wasn't listed in her bio on the show website, and if she really wanted to bake, a food science, hospitality, or culinary school background would make more sense. Of course, people can change their minds. Just because I have known what I wanted to do since, oh, the age of five, doesn't mean everyone else does. Before the show, she did work in the industry according to the food hospitality reference in on her show bio, so that should count for something. But then who knows what that really means? She could have been a food server and that could have been labeled "food hospitality."

My office phone rings.

"This is Josephine," I answer.

"Hi, Josephine, it's Elaine from the front desk. Skye Reeve is here for your ten o'clock meeting."

"Okay, I'll be right down, thank you."

I pick up my iPad and head toward reception. I'll talk to Skye in one of our chat rooms first, a place where you can sit and brainstorm. After I review her recipes, I'll take her into our elaborate pantry and see if anything else catches her eye, and we can kick around some more ideas after that.

I open the door to reception and find Skye sitting in an oversized leather chair. She has her eyes cast down to the floor, and I'm shocked to see she's wringing her hands as if she's anxious. What on earth could Skye be nervous about? She's dated on TV! She had her boyfriend tell her on camera that it "wasn't love." The mere *idea* of that makes me nauseated.

Nothing could be worse than that.

But talking about cupcakes? This is easy. It should be fun.

Skye lifts her head and catches me staring at her.

Shit.

"Um, good morning, Skye," I say quickly, smiling warmly at her. "I'm Josephine. It's so good to properly meet you."

Skye stands up, and oh, she is so *thin.* If Nonna saw her, she'd strap her to the kitchen table and force-feed her manicotti.

"Hi," she says, extending her hand to me. "It's nice to meet you, too."

I shake her hand and notice it's clammy.

"Sorry," she says, cringing as she pulls it away. "I'm a little anxious."

Did TV wreck her confidence so badly that she's nervous talking about cupcakes? I have the urge to put one of my cozy blanket scarves around her and make her a latte.

"You have nothing to be anxious about," I say. "Come on, let's go chat for a bit."

Skye bites her lip. "Um, okay."

"Would you like coffee? Tea?"

"A black coffee, please."

"Sure," I say. "Let's go into the break room."

I lead Skye to the break room, retrieve a cup, and slide a cardboard holder around it.

"Do you prefer dark roast or light?" I ask.

"Dark, please," Skye says, fiddling with the shoulder strap of her black Gucci bag.

She's so nervous I'm starting to feel jumpy.

I pour her a cup of dark coffee, put a lid on it, and hand it to her.

"Thank you, that's very nice of you," she says.

"Please, my pleasure," I say, pouring myself a cup. I take a moment to grab some cream from the fridge and pour a smidge into my coffee.

I feel Skye staring at me as I swirl the rich cream into the dark brew. I'm sure she's wondering why on earth I would add this kind of calorie count to my cup. She must think I need to lose fifteen pounds at a minimum, but I don't care. Unless I'm having my beloved latte, I can't drink coffee with anything but cream.

"Okay," I say. "Let's go brainstorm."

A look of panic flickers in her blue eyes.

"Skye?" I ask. "Are you okay?"

She blinks. Her expression changes to one of sunshine, similar to the one I saw on the show whenever she went out with Wanker Tom.

"I'm terrific. Let's get started!" she says eagerly.

Too eagerly.

I furrow my brow. I thought the apron story was weird this morning, but it appears things are about to get weirder.

We take the elevator down a floor to the breakout rooms. I've never had to use these before because when Angelique normally gives me assignments, I go straight to the test kitchen to work. On this floor, there are separate rooms with tables and chairs for private meetings. In the center, there's an open space with a big cushy sofa surrounded by bean bag chairs. It's very cool.

I find my name put up outside one of the rooms. "Here we are," I say, opening the door and flipping on the light. This room has a little sofa, two easy chairs, and a coffee table.

Skye sinks down into one of the chairs, and I sit down on the sofa across from her.

I open her file on my iPad and glance up at her. She has taken nothing out of her purse.

"Um, are you ready?" I ask.

Skye nods. "Yes."

Okay then.

I clear my throat. "All right. This is for the Valentine's Day issue. We're featuring your cupcakes and you as America's Sweetheart, loving your life after the show. What kind of cupcakes did you have in mind?"

"Um . . . chocolate?"

What? I study her. *Chocolate?* That's her answer? If she were a real baker, she would be rattling off her favorite flavor combinations or talking about her signature base recipe and what she likes to add to it.

"What type?" I ask.

"I don't know. I thought you could help me with that."

"Do you have a base recipe for your cupcakes that you want me to start with?"

"Base recipe?"

I freeze. Oh, dear God. She's not a baker. Skye knows *nothing* about cupcakes. There's no way in hell she could run a bakery unless it was in name only.

"I can develop one for you if you need one," I say, realizing this project will indeed be true development.

Skye's hands begin to shake. She drops her coffee cup, sending it splattering on the hardwood floor, and bursts into tears.

"I'm a fraud," she sobs, burying her face in her hands. "I don't know anything about baking! My agent told me I should pretend cupcakes are my passion so I would be cast on the show. Cupcakes are popular and people would associate their sweetness with me. And with my looks, it would be a no-brainer casting."

Heavy sobs wrack her body, and I don't know what to do except let her spill her heart out.

She looks up, and her mascara is smeared all over her face.

"Nothing has turned out like I thought it would. Nothing," Skye cries, and I have a feeling the dam has burst open. "I sat in that meeting yesterday wanting to scream. I don't know anything about baking. I've never baked anything in my life that didn't come from a mix. I don't want to own a cupcake shop. I thought I wanted to be a lifestyle reporter and the show would give me good exposure.

"But then I actually fell in love with Tom, and now I'm the biggest idiot ever," she continues. "I believed everything he said. Meanwhile, he was saying the same things to the other girl. *The exact same things!* America laughed at me. People have made fun of me on social media. They've been cruel. People say I asked for it by going on the show, but I had no idea it would be so *hard.* I don't ever want to be on TV again, but I have no other skills.

"My agent said this feature could possibly land me a baking show on a food channel, and I kept saying I don't know how to bake. She assured me I don't have to actually bake, just fake it, but I feel trapped! I've been *sick* over this, over the feature, over my future, over the way people see me as a dumb blond who is nothing more than Tom's reject. My life is *total shit.*"

Then she bursts into tears again.

"Tom is a wanker!" I blurt out.

She freezes. "W-what?"

"Tom is an absolute wanker, and that is lower than low," I say. "People are relieved for you, Skye. Don't you see that? That's why we want you for this feature. To showcase you because you were so sweet and lovely on the show."

"That was real," Skye insists. "Please believe me when I say that. The way I was with Tom, the other contestants, how I never said anything awful or catty to the other girls, even if they deserved it. That's me."

I see she is desperate for me to believe her. For someone to believe a real Skye exists underneath all the things she's done to try to please others.

"I do," I say.

"I think you're the only one," she says, jerking her hand across her face to wipe away her tears.

"Do you like cupcakes?" I ask.

Skye retrieves some tissues from her bag and looks at me confusedly, as if wondering how we went from talking about her mess of a life back to the topic of cupcakes.

"Um, yes, I do."

"Then that's another truth. You're a nice person. You fell in love on the show. And you like cupcakes."

Skye smiles. "I think you're the first genuine person I've met in a long time. You're really nice, Josephine."

"You can call me JoJo," I say. "It's what my friends call me."

"I'd like to call you JoJo, then," Skye says, taking a moment to blow her nose. "Oh, that's something they edited out of the show. I was a sobbing, snotty mess in the back seat of the limo after Tom dumped me. They had a psychologist there to help me deal, but of course, a camera, too. I kept blowing my nose and the producer said, 'This will be on TV, please try to cry cleaner. No snot.'"

"*Clean crying?* Who does that after a broken heart?" I ask, incredulous. "I was a snotty mess, shoveling cheesecake down my throat, when my ex dumped me."

"I couldn't have cheesecake because I had appearances and my agent was telling me I couldn't gain weight. It was a prime opportunity to land me a TV gig. She suggested a gossip talk show, but the idea of that made my skin crawl. I don't want to talk about other people I don't know. Not when I know how awful it's been for me."

"Skye, a food show would be completely different," I say, leaning forward. "A lot of celebrity chefs are handed recipes. They play their part, they *act* like an authority on food, and it all comes together with TV magic. You know how that works."

Skye runs a hand through her luxurious, beach wavy hair. "I can't be something I'm not. It has to be authentic to me, which means I won't be considered. I don't have a job. I don't want to do product placement on Snapchat or Instagram. I just feel . . . so lost."

"This is temporary. I promise you it is. You're only twenty-three! You have lots of time to figure out what you want to do. Would it hurt to do a cooking show for a while, if the opportunity came your way? If you could find a vehicle that represented your voice?"

For the first time since she arrived today, I see a hopeful glimmer in her blue eyes.

"Maybe," she says slowly. Then she winces. "But there's still the public. I know I can do a magazine article, but TV? I know I'm supposed to be on board with this, but for the first time in forever, I'm being honest. I don't know if I want to go back to TV, where everyone is watching me."

I have a flash back to last night, when Cade was talking about dealing with fans and backlash in the social media.

"I think I have someone who can help you," I say, as an idea hits me. "This may be totally unprofessional of me, so please say no if you want no part of this, but are you available for dinner tonight? I have some people I'd like you to meet. I think they can help you."

CHAPTER TWELVE

"JUDE AND CADE ARE ON THEIR WAY UP," SIERRA SAYS, reading a text message as I finish piping filling into the last cannelloni tube and place it on top of the tomato sauce on the bottom of my baking dish.

"Okay," I say casually.

But inside, I'm anything but casual.

My anticipation rises at the thought of Cade being here in seconds. He and Jude agreed to talk to Skye over dinner tonight about dealing with fans and social media. In return, I promised them a homemade Italian meal.

I frown. Of course, I didn't have time after work to make my own cannelloni shells, so I cheated. Hmm. *Nonna would not approve of this cheat at all,* I think.

I shouldn't be feeding my future husband boxed pasta. In Nonna's mind, that would be enough for him to reconsider this whole marriage-of-destiny thing.

I shake my head. Our crazy conversation about the apron is still lingering in the back of my mind. Thank God Cade knows nothing about it. He would probably ask his coach to be traded just to get away from the crazy girl whose nonna is claiming he will marry into the family because he saw her in THE APRON.

I reach for my ladle and pour the rest of my homemade tomato sauce over the top of the pasta, nearly laughing out loud at the thought of Cade trying to explain his reason for leaving to the coach. Yes. I'm very glad that we are in Denver and my family is a thousand miles away in Chicago.

A knock at the door signals their arrival.

Whoosh! The butterflies flutter madly in response. Last night was pure magic, and I want more of it. Our texts back and forth today were exactly like our conversation last night: intelligent and flirty. And while tonight is about helping Skye, I can't help but think I'm lucky to have more time with Cade, too.

"I'll get it," Sierra says, putting aside the whisk she was using to make salad dressing.

She goes to the door and opens it, and I turn to find Cade and Jude stepping inside our apartment.

My heart flutters. Cade is wearing a simple gray T-shirt and distressed jeans with brown chukka boots finishing off his casual vibe.

The second his eyes meet mine, a smile lights up his face, revealing that dimple in his cheek. Every nerve I have jumps when I see it. Cade makes his way over to me in the kitchen, and anticipation builds in me with each step he takes.

Finally, he's in front of me and, as I wonder how to greet him, Cade draws me against his body for a hug.

I relish the warmth of him, the glorious combination

of soft cotton fabric and hard muscle, and the rich scent of his skin. Oh, this feels so good. I close my eyes and breathe him in.

Cade dips his head down next to my ear.

"You look beautiful," he whispers to me, his sexy voice vibrating against my ear.

My pulse jumps with his compliment. Once again, I'm in my apron, and once again, he thinks I'm beautiful.

Joy sweeps over me. It feels so natural, so right, to be held in his massive arms, inhaling the sensual sage and citrus scent lingering on his powerful, athletic body.

Cade presses a quick kiss against my cheek, and his stubble scratches deliciously against my face. An image of us kissing flashes through my head, and heat rips through me.

To my dismay, he lets me go and stands straight up. Of course, it's for the better because my thoughts were teetering further and further into dangerous territory the longer I stayed pressed against him.

"It smells amazing in here," Cade says.

"Yes, you do," I say without thinking.

"What?"

GAH!

I feel my face burn hot. "Um. I mean, um, it's sauce."

Cade cocks an eyebrow at me. "I smell like sauce?"

"No! You smell hot!"

Shit! When did I turn into a babbling idiot? When?

"I smell like hot sauce?" he asks, his eyes shining wickedly at me.

"You're enjoying this way too much," I say, shaking my head. "I meant to say, you smell the tomato sauce for *cannelloni napoletani*," I say, adding the Italian emphasis on the words. "Which means cannelloni with meat and ricotta filling."

"Say ricotta again."

"What?" I ask.

"Just do it."

"Okay, ricotta," I say, using Italian pronunciation on the word.

"I love how you say it all Italian-like."

"You say it," I challenge.

"Ricotta."

"Wrong."

"I'm speaking English," Cade declares.

"Your pronunciation is incorrect," I declare. "I'll have to teach you the proper way to say it."

"Oh, is that so?" he asks, leaning against the counter.

I smile flirtatiously at him. "Yes."

Sierra returns to her salad dressing, and Jude stands on the other side of the breakfast bar counter.

"We're really counseling Skye Reeve tonight?" Jude asks while reaching for the antipasti I set out on the countertop. He selects a piece of prosciutto and pops it into his mouth.

"Yes," I say. "And I can't thank you enough for helping her tonight. She is having a rough time dealing with the trolls on social media."

"But she had to know this would happen by going

on the show, didn't she?" Sierra asks as she adds a bit of salt to her dressing. "JoJo, taste this."

Sierra grabs a spoon and dips it into her dressing, handing it to me. "Enough basil?"

I feel Cade's eyes on me as my palate goes to work.

"Yes, there's a nice balance of basil, but I still get the orange," I say. "It's good." Then I look at Cade, whose beautiful jade eyes are locked in on me. "What?"

"You," he says simply. "I love watching you work."

Sierra smiles and goes back to chopping some romaine for the salad. I turn away before I become a big melted puddle in front of everyone.

"Can I do anything to help you?" he asks.

I'm struck by how considerate he is. Marco would already be on the sofa with a beer popped open by this point.

"You can open the oven for me," I say.

"I see you don't trust me with anything complex," he teases.

"It's because she's smart," Jude interjects, as he moves next to Sierra to help with the salad. "Did he tell you he caught our microwave on fire last year?"

I slide my baking pan into the oven, and Cade shuts the door. I set the timer and turn to Cade.

"No, I haven't heard about this oven fire," I say, lifting an eyebrow at him.

"You can shut up now, Jupe," he teases.

Sierra turns around, pointing her knife at me. "You told him about *Jupe?*" she accuses, referring to the drunken night of texting that led to his nickname.

"No," I say, pointing at Jude. "*Jupe* told Cade about *Jupe!*"

Sierra begins laughing, and we join in.

"Okay, let's not revisit that part of history," Sierra declares.

"But it gave Jupe his nickname," Cade teases. "You know at practice, he'll only pass me the puck if I call him Jupe."

"Really?" Sierra asks.

Jude grins. "It's a lovely nickname, sweetheart. I had to keep it going."

I see the biggest smile pass over Sierra's face, and I know she treasures his little public nod to her.

Sierra clears her throat. "Okay. We were talking about Skye, remember?"

"Right," I say. I move next to Cade, and to my delight, he slides his arm around my waist. Goose bumps instantly prickle my skin in response to his touch. "Skye knew she was going on the show to get publicity. And she knew there would be some negativity because of it, but she was caught off guard by the reality."

"Sometimes knowing it and living it are two different things," Cade says. "You have to learn to ignore the trolls."

"See, that's the thing," I say. "I don't know if she wants to learn to deal with it or simply pursue something out of the limelight. I knew you guys could at least be able to give her some ways to cope if she decides to stay in television."

"I *told* you she was in it for TV," Cade teases.

"Okay. Yes. You were right about that. But Skye

really fell in love," I say firmly. "That part was genuine. Sometimes love happens when you aren't expecting it. Skye said she never dreamed she could fall for Tom, but she did."

I look up at Cade, and his eyes lock with mine.

"I guess that can happen," he says, his gaze holding on my face. "When you aren't looking at all, I mean."

Ohhhhhhhh!

"But she shouldn't let fear drive her decision," Jude says, interrupting our moment. "If her dream is to be on TV, she needs to follow through. Especially now that she has all this publicity."

Sierra grabs some wineglasses. "I agree. She can't let other people have that kind of power over her life. Hey, do you guys want some wine? I have some that is decanted."

"I love that my girlfriend is a foodie," Jude says, smiling at Sierra. "I get home-cooked meals and decanted wine. A vast improvement over boxed macaroni and cheese at home."

Sierra blows him a kiss and begins to pour some red wine into glasses for us.

The doorbell rings, and we stop talking.

"I'll get it," I say, knowing it's Skye.

I slip out of my apron and hang it on the wall hook I put up for it in the kitchen. I can feel Cade's gaze on me, taking in my jeans and chambray off-the-shoulder blouse.

Happiness fills me as I know he's staring. I add a little swing to my hips as I walk, just for his enjoyment.

I head to the door and verify it is indeed Skye before unlocking it and pulling it open.

"Hi, Skye, I'm so glad you could make it," I say. "Come on in."

Skye smiles warmly at me. "JoJo, thank you so much for inviting me over. You have no idea what this means to me."

"Here, let me introduce you to everyone," I say, ushering her inside. "Skye, this is my roommate, Sierra Crawford."

"Hello," Sierra says, flashing her a grin.

"Hi, nice to meet you," Skye says.

"I'm Jude," Jude says, walking up and extending his hand. "Sierra's boyfriend."

"Hi," Skye says, shaking his hand.

"And I'm Cade," Cade says, extending his hand to her, too.

"Cade, pleasure to meet you," Skye says, shaking his hand.

"We watched your season," Jude says. "How have the last few months been for you?"

I notice that Skye's smile wavers a bit, and I can tell she is unsure of how much to say.

"Whatever you say stays here," Cade reassures her. "I know you don't know any of us, but you have my word on that."

Skye sits down on a barstool and begins twisting the bracelets stacked on her tiny wrist. She looks so small and anxious. I swear Skye hasn't been eating right since this whole disaster happened.

I'm going to give her a double helping of pasta tonight and fatten her up on Nonna's behalf.

"Would you like a glass of wine?" I ask. "We have some Chianti open, or we have sparkling or bottled water."

"Wine, please."

Sierra pours her a glass and hands it to her.

"Thank you," she says, pausing to take a sip. "It's been very hard. Watching everything back has been excruciating. And having the whole world comment on what an idiot you've been is soul-destroying."

And then she opens up. Skye talks about how she thought it would be good exposure, but then, living in the bubble created by the show, she got wrapped up in Tom. She fell in love. Skye was blindsided when he dumped her and, worse, she couldn't talk about the experience to anyone.

I can't imagine what that would be like. When Marco dumped me, Sierra, along with my family, was the one who helped me get my life back together. I can't imagine trying to deal with heartbreak while being silent.

"When the show aired, everyone talked about me. From what I said to how I dressed. They even discussed how I kissed," Skye recalls, her face turning red. "Every part of me was analyzed. Mocked. I feel stupid saying this, but knowing it would happen didn't help. I feel like an idiot for putting myself up for it in the first place."

I notice Cade is studying Skye with a thoughtful expression.

"What do you like about being on TV?" he asks.

"I love hosting," Skye says, her eyes lighting up. "I like the energy of TV, how anything can happen on air. I love talking to people. Sharing stories and bringing something to people through that medium."

"You don't have to read what people say about you to work on TV," Cade says simply. "What do you gain from it? You aren't going to change their opinion. There are always going to be people who live to hate on you. I know because I'm hated in the league."

"*You?*" Skye asks, surprise in her voice. "People hate you?"

"Lots of them hate me. If I were to try to read all the negative comments about me, I'd never finish. But I know the person I am. The people around me know the *real* me. I stand by my play on the ice. I know I'm not a dirty player, even though a lot of people say I am. The bottom line is this: all that matters is that you're happy with the person you are. You can't give people who don't know you power over your life choices. I don't think you'd tell me to quit playing hockey because some trolls said I was an asshole, right?"

I stare at Cade in amazement. He's so *strong*. Cade knows who he is, he's secure in what people close to him think, and that's all that matters. It's another quality I find very attractive in him.

"You're right," Skye says. "I can't let people have that power."

"Don't let the wankers win," Jude adds.

"Or knobs," Cade teases. "Right, Jude? Wankers and knobs?"

"What?" Skye asks innocently. "Is knob an idiot?"

"Yes, you could say that," Jude says, grinning.

"*Jude!*" Sierra cries. She turns to Skye. "It can mean idiot, but really, it's British slang for *penis.*"

Skye bursts out laughing.

"Okay, good to know," she says. "Either way, it works."

The rest of the night is spent eating and talking. I don't get Skye to eat a double portion of pasta, but she does eat one, so I count it as a success.

It was nice getting to know the "real" Skye. She was outgoing and talkative, and while I know she won't ever *forget* what has been said about her, I think Cade and Jude have given her the courage to move forward.

Which is something she didn't have until tonight.

When it's time for Skye to leave, she says goodbye to everyone, and I see her out the door.

"Thank you so much for everything, JoJo," Skye says, holding my hands in hers. "You have given me hope I can get past all this."

"You will," I say confidently. "This article is just a start for you."

She nods. "I wish I could stay longer in Denver. Tonight is the best I've felt in months."

"We do have TV in Denver, you know," I say, smiling at her. "Maybe you need a new start in the Rockies."

Skye laughs. "One change at a time. Right now, I'm going to learn not to read everything that is written about me. Or at least begin to mentally toughen up."

"Okay," I say. "That's a good start."

She gives me a quick hug, and I embrace her, knowing I've made a new friend.

"I'll talk to you tomorrow when I'm back in LA," Skye says, nodding. "I'm already looking forward to coming back for our tasting."

"Me, too. Have a good flight home," I say.

She waves and heads to the elevator, and I go back inside.

"Hey," Sierra says, picking up her purse, "Jude and I are going to go out and get coffee. Do you want anything?"

"No, thank you," I say. I turn to Cade. "Do you want some?"

"Nah, I'm fine," he says. "See you guys."

"Later, mate," Jude says to Cade, and they head out the door, leaving us alone.

Cade moves over to me, and my breath catches in my throat. He slowly picks up my hands, carefully entwining his fingers through mine.

"Thank you for talking to Skye," I say, squeezing his strong hands affectionately. "It was very nice of you to share your insights with her."

"Normally, I'd distrust someone who went on TV with an ulterior motive," Cade admits. "But you were right about her. She admitted her reasons for being on the show, and she didn't have to explain any of that to us. Or admit how it all backfired and how humiliated she was. People hurt her so badly with those stupid comments. She was genuinely vulnerable. I see what you see now. But I was going to help her regardless."

"Why?"

"Because you asked me to."

My heart pounds rapidly against my ribs as Cade moves his hands up to my face, framing it.

"Do you know what it means to me to see how much you care about other people?" he says softly.

I can't breathe.

"You're special, and you have no idea that you are," Cade continues. "I see it in these gorgeous dark brown eyes of yours."

"What else do you see?" I whisper back.

"A girl that I need to kiss," Cade says, lowering his mouth to mine. "Right now."

CHAPTER THIRTEEN

Excitement courses through me the second Cade's lips brush against mine. He slowly eases my mouth open in an exploring kiss, just like the ones he gave me last night when I was on his sofa. I slide my hands up to the back of his neck so I can run my fingers through his hair as his tongue caresses mine.

A drugged feeling comes over me as Cade continues to kiss me in his sensual way. His hands are still framing my face, and his kiss makes me feel *treasured,* as if Cade is holding something precious. Something he's going to handle carefully and with caution.

With a jolt, I realize his kiss is reflective of how he wants to move with me. I'm special to him, but because of our pasts, he's going to handle us cautiously.

So neither of us will break.

Cade breaks the kiss and brushes his lips across the bridge of my nose. A contented sigh escapes my lips.

"I like the way you kiss," I say, moving my hands to

his face and rubbing my palms over his wonderfully sexy stubble.

"We could use kissing as a reward program," Cade says, smiling down at me.

"Reward program?" I ask, confused.

"You know, every time I pronounce a food correctly in Italian, I get to kiss you."

I arch an eyebrow at him. "That seems more like a reward for me," I tease.

"Oh, trust me, it's a reward for me, too," Cade says, lowering his head toward mine and kissing me again.

I melt into him, relishing the rugged sexiness of his facial scruff and the taste of Chianti on his full lips. Cade lifts his mouth from mine and gazes down at me.

"See?"

I smile. "I need to think of something special for you."

Cade takes his fingertips and gently traces them down the side of my neck causing my nerves to tingle in response. He slowly moves to my collarbone, skims along it, and then stops at my shoulder.

"You could keep wearing these off the shoulder blouses," he says slowly.

Then Cade lowers his lips and gently brushes them across the top of my right shoulder.

I'm on *fire*.

"Mmm," I moan.

Cade proceeds to kiss me along the top of my shoulder and then back up the side of my neck. I grow dizzy from his hot mouth moving against my skin.

"These blouses," he murmurs into my neck, "are *hot.* I love seeing your skin. I love kissing your skin."

His mouth reclaims mine, and I kiss him back in the same sensual way. Finally, I break the kiss and gaze up at him. I see nothing but desire for me in his eyes.

"I think that can be arranged," I manage to say.

"Then I'm going to bust my ass learning the Italian way to say ricotta. And every other word I can think of. It's worth it if it gives me the opportunity to see you in these sexy blouses."

I gaze up at him in awe. "You really find this top sexy, don't you?"

"I find the woman who is wearing it sexy," Cade declares. "I like how it only shows a hint of you."

I realize Cade is a "less is more" kind of guy, that he enjoys the provocative hints that clothing can provide.

And I find that quality in him very, very attractive.

"Wait until you see me in my outdoor wear," I tease, sliding my arms around his back.

"I can't wait to go fishing with you on Saturday," Cade says, locking his hands around my waist. "One of my greatest passions is the outdoors."

I bite my lip. I've never spent much time in the great outdoors as it has never appealed to me. Outdoor café with a latte? Perfect. But hiking in the woods and putting bait on hooks? It's a world I have no interest in, to be honest.

Doubt riddles me. What if I don't like it? What if I'm terrible at fishing? Will it be a deal breaker for Cade if I don't find an interest in his hobby?

"What's the look for?" Cade asks.

I blink. "What?"

"You're biting your lip."

I blush. "Just thinking about fishing and what to expect," I say. "I hope I don't ruin your time on Saturday."

Surprise flickers across his face. "How could you possibly do that?"

"I've never fished before," I say anxiously.

"Which is why I'm taking you," Cade says.

"But what if I'm terrible at this whole outdoors thing?"

"How can you be terrible at being outside?"

Oh, God, he really doesn't understand what a city girl I am.

"Listen," Cade says, "My goal is to be with you on Saturday. Catching fish doesn't matter."

"Okay," I say, but I still feel doubt in my heart.

"Josephine," Cade says seriously, "trust me."

I stare up at him and see sincerity in his eyes.

"I do," I say, which is absolutely terrifying to admit.

Because I know I'm supposed to be moving with extreme caution. My heart should be stopping at all the yellow lights. Obeying all of the yield signs.

But despite my brain's best efforts, I'm moving forward with little hesitation. Because I do trust Cade. I barely know him. But I know, *without a doubt,* there's more than chemistry between us.

"You're what matters," Cade says, pressing his lips against mine.

And as I kiss him back, I run another yellow light.

I'm falling for him.

And I just pray I don't end up crashing as a result.

I REVIEW MY PROPOSAL ONE MORE TIME BEFORE I HIT send on my email to Angelique. After talking to Skye and getting to know her yesterday, I have come up with three cupcake concepts to test in the kitchen: a whimsical cupcake playing on sugar and spice and everything nice, filled with a snickerdoodle cookie dough and topped with cinnamon buttercream; a decadent chocolate cupcake with a brownie batter filling, topped with dark chocolate whipped ganache; and a vanilla and cherry Funfetti cupcake topped with cherry buttercream and adorned with a customized conversation heart. The cupcakes are elevated, but yet accessible to the home cook wanting to put in the extra effort.

My finger hovers over the send button. This is my first creative proposal for Angelique, and I desperately want to show her I can not only do this, but do it well.

The cupcakes reflect Skye's tastes in food and the holiday. She reminds me of sugar and spice. Brownies are her favorite chocolate treat, so I had to do a cupcake with a nod to that. And we both agreed something pink for Valentine's Day was in order. Skye mentioned she absolutely loves Funfetti and that everything is better with sprinkles, so we decided to bake a cherry flecked vanilla cupcake filled with pink and red candy confetti and topped with a luscious cherry juice-infused vanilla frosting.

I know I'm going to have to defend the choice of

candy confetti. Angelique will *hate* it, but it's for Skye. It represents who she is and, more to the point, home bakers will think it's fun. It's perfect for kids, too. I go ahead and add this to my proposal:

Please note: Skye loves candy confetti and it's a whimsical nod to her personality. Fun and bright. I also think our readers with children will love making these together this Valentine's Day.

I sigh. My note won't make a bit of difference, but I'm prepared to put up a fight.

I almost laugh. *Fighting for Funfetti.* I should get that on a T-shirt.

I hit send on my email, and then I reach for my phone so I can text Cade.

In case you were wondering, you aren't the only one who fights on the job. I'm prepared to come to blows over the use of Funfetti in a cupcake if I need to.

Then I hit send.

Texting throughout the day has become routine. Cade has also continued waking me up with a phone call because he likes to hear my voice first thing in the morning. It's romantic, one of the most romantic things a man has ever done for me, and it's just another thing that makes him so different.

Caution.

The yellow light blinks in my head. I've been with Cade for three days. That's it. But his phone call is already a part of my daily life. As is texting him during the day and seeing him when I get home. Our easy conversation from that infamous cheesecake baking night hasn't stopped. It continues whenever we're together. We're eager to see each other; to keep discovering more; to share slow, sexy, exploring kisses . . .

I blink. I need to focus on each day with Cade as it comes. Nothing beyond that is guaranteed.

But my heart is tumbling. Cade is different from any other man I've ever met. He's brilliant. Strong. Secure. Passionate. Funny. Sweet. Sensual.

I'm drawn to him like I've never been drawn to anyone in my life.

I swallow hard. If I already feel this way, there's no going back for me, although my head is screaming to slow my feelings down.

What if he's seeing other girls?

I freeze, surprised by the thought. Oh shit, I mean, he probably is, right? No. Not after the way he kissed me. There's *no way* he's kissing other women like that.

Three days and you think you have a lock on one of the hottest eligible men in Denver? A badass professional athlete, no less?

Dammit! I hate both my head and my heart right now.

In fact, the only thing I trust about myself these days is my super-taster skill.

Buzz!

My phone jars me from my thoughts. I glance down, and it is indeed from Cade.

Funfetti is worth clocking someone for. Who doesn't like Funfetti?

I smile as I read Cade's words. I begin to respond but another text drops in:

I could show you some of my favorite punches this evening, if you like. Because you have to win. Funfetti lovers of the world are counting on you.

Ohhhhhhhhhh! He wants to see me again!
Butterflies are dancing with elation in my stomach.

Could be very helpful. I do have to grocery shop tonight, though. In exchange, would you like me to show you the proper way to pick out produce?

I just asked Cade to go *grocery shopping.*

I'm sure no woman has asked him to do that this early in the game. "Hey, hot hockey player, want to go see if Whole Foods has some fresh heirloom tomatoes?"

Buzz!

That depends. Do I get to push the cart?

Ahhhhhhhhhh!

I know if I were to look in my compact mirror right now I'd see a beaming smile reflected back.

I respond:

Of course you can push the cart. So is this a yes?

Buzz!

Hell, yes, it's a yes. Jupe never lets me push the cart. Or trolley, as he calls it. Come down when you're off work. We can get dinner and go look at produce. Play your cards right and I'll show you how to clock someone on the jaw, too.

I'm stupid giddy at this moment. We're going to dinner tonight! I'm about to reply when he sends me another message:

Going to skate at the rink with Jupe now. Gotta gear up for training camp next week. Excited for that. But more excited to see you and get your thoughts on lettuce.

Ohhhhhhh!

I type back that I'm just as excited and will completely change his view on lettuce tonight and hit send.

Ding!

I shift my attention to my email. Angelique has replied. I steel myself and open her response.

I do not pay you to come up with ideas using insipid *candy confetti*. This is why you are not given development projects.

**You obviously have a taste problem.
Please come to my office to discuss.**

Hot anger burns in me as I re-read her words.

While my romance with Cade is moving forward, my Funfetti cupcakes were just told to exit the freeway. Along with my apparently insipid taste.

But I'm not taking the exit ramp just yet.

Just like Cade does on the ice, I'm going to stand up for myself. My idea is good, it's perfect for Skye, and more to the point, *Bake It!* magazine readers would love it.

I rise from my chair.

If Angelique thinks I won't fight over candy confetti, she doesn't know Josephine Rossi.

Well, she's about to get to know the real me.

Right now.

CHAPTER FOURTEEN

I THINK CALMING THOUGHTS AS I HEAD DOWN THE hallway to Angelique's office. I can't go in livid. I need to present a mature, educated defense of my decision to use candy confetti.

I stop walking. It's almost comical when I stop to think about it. I'm passionately going to defend my choice of using candy confetti in a cupcake for a *baking* magazine. Our content is geared toward the casual home baker. If they wanted to make a chocolate gateau with dots of sauce, a chocolate powder crumble, and freaking foam requiring hours of work, special equipment, and expensive ingredients, they'd subscribe to *Joys of Pâte Brisée*, not *Bake It!* magazine.

I exhale. Okay. Time to fight for my cupcake.

I move forward and stand outside of Angelique's office. She's typing at her computer, probably sending a message to her fellow editors asking how to deal with an insipid underling who doesn't understand the importance of complexity and dramatic plating.

I rap on the doorframe. Angelique looks up.

"Come in," she says.

I enter her office and stand at the edge of her desk.

"Have a seat, Josephine."

I sit down. Angelique moves her laptop aside and leans forward toward me.

"May I be blunt with you?" she asks, peering at me through her chic designer glasses.

Ha-ha! I think calling my idea insipid wasn't exactly holding back, but hey, whatever you need, Angelique.

"Of course," I answer.

"I don't know if you have what it takes to be a recipe developer."

I sit dead still while a stream of choice Italian swear words flash through my head. *Bullshit,* I think as anger roils inside of me. *I do have the skills. And it's total crap for you to sit here and set out to destroy me just because I don't want to use edible 24-karat gold on my cupcakes.*

"Would you please elaborate on how you came to that conclusion based on one proposal?" I ask calmly.

Angelique's green eyes narrow for a millisecond. She doesn't like that I'm challenging her.

"Of course," she says smoothly. "Josephine, your proposal was, for lack of a better word, *disappointing.* I didn't expect such immature suggestions from someone at your level. It was actually stunning."

Fuse.Lit.For.JoJo.Explosion.

I take a moment to act as though I'm considering her words, which she completely misinterprets as acceptance.

"I know this is hard to digest," Angelique continues,

her voice grave. "But it's obvious your future is in testing and following directions. As your mentor, I would be doing you a great disservice if I let you follow down a path I don't think you'll ever see the end of."

And BOOM!

"You aren't my mentor," I say.

Angelique's eyes pop wide open in shock.

"Pardon me?"

"You're my assignment editor. I report to you." I pause for dramatic effect. "May I be completely honest with you, as you have been with me?"

Ohhhhhhhhhh, she's *fuming.* I can see her eye twitch.

"Of course," she says, but her tone implies otherwise.

"A mentor is someone who helps guide someone else to achieve success."

"That is what I'm doing," Angelique interjects. "I'm leading you away from career failure."

"No. A true mentor would *teach* and *inspire* me. You don't do that. And that's fine, you don't have to be my mentor, but don't say you are when you are not."

She twists her face up. Obviously if her agenda was to upset me or put her thumb on me, it's failing.

"Point taken, Josephine. But your proposal is childish. Sadly, I can't even blame Skye for that because I know she doesn't have the basic understanding of baking necessary to come up with those silly cupcake ideas. But you—I expected more from you."

"My proposal was based on three components," I counter. "It had to reflect Skye's personality since they are supposed to be *her* cupcakes. I can tell you right now, she'd rather set herself on *fire* than eat vanilla foam with a cupcake."

Ha! Angelique's ivory skin turns bright red, and I know I've pissed her off.

"Second, I was mindful of the demographic of our readers when I conceptualized these ideas. They are women. The median age is 52. They spend an average of 52.1 minutes pouring over an issue. In our 'Reader Comments' section, I see the words 'accessible' and 'fun' over and over. And while yes, we do have recipes that challenge the home cook and help them elevate a dish, they don't want a cupcake with 30 ingredients or one using flour imported from Italy. And while you think candy confetti is *insipid,* I think it would be *fun,* which was my third component. I wanted these to be simple, genuine, fun cupcakes, especially for readers cooking for their kids or grandchildren. By the way, Skye loves Funfetti. Her birthday cake is always Funfetti, so it's reflective of her, too. Therefore, I stand behind all of the ideas I submitted to you and, respectfully, ask for your reconsideration."

"Sounds like you've done your homework," a voice from behind me says.

I freeze. I know that confident voice.

It's Tiffany Kendrick, our editorial director.

I turn and find Tiffany standing in the doorway. She's been at the helm since the magazine was created. She's in her early forties and has short, choppy blond hair and impeccable style. She's wearing a crisp white shirt, a stack of bangles on her wrist and, as always, her signature Kendra Scott drop earrings.

"So, I take it you want a Funfetti cupcake for the Skye Reeve feature?" Tiffany asks, pausing to take a sip of coffee from a bright pink tumbler that says "BOSS LADY" on it.

"I do," I say, nodding my head.

"We've done Funfetti a million times before," Angelique says. "I'm trying to get Josephine to think outside the box a bit."

I shoot her a look. Are you kidding? She wasn't trying to get me to do anything but go back to testing recipes!

"But for Valentine's Day, Funfetti hits the spot for kids," Tiffany says. "And if it's Skye's favorite type of cake, the article would entirely miss the point if Funfetti wasn't included."

My heart pounds in my chest.

Tiffany Kendrick gets my vision.

"I agree," I say confidently.

Whoosh! The daggers in Angelique's eyes fly into my back, and I feel the sting of their impact.

"I'll green light that one. Why don't you send me your proposal, and I'll give it the once over," Tiffany says, essentially ripping the project out of Angelique's hands. "Skye Reeve was a big land for us. She's America's newest sweetheart, and our readers will love seeing her happy at last on Valentine's Day, even if it is with a plate of cupcakes. Funfetti makes her relatable. Josephine, I have a good feeling about this project in your hands. I'll work with you on this."

"But . . . it's my assignment," Angelique sputters.

Tiffany shoots her a knowing look. "And as we've

talked about before, while you have beautiful food knowledge and ideas, we need to make sure they fit *our* demographic."

Ooooooooooooh!

I glance at Angelique. She is the color of a tomato.

"I'm about to go into a meeting," Tiffany continues. "Josephine, could you shoot me that proposal right now?"

"I'd be delighted to," I say, rising from my chair. I turn to Angelique, who barely acknowledges my leaving.

As soon as I do, Tiffany shuts the door behind me. Ooooh! I wonder what that is going to be about. The policy of our workplace is "open doors for open minds," so it can't be good. My guess is Angelique is about to be dragged over the coals by Tiffany, and it's not going to be pleasant.

My brain is spinning as I head back to my desk. I know I've just made my work life hell with Angelique for all the days to come, but it was worth it. Tiffany Kendrick is going to guide me through my first development project. She's smart, she's driven, and best of all, she's mindful of who we are publishing for. Ahhhhhhhh! I'm so excited to get started!

I sit down in front of my computer and forward my proposal to Tiffany. Now I need to get into the test kitchen and work on today's assignment, which is testing chocolate chip cookies using muscovado and demerara sugars instead of light brown sugar and recording the results.

I log off my computer, grab my iPad, and head down the hall to get changed. Today is turning out to be a good day. I won my project. Angelique won't oversee me on it, praise the Lord. I'm going to be baking chocolate chip cookies all day, and I love the scent of them wafting from the oven, all the vanilla and chocolate and sugar. It's heaven.

And the icing on the awesome cake that is today?

Spending another evening with Cade Callahan.

I smile with contentment.

Right now, there are no yellow lights.

All I see is green ahead.

And I couldn't be happier about it.

CHAPTER FIFTEEN

"I'M SO EXCITED TO TRY THIS PLACE," I SAY EAGERLY, gazing around the patio.

But I'm even more excited to be here with you, I add to myself.

After my victory over Angelique today, Cade has taken me to Bones, a famous restaurant in the Capital Hill area of Denver. The temperature has dipped into the upper sixties, making it a beautiful September evening for eating outside on the small patio.

I glance back at Cade, who has a navy and gray plaid flannel shirt thrown over a white T-shirt. A backward navy Denver Broncos baseball hat covers his hair, and his stubble is fuller than usual.

Damn. His rugged look tonight is smoking *hot.*

I swear the temperature outside is climbing instead of falling because suddenly I feel the need to take off my cardigan.

The server comes by with our beers, and Cade puts in an order for steamed buns with pork belly filling. He orders lobster ramen as his entrée and I follow his lead because it sounds way too good to pass up. As soon as the server walks away, Cade turns his attention toward me.

"Josephine?"

"Yes?"

"I brought you here for a very important reason. I have to know something about you before we can move forward, and this is the perfect place for you to answer my question."

I know he's teasing me by the sparkle in his eyes. Cade reaches for my hand across the table, and pure electricity surges through me the second his masculine hand wraps around mine.

"Okay," I say, nodding gravely.

"You have to answer honestly."

"Honesty is paramount to any relationship, of course."

Cade's face freezes in response to my words, his smile replaced by a serious expression.

Oh shit, shit, shit, why did I say *relationship?* We are supposed to be going slowly, and here I am tossing that word out on our first night out at a restaurant? Why did I say that, why?

"I mean, in any kind of relationship, not just romantic, of course," I say, the words flying out of my mouth. "I'm not saying we're in a relationship. I get that. I just want you to know I believe in honesty. Everywhere. All the time. I don't like lies and—"

"Josephine," Cade interrupts, squeezing my hand in a reassuring way. "I agree with you. Honesty is important in a romantic relationship. And I'm glad to hear you say that."

"I'm sorry," I say, averting his eyes. "Sometimes I just start talking and I don't shut up. It's the way I grew up. To be heard in my family, you just had to start talking and say as much as you could before someone began talking over you."

"I don't think it's that," Cade says.

I glance back at him, and I see he's staring at me.

"How would you know?" I ask.

"I think you're passionate, and when you feel a certain way, you come out and say it. If I was staring at you, it's because I've never been with a woman who really *says* what she *means.* You're a first for me."

My heart holds still as I drink in his words. He's revealed something about his ex Cassidy here, I know it. But I also know I don't want to talk about her tonight.

Not when we're discovering who we can be together.

"Okay, then I take it back," I say, smiling at him. "When I care about something, when I'm invested, I'm passionate."

"So you're invested in me?"

My head screams to be coy, to be safe. Flirt with him, don't answer his question. Ask him to answer it first.

"I'm invested," I say, my heart answering for me.

Cade's jade eyes linger on mine.

"Good. Because I'm invested, too," he says, running his fingers over the top of my hand.

Ahhhh!

"And because I'm invested, my question is important."

"And the question is?"

"Do you slurp your ramen?" Cade asks, his expression serious.

"Wait," I say, studying him, "your serious question this whole time has been about *ramen?*"

Cade releases my hand and adjusts his baseball hat. "Well, while honesty is paramount, so is how a woman eats her ramen."

I burst out laughing. "You kill me. All you wanted to know is how I eat ramen and I'm going on about relationships and honesty. I should be mad at you!"

He grins wickedly at me. "But you aren't."

No, I think, *I'm not.*

"Well, honesty obviously means nothing compared to ramen. You have to use your chopsticks. And, yes, I *slurp.*"

Cade twists his face into one of reflection. "So you slurp?"

"Absolutely. In Japanese culture, if you don't, you're insulting the chef." Then I lean across the table. "Do you slurp?"

Cade leans closer to me so we're inches apart. The sexy soap scent lingering on his skin drifts toward me, and my heartbeat quickens in response.

"I slurp," he says, lowering his voice.

"Good to know," I say, anticipation building in me.

"It is. I like a woman who isn't afraid to get serious with a bowl of ramen," he says, moving closer so our mouths are about to touch.

I close my eyes when his hand gently touches my face, caressing it. A shiver shoots down my spine as I feel his palm on my skin.

Oh God, I never dreamed a conversation about slurping could be so hot.

Cade's full lips descend on mine, and my body burns white hot from his brief, soft kiss.

Then he lifts his head.

"So we're ramen compatible," Cade declares.

"Check it off the list," I say.

"Consider it checked," he says, leaning in for another quick kiss.

I drink in every second of our brief kiss, the taste of beer on his lips, his sexy scent, the way his hand constantly caresses my skin whenever his lips find mine.

Cade lifts his head and studies me with his gorgeous eyes.

"How did it take me so long to see you?" he says, his voice etched with amazement as he reaches for my hand across the table again.

"We weren't ready when we first met," I say softly.

But I'm ready for you now, I think as I stare into his eyes. *And I think you're ready for me, too. As long as we move slowly.*

The server reappears with our steamed buns, interrupting our moment.

"Thank you so much," Cade says, smiling at the server.

"You're welcome. Enjoy," she says, retreating to the next table.

"You can't go wrong with these," Cade declares,

inclining his head toward the appetizer sitting between us.

I arch an eyebrow at him. "Are they fluffy on the inside? Like a pillow?"

A smile lights up his face. "Heck, yes."

I giggle. "And the pork belly?"

"It melts in your mouth."

"You're talking an educated game, Cade Callahan," I tease.

Cade stares seriously at me. "Test me. If I'm right, I'll earn another star, which means I get to kiss you. And I have no doubt I *will be* kissing you after you try it."

Ohhhhh!

I put one on my plate. Cade doesn't move. He simply watches me, waiting for me to take a bite.

I pick up a bun, which is open like a taco with pork belly in the center and a dash of hoisin and green onions on top. I decide I want a pure bite first, so I resist the urge to dip it in the sauce provided with it.

I take a slow bite, and I moan in pleasure.

Cade's eyes flicker.

"Mmmm," I murmur. "Oh, God."

I set the rest of my pork bun down and enjoy my bite.

"And the verdict?" Cade asks.

"This," I say slowly, "is *perfection.* Such a wonderfully fluffy, soft bun. The pork belly is succulent. The bit of green onion adds brightness, and there is just the right amount of hoisin glaze."

"I didn't oversell it," he says, a hint of a smile tugging at his mouth.

Damn, he's sexy when he flirts.

"No," I say.

"So I get a kiss."

He leans in, but I put a hand up to stop him.

"I'll taste like hoisin and onions," I protest.

"I really don't care," Cade insists, moving in for his kiss.

I giggle as he brushes his lips against mine.

He lifts his head and looks at me. "You taste perfect."

Ohhhhhh, falling, falling, falling, down the rabbit hole with no way to stop it.

We continue to talk while we eat our steamed buns, and I'm afraid I won't have room for the lobster ramen that will soon come my way.

"These are addictive," I say.

"I know. It's a good thing I skate because I eat here a lot when it gets cold. I love ramen when it's cold out."

"Me, too. It's a great comfort food."

"I thought your comfort food was pasta," Cade teases.

"Oh, yes, because I'm Italian my go-to foods must all be pasta-based," I say dryly. Then I grin at him. "My favorite comfort food is soup. I love soup. But I do love a good ravioli, too."

"Is that what we're going to make on Saturday?"

Swoon. I love that he's looking forward to our night of pasta making after our great outdoors adventure.

"Yes," I say. "Making homemade pasta is one of my favorite things to do. I use the same recipe that has been passed down in the Rossi family since they came over to Chicago from Italy."

"I can't get over the history of that cheesecake recipe, that link to your past," Cade says thoughtfully. "That would make an interesting book. Think about it. Tracing the recipe and the people who made it and what was going on in their lives at the time. I'd love to study that. Does Nonna have all the family recipes collected?"

I don't say anything for a moment. I'm touched that Cade not only remembers the story I told him but has a genuine interest in it.

Which means he has a genuine interest in me, too.

"Yes, Nonna is big on passing down the family recipes," I say. "She's the gatekeeper of the Sunday gravy. It's a big family secret. Only certain Rossi women get to learn that recipe."

"What's Sunday gravy?"

I grin at him. "You're so not Italian."

Cade laughs, and the sound causes warmth to radiate down my spine.

"Yes, my family doesn't do this Sunday gravy thing. Explain."

"Sunday gravy is for the big meal that night. It is a meat-based red sauce, and it takes about four hours to cook. Nonna says it's a sauce of love best cooked while drinking red wine. She waited to teach me the recipe until I turned twenty-one so I could drink with her in the kitchen." Heat creeps up my cheeks. "I got so drunk that afternoon I passed out before dinner."

A gorgeous smile lights up his face. "Your nonna drank you under the table?"

I nod. "Yes, how embarrassing is that?"

"But you know the secret," Cade says, his eyes dancing.

"I do."

"Will you teach me sometime?"

"I could, but you aren't ready now. If you're setting a microwave on fire, you aren't ready for Sunday gravy."

An embarrassed expression filters across his gorgeous face and oh, is he cute when he's self-conscious.

Cade pushes down on his baseball cap. "That was an accident. And so was scorching Jupe's precious Pot Noodle cup."

"You scorched a *noodle cup?*"

Now Cade looks really embarrassed. "Um, yeah. I kind of forgot the water when I nuked it."

"Oh, the smell must have been *awful!*" I cry, delighted that super smart Cade is a total disaster in the kitchen.

"Stop it," Cade says, grinning sheepishly as he shakes his head. "The kitchen is not my place."

"Then you are not ready for Sunday gravy," I declare, shaking my head. "I'm not sure you're ready for ravioli. We might have to start with Pot Noodles."

"No, you promised me pasta," Cade says firmly.

"I did," I say. "And you will get your lesson because I'll never say things I don't mean to you."

Cade's eyes lock on mine. "I believe you," he says, his voice quiet.

The sounds of the city street and the conversations of others on the patio fade away. I realize how important it is to Cade that I am always honest with him. Cassidy must have hurt him with a lack of honesty, but like I said, this isn't a night about her.

It's about Cade and me.

"I won't," I say, speaking from my heart.

No further words are needed to be said. Cade continues holding my hand, his eyes locked on mine, and he's the only thing that exists in my world at this moment.

As terrifying as the thought is, I might reach the bottom of the rabbit hole by the end of the night.

I'm falling for him faster than I've ever fallen for anyone.

While I should slam on the breaks, slow myself down, stop for that yellow light, I don't want to.

I stare back into Cade's jade eyes, the ones gazing at me with nothing but sincerity, and I know I have no intention of stopping my heart tonight.

The only question remains is how far I will fall.

And if Cade is falling with me.

CHAPTER SIXTEEN

I TAKE ONE LAST SLURP OF MY LOBSTER RAMEN AND SIGH loudly. That was the most incredible bowl of ramen I've ever had in my life.

And being able to slurp with abandon because the sexy man in front of me likes my food passion?

Bliss.

"The content, end-of-the-bowl sigh?" Cade asks, slurping from his bowl.

"Let's see," I say. "Perfectly poached lobster claw and tail meat served in liquid gold beurre blanc that is as smooth as velvet? Yes. That was a contented food sigh."

Cade sets his bowl down and wipes his face with his napkin. "It's freaking phenomenal, isn't it?"

"I already want it tomorrow," I joke.

"It's addictive," Cade says, his eyes shining.

"Very," I agree, already hoping Cade will bring me back.

This has been the best date I've ever had. We've laughed. Flirted. Held hands. Kissed across the table.

But best of all, I've been *myself.* Whether that means telling Cade I'm invested or slurping from a bowl in front of him, I'm *me.* Not monitoring my moves. Not afraid to spill broth on my chin. Free to talk about making Sunday gravy or asking him to clarify a history point he's talking about because I don't remember it from school.

This is real.

And I want more of it.

Cade picks up the bill holder and gets out his wallet.

"Thank you for dinner," I say. "My treat next time."

He stops and stares at me. "Your treat?"

"Well, it's only fair."

"I don't know if you've heard this, but professional athletes are compensated very well. You don't need to treat me."

"Yes, I'm aware you get paid an obscene amount of money to take shots on goal and irritate the hell out of opposing players," I tease, "but that doesn't mean I can't treat you, too."

Cade removes some cash and tucks it inside the leather holder, closing it.

"I like how genuine you are."

"I don't know any other way to be."

His eyes lock on mine again, and my pulse quickens in response.

We get up to leave, and Cade puts his hand on the small of my back as we head out. Oh, I love how his hand always finds a way to keep in contact with me.

We walk out into the street, and Cade reaches for my hand, entwining my fingers with his. I'm aware of people taking pictures of him, but he seems oblivious to it.

"So we're going to the grocery store next?" Cade asks.

"Well, it has fallen on my shoulders to not only teach you how to make pasta, but also how to shop for produce."

"Don't forget Sunday gravy."

"Let's start with Microwaving 101."

Cade laughs and puts his arm around my shoulders, drawing me to him and brushing his lips affectionately against my temple.

"Let me guess where you shop. Whole Foods?" he asks.

"That Cornell education has served you well," I tease.

We get into Cade's BMW X5 M, and I still can't get over the fact that his luxury SUV costs more than triple my salary. The SUV is modern, rugged, and sexy.

Just like Cade.

Suddenly my *Golden Girls* ringtone fills the air.

Gah!

"It's my tone for Nonna," I explain. "Let me shut it off."

"Oh, hell no," Cade says as he pulls out into the street. "I want to talk to Nonna. Put it on speaker so I can meet her."

Oh, God. No, no, no! Nonna would totally embarrass me.

Or worse—she could bring up the damn apron.

Shit!

"Um, no, we're on a date," I say, fumbling in my large bag, desperate to shut off my phone. Damn it. I'm getting a small purse with my next paycheck so when I desperately need to shut off my phone, I can actually do it.

Cade clears his throat. "I'm sorry. I shouldn't have asked you that."

The phone stops ringing. I glance over at him, and his light-hearted expression is gone.

"What?"

"Going slow and taking our time doesn't mean conversations with your Nonna during our second date. I never should have asked that. I'm sorry if I put you in an awkward spot. I promised myself I wouldn't jump into things, and here I am, repeating the same freaking mistake."

Oh, no. This is worse than Nonna bringing up the apron. I know we agreed to proceed with caution, but misinterpreting my resistance may bring him to a full stop.

"It's not that," I say, pulling out my phone. "I was afraid she'd say something to embarrass me. I didn't want her to say something to scare you off."

Cade pulls up to a red light, and my heart sinks, wondering if that is where we are now, too.

Stopped.

"What?" Cade asks, a confused expression passing over his face.

Heat burns in my cheeks. "My family is different. They get all in your business. I didn't want to put that on you or have them say something that would leave you wondering how to get out of our date on Saturday."

"Josephine," Cade says, his eyes lingering on my face, "that's not going to happen. No matter what they say."

My heart remains in the pit of my stomach.

"You can't guarantee that," I admit fearfully.

"Yes, I can," Cade says. "Do you not see I'm *crazy* about you? I have to remind myself to slow down. Because I'm not going to mess this up, not like last time—"

He stops abruptly, and I know he's determined not to make the same mistakes he did with Cassidy.

The light turns green, and Cade shifts his attention to driving. In the meantime, I decide to take the risk and call Nonna. When she answers, I put her on speaker.

"JoJo!" Nonna cries excitedly. "I thought I missed you."

Cade's eyes widen the second he hears Nonna's voice. I know I'm proving to him in this moment just how much I like him.

"Nonna, I have you on speaker," I say.

"Why? Are you cooking?"

"No, because I'm out with Cade. We're going to the grocery store."

Silence.

"What? JoJo, why are you going grocery shopping on a date? Are you trying to lull him into a coma? If you are wearing sweats, you have learned nothing from me!"

A huge smile lights up Cade's face.

"Nonna, this is Cade," he says. "It's nice to meet you."

"Hold on, I'm going to do a Connectivity Video Connect," Nonna announces. "Donna-Marie! JoJo is out with Cade. I'm going to do a video chat. Come here so we can both talk to them."

Oh, shit.

Then Nonna hangs up.

"I warned you," I say. "My family is all kinds of crazy."

"I like them already," Cade says, grinning. "Your Nonna is your mom's mother-in-law?"

"I'll need to make you a flow chart, but yes. She lives with them and so does my grandfather, Pop. My brother Anthony lives two doors down with his girlfriend, which mortifies Mom because she wants them married. And Christopher, my other brother, is attending Loyola and lives near campus but comes home for dinner and laundry."

Buzz!

I sigh. It's Nonna with her promised Connectivity Video Connect request.

I hit accept and Nonna—along with my mom—appears on my screen.

"Hi, Nonna. Mom," I say, forcing a smile on my face.

"Why are you grocery shopping?" Nonna asks, getting straight to the point.

"Because I need food," I say simply. "And Cade was nice enough to offer to go with me."

"Let me see Cade," Nonna says.

I point the phone camera at Cade while he drives.

"Hello, Mrs. Rossi," he says. "It's a pleasure to meet you. Sorry I can't see you right now."

"Ohhhhhhhhhhh, but we see you," Nonna says appreciatively. "You're *nice.*"

My face flames. Nice is her word for *hot.*

Then Mom bursts into tears.

"He's so good looking. She's never coming back home," Mom wails.

Shit!

"Mom, stop it. You *knew* I was staying in Denver when I moved here last January," I declare.

"No, no, I thought you'd eventually come home, but I see you're already *grocery shopping* with Cade. You'll never come back now. Not if you're already so comfortable you can do mundane things by the second date!" Mom sobs.

Gah! I turn the phone back on myself.

"Donna-Marie, did you look at him? I wouldn't come back from the North Pole if I had a man like that," Nonna interjects. "Niiiiiiiiiiiicccccce. Whew."

Good Lord. Mom is crying, and Nonna just declared Cade niiiiiiiiiiiicccccce.

Cade will mysteriously come down with the bubonic plague by Friday night.

"Yes, we're shopping because, like I said, I need something called *food.* And I'm teaching Cade how to buy produce while we're there."

Nonna raises her eyebrows.

"That could be fun," she says slowly. "Depending on

the produce being discussed. Be sure to see how fresh the cucumbers are, JoJo."

Cade snorts the second he hears that comment, and Nonna winks at me in return.

My face is on fire.

I've decided I want bubonic plague now.

"Who are you talking to and why are you crying?" Dad yells in the background.

"We're doing a video chat," Nonna yells back, as my family is incapable of merely talking to one another. "The famous hockey player is on it!"

"Cade Callahan is with my daughter right now?"

"She'll never come back to Chicago. She'll stay with her hockey player. They are already *grocery shopping*, Louis! Do you know what that *means?*"

I need something quicker than bubonic plague.

"Do you all realize Cade can *hear you?*" I shout.

Silence, merciful silence finally fills the air.

Thank God.

"I want to have a word with him," Dad says.

So much for that.

I glance at Cade, who looks surprised.

My dad appears on the screen.

"Hi, Daddy," I say.

"I want to talk to Cade," Dad requests again, never one to beat around the bush.

I glance at Cade, who nods in agreement.

"Hello, Mr. Rossi. It's a pleasure to meet you," Cade says, his eyes still straight ahead as he turns into the Whole Foods parking lot.

"I'm going to ask two things of you. One, be good to

my daughter. She's a good girl, and she deserves to be treated well, which she never got from that last idiot she dated."

"I couldn't agree with you more, sir. Josephine is amazing. She's very special, and I swear to you I will treat your daughter with respect. You have my word."

His promise to my dad fills me with warmth. I know how Cade is, and I know he will keep his word to my dad—and me.

"Good, that's what a father wants to hear."

"What is your other request, sir?" Cade asks as he pulls into a parking space and shifts the SUV into park.

"Please do not beat the crap out of Landy Holder like you did last year," Dad says, referring to a player on the Chicago Buffaloes hockey team. "You deserved your time in the box for that hit."

Then my dad laughs, and Cade laughs with him.

"Yes, sir."

"New request. Call me Lou."

"Yes, Lou, I will."

"Well, I can't believe you kids are going to the grocery store for fun, but hey, whatever you want to do. Love you, JoJo. Come on, Donna-Marie. Leave them alone now and that goes for you too, Ma," Dad orders. "Get off the phone."

"Bye, Dad," I say, turning the phone back on me. "Mom, I'll call you tomorrow. Love you both."

I swear he's the best dad ever for getting my over-emotional mother off the phone.

Cade takes the phone back from me and is face-to-face with Nonna.

"Nonna, I've heard so much about you and how much you mean to Josephine," Cade says. "It's an honor to meet you."

"You call her *Josephine?*" Nonna asks, arching an eyebrow.

"Yes, I do," Cade says.

"Interesting," she says slowly, and I know I need to ask her what she means by that later. "My son is right when he says JoJo is very special to us."

To my surprise, Cade reaches for my hand and entwines his fingers around mine as if to tell me he agrees with her.

"I understand why," Cade says. "Because I think she's special, too."

Oohhhhh!

Nonna beams at him. She likes Cade, I can tell.

"Ma! Off the phone!" Dad yells in the background.

"Holy Cannoli, will you stop yelling, Louis? I'm coming!" Nonna yells before turning back to us. "Go do your grocery shopping, but JoJo, do something fun with this boy later, will you please? Although I don't have to tell you what I think you should do for fun with your niiiiicccccccccce boy. And it's not board games."

Then she winks at us.

"Nonna!" I gasp, mortified.

"Ciao!" She grins mischievously. Then she disconnects the call.

"Oh, God," I groan, dropping my phone in my lap and covering my face with my hands. "I'm so sorry."

"Sorry? For what?"

I peek at him through my fingers. He doesn't want to run for the hills after Nonna's last comment?

Of course, it would be rude to dump me at the Whole Foods in Cap Hill. Cade's a nice guy. He'll at least let me get some groceries before dumping me at the apartment building.

Cade pries my fingers open so he can see my face.

"Your family is *great,*" he declares, his eyes shining brightly. I lower my hands and stare back at him. "I love Nonna. She just says whatever the hell she thinks. That's awesome."

"What? No, it's not! Her mental filter broke after she turned sixty! Did you honestly like that cucumber remark?" I blurt out.

"*Heck, yes,* that was hilarious."

"Right."

"Truth."

A hint of a smile plays on his full lips, and I know this whole episode hasn't fazed him.

"What about my dad telling you not to hit Landy Holder?"

Cade grins wickedly at me. "I'm afraid I can't promise that one. I always piss him off when we play each other, and we end up going at it. But you can tell your Dad I think Landy is a great guy off the ice. I got to know him this summer at a training camp sponsored by the sports drink we both do promos for."

Okay. He loves Nonna and is cool with my dad, but what about the worst of it?

"And my over-dramatic, over-emotional mother who thinks I'll never leave Denver because of you?"

Cade reaches for my hand.

"She misses you. I imagine she thought you'd go to Denver, eventually come back, get married, and buy a house two doors down like your brother so she'd see you every day. Your leaving must have been hard for her. The fact that you are starting to date in Denver makes it all the more real for her, that's all."

Once again, I'm struck by how much Cade truly listens to what I say and how perceptive he is. The fact that none of this nonsense right now bothers him and he can look past all the crazy and see me, tells me once again what a good man he is.

"I think you're the special one," I say, squeezing his hand in mine.

Cade leans forward and kisses me, a slow, sweet kiss that sends happiness through me.

He breaks the kiss. "Okay. I can't kiss you anymore or I won't want to go shopping. I will want to take you home and make out with you, and then you'll starve to death and your family will hate me."

"Hmmm, I see why you understand my over-dramatic mother so well."

Cade grins at me. "The sooner we shop, the sooner I can take you home. So we can not play board games."

"While I'm in favor of not playing board games with you," I say, flirting with him, "you aren't getting out of your produce lesson so easily. But we're skipping *cucumbers.*"

Cade bursts out laughing, and I join him.

As we get out of the SUV and walk toward the store, I know I've found something special with Cade.

I glance up at him, looking so masculine in his baseball hat, facial scruff, and plaid shirt, and know every time I'm with him, I give him more of my heart.

There's no one else I want to give it to.

The thought gives me pause.

No matter how amazing Cade is, I still need to proceed with caution. Besides Cade has made it clear he still wants to move slowly, too. I just pray his feelings, however hard he tries to slow them down, are growing in the same way.

CHAPTER SEVENTEEN

Today's Purpose and Passion Statement:

Today I will meet with Tiffany with the purpose of getting feedback on my recipe ideas. This is a huge opportunity to learn from her and I'm going to take full advantage of it. I'm going to ask questions and seek her advice for following my career passions while I have this golden opportunity in front of me. I'm also going to give a full report to Skye regarding any changes and make sure she's comfortable with those, too.

I repeat my purpose and passion statement in my head as I sit down at my desk first thing on Wednesday morning. Today is going to be a *great* day.

I can already tell.

I'm tired from lack of sleep, but staying up late to make out with Cade was more than worth it. I didn't want him to go home last night. We've just discovered each other, but after spending every day with him since Sunday, I already find myself missing him when he's not around.

How can I want to be with him all the time so soon?

Because it's right, my heart whispers.

My face flushes with happiness. It *is* right. I'm so convinced of that, more than ever after our date yesterday. The way we laughed and talked. How he survived my family and oh, the way he caressed me as his lips found mine . . .

I'm letting myself fall.

I think about how I was so sure I was going to act differently this time around. That going slowly was what I needed to do. But now I'm not so sure.

I should have gone slower with *Marco.* I should have used every yellow light to slow down and get to know him better before falling in love with him.

But maybe I don't need that with Cade.

He's not Marco.

Maybe I *can* trust him with all of my heart.

Beep!

I glance at my computer screen and see a new email from Angelique in my inbox. I swear she must have been keeping watch for me so she could send me an email as soon as I sat down. I steel myself and click on it:

From: Angelique.Whitmire-Hox@bakeit!magazine.com
To: Josephine.Rossi@bakeit!magazine.com
Date: September 6
Subject: Assignment

Josephine. While I realize you are working with Tiffany on the Skye Reeve cupcake project, you will continue to receive your regular workload from me. You completed your sugar assignment in regards to the chocolate chip cookies yesterday, however, I feel it would be best to replicate the entire project again to ensure your results are indeed *accurate* because I question the results you achieved. I have also assigned you to do the next part of the cookie test, which is to test various chocolate chips and record the results.

Angelique

By the time I'm finished reading, I'm fuming. There was nothing suspect about my results with the sugar testing yesterday. She's making me replicate it because she's pissed. Why didn't Greg Martin get the chocolate chip assignment? Usually we split the ingredient testing and recipe testing assignments. I can see this will be my punishment. I'll get every ingredient trial this week while Greg gets all the new recipes to test.

Fine. I can play her game. I can test chocolate chips with a smile on my face to spite her crumble and foam-loving self.

I gather up my stuff and head down the hall to Angelique's office. I rap on the door, and she looks up from her laptop.

"I received my assignments. I'll get started on the sugar comparison after I meet with Tiffany," I say.

Angelique smiles at me. "I'm glad to hear that

because your results were so *disappointing.* I knew you had errors the second I read them."

"Oh, I don't think they were wrong, but I'm glad to do it again to prove I'll secure the same result," I say cheerfully.

Ha-ha! Angelique's nostrils flare telling me she's *pissed,* but she quickly recovers and clears her throat.

"Don't be overconfident, Josephine."

"I don't think believing that your proven, recorded result is correct is being overconfident, Angelique."

Angelique narrows her eyes and stares me down. I don't flinch.

"Go meet with Tiffany," she says and resumes typing on her keyboard.

I walk off, thinking I'm so glad I'm confident enough to stand up for my work. If I have to spend the next few months testing ingredients, I'm game. As long as I have this development project with Tiffany, my purpose is met.

And with that thought in my head, I head off to meet with Tiffany.

"I HAVE TO SAY," TIFFANY SAYS, PAUSING TO TAKE A SIP of coffee from her *BOSS LADY* tumbler, "I love these cupcake ideas. They're so whimsical."

"Thank you," I say, feeling pride in my concept.

"I also like how you explained your thought process in your email. I got inside your head for a little bit,"

Tiffany says. "I think you have a playful personality when it comes to your baking, am I right?"

I nod. "I do. With my background, I know a lot of people think I should want to work in a five-star restaurant doing precision pastry, but I find no joy in being confined like that. I want the freedom to use ingredients that speak to my heart. I want people to not necessarily 'oooh' and 'ahhh' over my baking complexity, but think, 'That looks fun, I want to try it!'"

"You seem to know yourself very well," Tiffany says. "Unusual for someone so young. Usually, people your age think they know what they want but are still finding themselves. You, however, seem to know."

"I do know the path I want to take," I say. "I want to be a developer and ghostwrite recipes for cookbooks. That's why I'm here. I want to learn everything I can. I'm very excited to be able to have you oversee me on this project."

"Do you know what I like about you? You're really hungry for this. Your playfulness with baking is exactly the breath of fresh air I want. Whimsical and accessible."

She gets me. It's like Tiffany is inside my head, seeing everything that is whirling in there in regards to my career passions.

"Let me guess, you have a stack of ideas stored in that head of yours."

"I do."

"Tell me two of them."

I tell her about my recent Italian desserts cheesecake fusion idea and then follow up with another one.

"I would love to do a cupcake feature called 'Cupcakes and Cereal,'" I explain. "Each cupcake would feature a different childhood cereal. Cinnamon Toast Crunch, Honeycombs, Cookie Crisp, Fruity Pebbles, Lucky Charms, Trix. I'd like to use my own unique spin on this kind of nostalgia baking. I've studied the back issues. We haven't run a piece with either of these ideas."

Tiffany looks thoughtfully at me. She reaches for her pen and scrawls something on the notepad in front of her.

"I appreciate that you do your homework. You believe in yourself, and you're aggressive enough to go after this. If I like what you do with Skye's cupcakes, we'll discuss another development project. I'm going to turn you loose now with the Valentine's Day project. Why don't you come back next Monday and tell me how it's going? You can schedule your appointment with Monica," she says, referring to her assistant.

Ahhhh! I'm so ecstatic I could burst.

I rise from my seat, smiling at Tiffany. "Thank you so much for your belief in me."

"Hey, when I find talented young people, I like to *keep* them," she says, smiling back. "It's wise investing."

"Well, thank you for taking the time to mentor me," I say. "And for giving me this opportunity."

I head back to my desk so I can check my messages before starting a batch of Skye's cupcakes and another sugar trial.

And so I can text Cade and tell him about the meeting.

I reach for my phone and see I have two new messages: one from Cade and one from Skye.

I open Cade's first. I love how I always start my day by talking to him. I look forward to our little exchanges throughout the day.

Thinking about you. Text me when you can to tell me how your meeting with Tiffany went.

I smile to myself. I've found a good man in Cade.

I text him back:

Just got out. Tiffany believes in me and wants to see me grow. If these cupcakes go well, she'll let me do another development piece. I'm so happy!

I hit send and he replies right back:

That's fantastic! I'm not surprised though. She'd be an idiot not to see your talent. Proud of you. We should celebrate tonight.

Oooh!

I decide to flirt with him:

How so?

Cade responds:

By not playing board games.

My face immediately grows hot as I remember making out with him last night.

Another message from him drops in:

Kidding! I wouldn't invite you over just to not play board games.

Now I'm grinning. I type back:

Well, that's disappointing. I like not playing board games with you.

Another text comes through:

Stop it. I'm trying to behave. Dinner?

My fingers fly across my iPhone:

I'm not coming downstairs for scorched Pot Noodle, Cade Callahan.

There's a pause and then a reply:

You made me spit coffee out on Jupe's dashboard. He's not pleased with either of us. But I'll surprise you with the one dish I can make.

A giggle escapes my throat, and Emily Sharp, the

girl at the desk next to me, glances my way. I recompose myself:

Tell Jupe I'm sorry. And I'll see you tonight. With a fire extinguisher just in case.

I hit send, and I know I'll get an instant response:

HA very funny. But smart on your part.

I say goodbye and flip over to Skye's message:

JoJo, can I ask you a huge favor? I'm thinking about what I want to do for the REAL ME, and I think a good start would be blogging. Writing about life straight from my heart. Would you mind reading my draft and telling me what you think? Whenever, no rush. I emailed it to you. Xo

I access my Gmail and find the message from Skye sandwiched in between emails from Williams-Sonoma and King Arthur Flour.

I click open the attachment and read:

REALITY BLURRED

First of all, thank you to everyone who followed me on my journey on Is It Love? While it didn't end in love for me, I realize this is exactly what was supposed to happen. Looking back on the whole experience and knowing what happened after the show aired, I understand now that the cameras blurred my reality. I put my head aside in favor of my heart while I was on TV.

I pause for a moment. An uneasy feeling runs through me. I feel like she is speaking to *me* with these words. I force myself to continue:

What I realize now is that I was swept up in the idea of love. Tom Broaden was gorgeous, successful, witty, bright—everything I had ever wanted. I didn't go on the show with the idea I'd fall in love. I put my brain in charge at the beginning. But somewhere between the romantic dates and magical kisses, I shut my brain off. I let my heart do the driving, and I made the mistake of putting my brain in the backseat. I knew he was different. He was special. I fell immediately, something I had never done before. But after Tom told me it wasn't love, I realized I had never listened to my head. Not once during the whole process.

One thing is clear to me now: you can't fall in love within days of meeting someone. Real love takes time. It takes time to truly know someone. You can't do that in a week. You can't even do it in six weeks, which is the length of time I was on the show. Lasting love isn't instant.

My stomach sinks as I read her words. Skye did everything I'm doing now. With a sick feeling washing over me, I continue:

I will never make that mistake again. After watching the show back, I see how in love I was with Tom. How eagerly I jumped all in. How wrong that was. Next time, I'll take my time.

Just like true love does.

I stop reading. I swallow against the lump that has formed in my throat. This time, it's not Tiffany reading what is in my brain. It's Skye. And I was meant to receive this warning.

Cade is everything I want. It's *magic* when we're together. He's sexy, caring, smart, and funny. Successful. Driven. He loves my passionate side.

But I can't be this stupid. Not after Marco.

The message is clear.

Cade wants to go slowly, to see if this could eventually be love for him. He's *told* me that. He's not going to make the same mistake and rush in. And I shouldn't either. While my heart is screaming at me to go all in, I can't listen to it. I can't.

I need to be careful. I need to proceed with caution. Even if my heart wants me to open up, I need to remain silent. I need to think in terms of one date at a time. I can't think of anything beyond that, no matter what my heart tries to tell me.

Because while Marco *hurt* me, I have a feeling if Cade were to walk away, the damage would be far, far worse.

It would devastate me.

And I can't let that happen.

CHAPTER EIGHTEEN

TODAY'S PURPOSE AND PASSION STATEMENT:

Today's purpose is to learn all about one of Cade's biggest passions: fishing. We're headed up to Boulder early this morning for fishing on a private pond. I know this is a big deal for Cade to share this part of himself with me. I just hope my lack of outdoor experience doesn't ruin his day. But tonight we're making pasta together, and I'm very excited to share my passion with him. I mean pasta making passion. Not passion-passion. Although as I type this, that doesn't sound like a bad idea either . . .

I HIT SAVE ON MY FILE, ELECTING NOT TO PRINT THIS personal statement and hang it in the kitchen for obvious reasons. I close my laptop and grab my canvas tote bag. It's still black outside, as it's like six in the morning, but Cade wanted to be in Boulder by seven, so here I am.

City girl Josephine Rossi, preparing for an adventure in the great outdoors.

With a beautiful man I can't stop thinking about.

I get up from bed and check my reflection in the mirror one more time. I'm dressed in jeans and a navy T-shirt, with a red and navy flannel shirt thrown over the top. I've pulled my hair up into a high ponytail, and I am wearing my usual bare minimum of makeup. I find I need less these days. I really have a glow about me. My eyes are sparkling. My cheeks naturally flush. I'm happy and excited.

All because of Cade Callahan.

While I *know* every date with Cade is just that, a date, I hope with all my heart that his feelings are progressing like mine have started to. But while my feelings are growing, I need to remember to heed Skye's warning and stay cautious.

I throw a bottle of sunscreen into my tote and head into the living room. As I do, my phone vibrates inside the bag.

I grin, knowing it is Cade.

I retrieve my phone and read his text:

If you happened to order a fishing guide for today, he's right outside your door.

Oh, *serious* swoon.

I open the door and find Cade standing before me, looking all kinds of *hot* in a gray Henley with a white T-shirt peeking out from underneath and khaki shorts that reveal his muscular legs. His facial scruff is full, like he hasn't shaved, and his longish dark locks once again peek out teasingly from underneath his maroon Denver Mountain Lions baseball hat.

And once again I get butterflies at the mere sight of him. While locking the door, I can feel Cade's eyes lingering on my face.

"You look sexy, Josephine," Cade says, his voice low.

I feel myself blush as I slip the key into my bag.

"Didn't you say my off the shoulder shirts were sexy?" I tease.

"Of course they are," Cade says as we walk toward the elevator. "But this . . . you in flannel and a ponytail. You look beautiful at this awful hour . . . and you're going fishing with me. All of this is a turn-on."

Then, as if to punctuate the point, he stops walking, draws my body to his, and presses his mouth to mine with urgency.

I burn with heat the second his mouth claims mine. His stubble scratches against my face, I taste mint toothpaste on his tongue, and I smell the glorious scent of his soap that lingers on his tan skin.

Cade breaks the kiss, and I draw in a breath of air. He slowly traces his thumb over my lower lip, and my body shivers in response.

"You are very hot right now," he says, his voice low.

I'm about to suggest we skip fishing when he takes my hand in his.

"Come on, let's head out for Boulder."

He leads me to the elevator and presses the down button.

"Do you know I've lived here for nine months and I've never been to Boulder?" I ask.

Cade shoots me a quizzical look. "Really? It's only forty-five minutes from here."

"I know, and I'm sure it's a happening town what with the University of Colorado there, but this is the first time I've ventured outside of Denver."

"Then I'm glad we're taking this adventure together," Cade says, his eyes locking on mine.

Adventure, I think, staring up at the handsome face I'm getting to know. I'm going on an adventure, but not in the way Cade is thinking. I'm taking an adventure with Cade. With romance.

And, most of all, with my heart.

"CADE, THIS DRIVE IS *BEAUTIFUL*," I SAY IN WONDER, staring at the mountains surrounding us on this gorgeous September day. The sun is bathing the mountains in a golden glow, and it's a spectacular sight to behold.

Cade nods as he keeps his eyes on the road. "That's why I love coming out here. Boulder is at the base of the mountains, so you get this fantastic view. You should see the Flatirons," he continues. "You can hike trails up sandstone formations. It's fantastic. In a few weeks, the trees will be crimson and gold. That is when it is really breathtaking."

"This is my first autumn here," I say. "I'd love to see that."

"Between October fifth and twentieth is the best time to see them, because the first snow will fall and you can get the colors of the trees against the snow-capped mountains. I don't have my game schedule memorized, but we'll come back and hike and take pictures of it sometime."

We'll come back.

Happiness fills every part of me as those words replay in my head.

"I'd love that," I say, smiling. Then I remember I'm terrible at outdoors stuff. "But, um, I've never hiked before."

Cade takes another bend in the road, heading to our destination, which he said is a teammate's house that is situated on a private fishing pond.

"Really?" Cade asks. "Not even once?"

"Nope."

"I grew up hiking in the Hudson Valley. We did it all the time as a family when I was young. And my favorite spot you could handle. The FDR National Historic Site. I walk that trail a lot when I'm back home. I think of how beloved Roosevelt's home was to him," he says, his voice growing with enthusiasm as he refers to the legendary American president. "Springwood was his lifelong home and central to who he was. Eleanor Roosevelt said he went there for rest. Peace. Strength. It was so important to him that he returned more than 200 times during his presidency. Can you imagine being so connected to a place like that?

"You feel the past as you walk in the present," Cade continues eagerly. "I think of how many decisions he made overlooking those grounds. The leaders who came there, like Winston Churchill and King George VI. What they talked about changed the world. And that is powerful."

I study him in awe. Cade is so passionate about history and what it means, and he has an amazing ability to connect with that. He's *mindful* of it. I picture him walking those woods, thinking of the history on the grounds before him, and appreciating the power of a place in the heart of one of our greatest leaders.

He abruptly stops talking.

"Shit, I'm sorry," Cade says, frowning. "That was probably more than you ever cared to hear about FDR outside of American history class."

"No, no, I love hearing you talk. You have no idea what a pleasure it is to hear you speak about your passion."

Cade doesn't say anything as he turns into a neighborhood with older, bigger homes, spread out between each other on acres of land with the mountains looming as a gorgeous backdrop.

"You're a sweetheart to say that."

I furrow my brow. "No, I mean it. I don't say things I don't mean, remember? I can't *wait* for you to start working on your book, Cade. It will be written in the same energy you have when you share your love of history. You make me want to walk that trail. I want to see it all through your eyes."

"Thank you," Cade says.

"For what?"

"You understand me."

I don't say anything, but say everything by reaching for his free hand and placing mine over his.

Cade squeezes my hand, and nothing needs to be said.

Even though it's early, and we have such a long way to go, this feels right.

Unlike anything I've ever felt before.

"So you've never hiked a trail?"

"Um, let me think. No. Unless it's the trail from the front to the back of Williams-Sonoma," I tease.

Cade's face lights up in a beautiful smile.

"Then we have another adventure ahead of us."

Oooh!

"Well, if we're planning all these adventures, I guess I need to get on it and come up with one for you," I say.

"The trail of upscale kitchen wares?"

"Maybe. Maybe not. I'm full of surprises," I declare.

"That you are. You continually surprise me," Cade says.

"What? How? I've never been called surprising in my life."

"Boy, you really don't see what I see, do you?" Cade says, turning his BMW down another road.

"What do you see?" I ask, feeling brave.

"That answer will have to wait until later because we've arrived."

Damn it.

Cade turns into a long circular drive, and his teammate's house comes into view. Not at all what I expected, either. It's an older home, I'd guess built in the mid-sixties or seventies, a split-level style nestled among lots of trees. It doesn't look like something a young, single professional athlete would own.

"And this would be Maxime's house," Cade says. "Or *Maxine,* as we call him in practice."

"Oh, I bet he *loves* that," I say.

Cade grins. "Yeah. We call him *Maxine* to piss him off. He's from Belgium. His name is Maxime Laurent. Max is a good guy," he says, stopping right behind a Jaguar F-Pace luxury SUV. "I wouldn't be close to him if he weren't."

I nod, as I feel this is true. Cade surrounds himself with good people. Like Jude. So I'm guessing Maxime is the same.

"This doesn't look like a house a player would have," I muse aloud. "This is a family house. Besides, it's so far from Denver."

"Once you meet Max, you'll get it," Cade explains, shutting off the engine. "This is his Springwood."

And as I get out of the car and look at Cade, with the sun of the new day shining down on him, I want nothing more than for him to find his own Springwood, too.

"Come on," Cade says, taking my hand and walking me to the front door. "We'll let Max know we're here, then we can get our fishing stuff and head around to the back."

Cade told me Maxime has his own private pond in his backyard, so we have the luxury of fishing in privacy today.

We reach the door, and Cade rings the doorbell. I hear multiple dogs barking and then some French being spoken, and then the barking stops. The door opens, and my eyes widen as I see Maxime for the first time.

If I didn't know better, I'd think he was a model, not a hockey player.

He's not as tall as Cade, but I'd say 6'2. Mid-twenties. Maxime's hair is thick and wavy and a stunning blend of blond and brown. His eyes are a piercing blue-green shade, and he smiles when he sees us.

"Cade, glad you could come out," Maxime says with a heavy French accent, and I find I have to concentrate to understand him. "Come on in."

As we step inside the house, I see the interior has been updated. The floor plan is airy and open, filled with lots of windows and pale gray walls. The sunlight is now cascading through, shining on the gray-toned wood floors.

"Thanks for letting us fish on your pond," Cade says as he gives Maxime a fist bump. "Max, this is Josephine Rossi. Josephine, this is Maxime Laurent."

"Nice to meet you," he says, extending his hand to mine.

"JoJo," I return, shaking his hand. "Pleasure to meet you, too."

"Cade talked a lot about you when we were skating this week," Max says, smiling at me. "He never talks about anything interesting, so it was a welcome change," he teases.

I like Max already.

"I'm only nice to you because you have a fishing pond," Cade insists. He bends down to pet one of the two big, identical, long-haired black dogs sitting behind Max.

"Your dogs are beautiful," I say, studying them.

"Thank you. They are *Chien de Berger Belge.* Belgian Sheepdogs," he immediately translates. "The one putting up with Cade is Amé. This one," he says, bending down and ruffling the other dog's thick fur, "is Henri. You can pet them. They're good dogs. Aren't you, Henri?"

Max stands up as I bend down to let Henri sniff my hand, and once he does, I pet him, stroking his long hair with my fingers.

"Make yourselves at home," Max says. "I'm going to take these two up to the Flatirons today for a walk. We'll be gone for a while. I want to go before the trails get crowded. There's *good* coffee in the kitchen, Beyers from Belgium, help yourself."

I stand up and watch as Max throws a baseball hat over his luxurious locks, tosses a flannel shirt over his white T-shirt, and grabs two leashes sitting on the hall entry table.

Cade gets up and smiles. "Max thinks our American coffee is shit."

"It is," Max says easily. "Oh, and in return for using my pond, I expect fish and chips for lunch when I get back."

"Now you sound like Jupe," Cade says, laughing.

Max laughs with him. "I miss fish and chips. You can't get a decent chip in the States, they aren't cut right, I can't eat them without mushy peas," he says in a fake British accent to mimic Jude.

"Mushy peas?" I ask, curious.

"I'm surprised he hasn't forced Sierra to figure out how to make them," Cade says.

I grin. "Because she hates peas, that's why."

"That's *hilarious.* I'm so giving him shit about that later."

"I'm still giving you shit about thinking Americans know what a good cup of coffee is," Max adds over his shoulder as he heads out the door.

As soon as the door shuts behind him, I turn to Cade. "I can see why you're friends with him. He's nice."

"He's a great guy. I think they'll name him alternate captain this year," Cade says. "They should. He's a quiet leader. That's why he likes to live out here. It's private, and that's how he likes to live off the ice."

Cade takes my hand and leads me into the living room. We move past a comfy-looking, black sectional and to a set of large windows that give us a view of huge deck out back. Towering trees frame a private pond, and it's beautiful.

"This is all his?" I ask in amazement.

"Yeah. Come on," Cade says, opening the door that leads to the deck.

We step outside and onto a huge patio where there's another sectional seating area. To my left, I see a breathtaking view of the Rockies. I hear nothing except the sounds of water lapping in the pond, birds chirping, and wind gently moving the leaves in the trees.

We don't say anything for a moment, content to take in the view and let the autumn sun warm our skin.

"This is why I love Colorado," Cade says eventually, breaking the silence. "The openness, the rugged beauty, the peacefulness of the sunrise over the mountains."

I nod. "It's so different from Chicago," I say. "I never thought I could fall in love with another place outside of home, but when I see this, these views, and that I get to see what nature created every day, it does speak to me in a way I never dreamed."

I glance at Cade. *Like you speak to me,* I think, staring up at him.

A mischievous smile slowly spreads across his face. "I'll make an outdoor girl out of you yet."

"Okay, you just hold on there, cowboy," I say, giggling. "I don't even know how to put a worm on a hook. Or do we even use worms?"

Cade throws his head back and laughs. "Hold on. I'll get my gear."

I watch as he heads back inside the house, and I wrap my arms around myself as a feeling of complete joy washes over me.

I never dreamed I'd be here. I'm in the Rockies. About to fish. Surrounded by trees and mountains and a glorious sunrise in Colorado.

With a man I'm falling rapidly for.

Nine months ago, my future was set on a different path. I moved here to start my dream job. I thought Marco would eventually join me. We'd get engaged. Enjoy life in Denver before relocating back to Chicago.

I remember I was devastated when that all fell apart.

But now I understand why it did.

I wasn't meant to live that life.

But I might be meant to live one with Cade.

I hear the door open and turn to find Cade returning with two fishing poles, a net, and a tackle box. He's in his element. Cade's rugged and outdoorsy, and I know this brings him as much pleasure as baking does me.

"Do you want a cup of Max's 'this-is-not-crap-American-coffee' before we get started?" he asks as he walks up to me.

"No, I'm still good from the lattes we got before we hit the road," I say.

"Okay, let's do this," Cade says.

I walk down the steps of the deck to the grass below. Cade follows me and puts the gear down by the edge of the pond.

"I've never held a fishing pole," I admit.

"I have serious issues with how you were raised," Cade teases.

"Come on. Do you see Nonna fishing?"

"No, I see Nonna baking cannoli shells and drinking wine."

"There you go."

He smiles, and I smile back. Then he bends down and picks up a pole, checking the end of it. "Okay, this has a little weight on it. Come here, you."

I move next to him, and Cade slides behind me, pressing his chest against my back and putting the pole in my hand. He bends down lower so he can speak into my ear.

"Okay," he says, his voice murmuring sexily against my skin, "body position is key."

Heat burns through me. Who knew fishing could be hot?

Cade puts his hands on my hips and gently swivels me forward.

"You need to be square, just like this," he instructs.

Oh, dear God. How can I think about fishing now? *How?*

"This is a spincast reel," Cade says, putting his hand over mine and demonstrating how to reel and use the release button. We practice dropping the line and reeling it back up.

Cade explains how to cast the line into the water. "Have your hands at waist level," he says, lowering them down. "Now, you're going to hold the release button while you pull your arm back, okay?"

I nod as Cade and I move the rod together, straight back, and then forward.

"Release it," he instructs at the right moment.

I watch as the line flies to the center of the pond, then, plunk! It hits the water.

"We did it!" I say gleefully.

"Your first cast. There you go," Cade says. "Now reel it back in."

"That was so cool!"

"Wait until you catch something," Cade says.

I bring the line in, and Cade takes the pole from my hand.

"I'll put a lure on it," he says, moving over to his tackle box.

"I can't wait to try it again," I say.

I spy Cade's other pole lying on the ground and pick it up while he works. I can't resist wanting to try casting on my own, so I follow his steps. First, I hold the release button. Then, I carefully flick the pole back. Next, I swing it forward while releasing the button.

But instead of the pole coming forward and the line casting out, it sticks. I instinctively flick the pole again.

"*Dammit!*" Cade yells, breaking the calm. "Son of a bitch!"

I whirl around and see my fishing line attached to Cade's leg.

The metal hook is through his knee.

"Oh, my God!" I drop the pole and rush toward him. Nausea runs through me as I see the metal hook attached to his kneecap, in one side and out the other.

I freeze. There's a hook through his knee! I put a fishhook in Cade! It's so gross. I'm going to be sick. I can't look at, I can't, I can't, I'm going to throw up—

"Josephine, it's okay," Cade says calmly. "I can get it out. Go to the tackle box and get the pliers so we can cut the line. Can you do that?"

I'm dizzy.

Everything is spinning.

Cade's lips are moving, but I don't hear anything.

My vision is fading.

And I think I'm about to pass out.

CHAPTER NINETEEN

I BLINK, CONFUSED AS I FIND CADE LEANING OVER ME with a worried expression on his face. I see the sky and clouds and what? Am I on the *ground?*

"Thank God," Cade says, gently stroking my hair with his hand. "You scared the shit out of me, Josephine!"

"Wh-what happened?" I ask. I'm so confused as to why I'm looking at the sky. I feel weak, as if all the energy has been sucked right out of me.

"You passed out," Cade explains. "I caught you before you hit the deck."

"Oh, God," I say, mortified beyond belief.

"How do you feel?"

I close my eyes and decide not to answer with "embarrassed."

"Weak."

"You need to lay here and rest. Don't move. Don't even try to sit up, okay?"

I nod because getting up seems impossible at the moment.

Then I remember what we were doing before I felt sick.

Cade.

Fishhook.

In his knee.

"Did you get the hook out?" I blurt out, concerned.

"What? No," Cade replies, shaking his head.

"Cade, get it out!" I cry, growing upset. "Your knee, I hurt you. I'm so sorry. I'm so, so, sorry!"

"Hey, hey, hey, I'm fine," he says firmly. "I'm more worried about *you*."

"Please go get the hook out. Please. Now. I can't stand it."

"Close your eyes. I don't want you to see me in case it makes you sick again."

I shut my eyes and focus on breathing the crisp autumn air. I hear Cade get up, noises like he's rifling through his fishing box, then the back door open and close.

As I lay in silence, I realize what a freaking mess I've made of our date, and I feel sick to my stomach all over again.

I lodged a fishhook through his *knee*. What if he's hurt? What if he can't play hockey in camp next week? Panic grips me. Oh, no, no, I pray that's not the case.

Then, if that weren't enough, I passed out in front of him. I've never passed out in my life! So instead of getting the hook out of his knee, he's had to catch me, with a *fishing pole* attached to his leg, and bring me back to consciousness.

And we've been outdoors for oh, all of about ten minutes?

I fight back tears. Being outdoors is important to Cade. It's part of his *soul,* and I'm a miserable failure at anything involving nature.

No wonder he wants to go slowly. Cade can get out of this now and find a girl who won't destroy his career with a fishing pole, who already knows how to hike, and who won't pass out during a date.

I know his ex, Cassidy, loved nature. Their social media footprint still exists, and when I Googled him I saw pictures of them hiking, going out on lakes, kayaking. In other words, a glamorous, adventurous couple.

Cade has gone from a beautiful blond who knew how to zip line to a baker who is lying on the deck of his friend's house because she freaked out over seeing a hook embedded in his knee.

I hear the door open and close again, and I open my eyes as Cade walks toward me. I try to sit up, but get woozy, and he lunges forward to help me lie back down.

"No, don't get up," he instructs. "All I want you to do is lie here."

"How is your knee? Do you need to go to a hospital?" I ask urgently. I glance over at it, and see it's wrapped in white gauze and oh, I'm about to cry.

Cade furrows his brow. "What? *Why?*"

"Will you be able to skate at camp next week?" I ask, my voice growing thick.

"Hey, hey, there's no need to get upset," Cade says, stroking my hair gently. "It's superficial. I'm fine, absolutely *fine.*"

"You're not just saying that?"

"No, I promise I'm good. I wouldn't lie to you, remember?"

Cade shifts so he's behind me and gently lifts up my head and rests it in his lap. I gaze up at him, and he's staring down at me with the sweetest expression on his face.

"Okay," I sniffle. Then I clear my throat. "I'm sorry I ruined our day."

"You didn't ruin our day. What are you talking about?"

"Cade. Please. I'm a disaster outside. You just experienced it firsthand!"

"You are not," he says, bending down and brushing his lips against my forehead.

Relief runs through me. Okay. This isn't going to send him running.

At least not today.

And if I'm taking a page out of Skye's playbook, that's all I can grab onto right now.

"I'm kind of flattered, actually," Cade says, interrupting my thoughts.

"What?"

"That you are trying to *hook me* so early in the dating game," he teases, his eyes shining mischievously at me.

Oh, I adore him.

"Stop," I say, trying to repress a smile.

"You want to *reel me in.* Trying to get me *hook, line, and sinker.*"

That does it. I burst out laughing, and Cade joins me.

"There," Cade says, smiling down at me and brushing his fingertips affectionately against my cheek. "That's what I wanted to hear."

"This doesn't bother you?" I ask bravely. "That I suck at outdoorsy stuff?"

"Does it bother you that I don't know how to cook a freaking Pot Noodle?"

"Nope."

"Same."

I reach my hand up and stroke the facial hair on his face.

"Maybe I should just sit on the deck and watch you fish," I say.

Because a repeat performance of what just happened is the last thing I can deal with.

"Why don't you continue to lie here, and in about a half-hour, if you are up for it, we'll do it again. And I'll make sure there is a lure on your hook before you pick up the pole."

"Okay. But stand far away from me so there's no chance I can hurt you."

"I don't think you would hurt me, Josephine."

My breath catches in my throat. Cade is staring down seriously at me, and I know he's not talking about fishing.

"Besides," Cade says, lowering his hands to my hip

bones and running his fingertips sexily across them, "I'll need to put you in the proper position, remember?"

My pulse burns white hot as his hands skim back and forth across my hips.

"Yes," I say, desire filling me.

And as he bends over and presses his full lips to mine for a slow, sensual upside down kiss, I realize the great outdoors with Cade is the *only* place I want to be.

CHAPTER TWENTY

My opinion of the great outdoors has vastly changed today.

I love it.

Or, rather, I love sharing it with Cade.

Warmth radiates through me while I get ready to make pasta dough with Cade for dinner tonight.

While I'm still mortified about the fishhook and fainting episode, the rest of the date turned out to be incredibly romantic. Cade stayed with me on the deck until I could sit up, kissing me, stroking my hair, and comforting me until my energy returned.

Then we gave fishing another shot, with Cade guiding me the whole time. His hands on my hips, shifting me into position and adjusting my form. His voice in my ear. He was so excited when I started casting on my own, and I was ecstatic when I got a bite on my line. With Cade's help, I reeled in my first fish—a trout! Of course, we had to take pictures of me holding it before I released it back into Max's pond.

I understand the enjoyment Cade finds in fishing. It's quiet and peaceful. While Cade might not have found his version of FDR's Springwood yet, he can renew himself by spending time outdoors until he does.

Now it's my turn to share something of myself with Cade: my passion for making fresh pasta.

I smile as I ready the ingredients. After returning from Boulder, we went our separate ways to prepare for tonight. First, I indulged in a hot bubble bath. Afterward, I put on my Yves Saint Laurent Black Opium moisturizer and perfume, making sure I sprayed the tops of my shoulders as Cade loves that spot on me.

I slipped into a pair of white skinny jeans and another off-the-shoulder blouse, this time a nude-colored one that looks beautiful against my olive skin. I wound my hair up into a loose chignon at the nape of my neck, and I put in my white pearl Kendra Scott earrings as my accessory. I finished by applying my standard makeup: a touch of mascara, some eyeliner, and my signature rosy-pink lipstick. Now I'm ready for the second half of our date.

I place the board I use for making dough on the countertop and feel the butterflies dance excitedly in my stomach as I anticipate the evening. Sierra is spending the night downstairs with Jude, so we have the place to ourselves.

Buzz!

I reach for my phone and see it's Cade.

On my way up. Can't wait to see you.

My heart soars as I read his words. He's just as eager to continue this date as I am. As if the hours we spent alone together today weren't nearly enough.

Within minutes there's a knock at the door. I eagerly open it and let Cade in.

My pulse quickens the second I see him. Gone are the casual flannel shirt and shorts that he had on earlier. Cade's now dressed in a long-sleeved, pale blue dress shirt, one that is opened sexily a few buttons at the neck to reveal his skin, with dark jeans and black dress shoes.

He's gorgeous.

Cade's jade eyes grow intense as they move over me, skimming down my off-the-shoulder blouse to my waist, and his jade eyes grow intense by the time they meet mine.

"You look gorgeous tonight," he says as he slides his hands up to my face.

He kisses me slowly, lingering, his tongue teasing me a bit before he stops.

I gaze up at him, at the beautiful soul who is capturing my heart, and frame his handsome face in my hands.

"And you look very handsome," I say, caressing his skin and feeling his stubble underneath my fingertips.

I give him a quick kiss on the lips, and we move into the apartment. I shut the door, and after I do, Cade winds his muscular arms around my waist and draws me closer so I'm snuggled up against his massive chest.

I can't get over how right this feels, how familiar, how amazingly perfect I fit in Cade's arms.

Like this is the place where I'm meant to be.

"Handsome enough to learn your pasta recipe?" he asks, interrupting my thoughts. Then he drops a sweet kiss on the top of my head.

I smile as the wonderfully crisp fabric of his dress shirt presses against my cheek.

"Oh, you're more than handsome enough to learn my recipe, if that were my criteria, but it's not," I declare.

Cade steps back from me, his eyes flickering with amusement.

"So why are you sharing your pasta recipe with me then?"

"Someone needs to teach you how to cook a dinner that doesn't risk a microwave being blown up. But you must be brave. Not only are you going to learn to make dough, but you will have to boil water. On the *stove*."

Cade rubs his hand over his face. "Shit. Things just got *real* in here."

I can't help it. I crack up, and he does, too.

"Oh, it's so real. I take my dough very seriously. It's my art. We should get started, because it has to rest for an hour before we can run it through the pasta roller."

"Do I get to run the roller?"

"Prove yourself with the dough first, and I'll think about it," I tease.

"You sound like Coach Kelly," Cade says, referring to the head coach of the Denver Mountain Lions.

"Yes, I'm your pasta coach," I quip.

I take his hand in mine and lead him to the kitchen.

"Hey, where's your apron?" Cade asks as he heads over to the sink.

I grin. "I don't wear aprons on date night," I say.

"Ah, I see," Cade says, turning on the water.

While he washes his hands, I pour us two glasses of chardonnay.

"White wine?" Cade asks, eying the bottle.

I nod. "Yes. I pair the wine with the sauce, and this one goes perfectly with *Raviolo al' uovo,*" I explain. "The ravioli is filled with fresh ricotta cheese, but tucked in between the sheets of pasta is a golden egg yolk, placed right on top of the ricotta. You simmer the pasta for a few minutes, then transfer it to the pan with the sauce, which tonight will be sage brown butter. The ravioli is heated in the sauce and then served. When you cut it, if it's prepared right, the egg yolk will flow from the center, creating a sauce of liquid gold on the plate. Nothing is sexier than a taste of the delicious pasta, that creaminess of the ricotta with that rich brown butter. Every bite is pure *decadence.*"

I stop speaking and realize Cade is staring at me.

"You're incredibly sexy when you talk about food," he says slowly.

"Food can be very sexy," I manage to say as heat fills me. "It's texture. Color. Taste. Aroma. Eating should be a sensory experience. Something to be savored. Enjoyed."

"I see," Cade says, his eyes flickering.

Oh, God.

Neither one of us is thinking about food right now.

I turn to my pasta board, and Cade moves next to me, his powerful arm brushing against mine as we stand in the galley kitchen. The chemistry between us is so intense I can barely focus.

"Okay, the first thing we're going to do is measure the flour on the board," I say, putting flour in my measuring cup. "We want to create a large well in the center for the eggs."

I dump the flour on the surface and move it around with my fingertips to create a well, fully aware of Cade's body leaning into mine as I work.

"I want you to crack the eggs into the center of the well," I say to Cade. "Crack all those that I have in that bowl there," I say, inclining my head toward it.

"Okay," he says, reaching for an egg.

Cade cracks it against the side of the bowl, and then dumps it in the center, repeating the process with the remaining eggs. I add olive oil and water, and a pinch of truffle salt for extra depth of flavor.

"Now we're ready to incorporate the ingredients, but we don't want to break the well," I say, picking up a fork and beginning to move the flour carefully into the center. "Otherwise you'll have eggs running across the board."

"Here," I say, handing Cade the fork. "You try."

Cade takes the fork and stares at it as if he's afraid to use it.

"It's flour and eggs. It won't hurt you," I tease.

"Right."

I can't help but smile. He's as out of place here as I was this morning at the pond.

He takes the fork but gets too ambitious and cracks the well, sending egg running.

"Dammit," he cries, dropping the fork. "It's oozing out!"

I move my hand and catch the egg mixture, pressing it back into the center and reforming the flour.

"Cooking is messy and imperfect," I say easily, wiping my hands on a towel. "Which is what I love about it."

"I didn't ruin it?" Cade asks.

"No, not at all," I say, smiling.

I take the fork and begin to work it together.

"Now we can knead it," I declare. "I love this part. You are bringing all these elements together and making them into something beautiful, something that provides you endless creative opportunities when finished. Give me your hands."

"What?" Cade asks, confused.

"Give me your hands," I repeat.

He extends his hands, and I put them over the dough, pressing my hands over his.

"You have to put your weight into it," I say, moving his hands in the motion of kneading. "We're going to use your palms and fold and knead. We want to stretch the dough."

I show him what to do. His hands are so big and strong that touching them is completely undoing me.

This experience is sexy. Intimate. Unlike anything I've ever done before.

"Does this feel right, Josephine?" Cade asks.

I glance up at him. He's no longer kneading but staring at me with nothing but heat burning in his eyes.

He's not talking about pasta dough.

"When it's done, it's smooth," I manage to say. "It feels like velvet underneath your fingers. That's when it feels right."

"Like this does?" Cade asks.

I have never felt sexual tension like this in my life.

"Yes," I whisper. "Like this."

Suddenly his mouth is on mine, hot, seeking, completely desperate for me. His hands are moving everywhere, and I rake my fingers through his hair, not caring that flour and dough are getting all over the place. He rolls me back against the counter, kissing me desperately, his tongue taking me with urgency.

In one swift move, he lifts me up to the countertop, sending dough and flour crashing as the board slips and falls to the floor. Flour and dough splatter us, but we don't stop. I wrap my legs around his waist while his hands undo my hair. His scorching kisses continue to burn my lips.

He rips his mouth away and presses it against my neck, his tongue dancing across the top of my shoulders. I shudder violently against him, my hands clutching at his dress shirt as a primal need to rip it takes over.

His mouth continues to burn against my skin while his hands climb up my ribcage. I tighten my legs around him, desperate for one thing.

Cade abruptly stops kissing me and jerks his head up. He puts his hands on my face, his eyes locked on mine, his breathing ragged.

"I want you," he says urgently. "I want to make love to you. I want it so badly I can't hold back, I can't. I didn't plan for this tonight. But after being with you today, seeing your passion, feeling what you feel, knowing how beautiful you are, I can't hold it inside. I need to be with you. *Only you.*"

My heart pounds furiously against my ribs as I take in his words. *He's attracted to me for my soul.*

Just as I am to his.

I search his eyes and I see desire, but not just for my beauty. But for the passionate woman I am *inside*. When Cade said he wanted all of me, he means more than physical.

I cup his face with my hands. "I want this. So much," I say, staring deeply into the eyes of the man I'm falling for, knowing I'm making the choice to live in the moment. "I want you, too."

Cade replies by passionately kissing me. I moan in protest when he breaks the kiss, but he ignores me and scoops me up from the countertop and carries me down the hallway. He takes me to my room, and we both fall back onto my bed.

His hard, muscular body presses against me, pinning me to the mattress, and our bodies entwine together with us fumbling with our sticky hands and flour-dusted bodies to remove clothing. I unbutton his shirt, moving my hands over his gloriously defined muscles and across the sexy Asian lettering tattooed along his ribcage. Heat surges through me as I do, and I begin kissing him all over. He's sculpted and hard and I don't want to stop touching him.

Cade removes my shirt and pushes himself up to gaze down at me, and my chest rises and falls at a rapid rate when he begins teasing me by tracing his fingertips over the delicate lace covering my nude strapless bra. I'm trembling with need for him. To feel all of him. To see what we are like together.

"Do I need protection?" Cade asks.

"I'm on the pill," I say, running my hands over his powerful arms, the ones that are going to hold me tonight.

"Good," he whispers, moving his hand around my back.

White heat shoots through me as he removes my bra. Cade stares at me for a moment, his eyes moving over me as I lie before him.

"You're perfect, Josephine."

Then, to my surprise, he lowers his mouth and places a gentle kiss between my breasts.

Over my heart.

Tears fill my eyes from the pure sweetness of his kiss.

I know, without a doubt, I'm not just having sex with Cade tonight.

I'm going to make love to him.

As we kiss and our bodies entangle again, I know I've hit the bottom of the rabbit hole.

I've fallen for Cade.

And there's no going back now.

CHAPTER TWENTY-ONE

I'VE NEVER HAD SEX LIKE THIS IN MY LIFE.

I stare up at Cade, who is gazing down at me, after we've finished making love for the first time.

He brushes his lips tenderly against mine, and I cup his face in my hands, lovingly kissing him back, blown away by what has happened between us.

Because this was, without a doubt, the most passionate, steamiest, most fulfilling sex I've *ever* had.

Cade rolls over onto the pillow next to me, and I turn so I can study the man who just loved me in all the right ways. Who made sure I reached earth-shattering heights of pleasure, who gave as much as he took, whose body was filled with raw passion and tenderness.

All for me.

Emotion fills my heart. That is what making love is, a connection of souls and a pure, overwhelming need to express our feelings by becoming one.

Cade reaches for me and pulls me into the crook of his arm, and I nestle against his chest, his skin hot against my cheek, his heart still pounding inside his chest.

His hand moves protectively down my shoulder, his fingertips dancing along my skin, his lips brushing sweetly against the top of my head.

"Josephine?"

I prop my head up on his chest so I can look at him. His hair is all tousled, and I see bits of dough stuck in it, but never has Cade been more beautiful than he is in this moment.

"Mmm?" I ask, pausing to drop a kiss on his muscular chest.

"That was the hottest sex I've *ever* had."

I don't need a mirror to know I'm beaming.

"It was for me, too."

He runs his fingers through my hair, pausing to pick out a piece of pasta dough and flick it aside, which makes us both laugh.

"Also the doughiest sex I've ever had," Cade quips. "I had no idea pasta sex was so freaking *hot.*"

I giggle. "Pasta sex."

"We'll keep it in the rotation."

Elation fills me. Making love to Cade has confirmed everything my heart is feeling.

This is right.

We're right.

"Well, I'm glad to see my recipe for pasta is multi-purpose," I joke.

"Heck, yes," Cade replies.

"You realize we don't have dinner now."

"I'll take care of it."

"Pizza?" I tease.

"Well, I don't want to barge in and get the Pot Noodle cups from Jupe right now so, yes, pizza."

I run my hand lower, over to his tattoo along his ribcage.

"What do your tattoos say?"

"I don't know if I can tell you. It's classified information."

"Oh, the Cold War is back," I tease.

Cade grins sexily at me. "Who knows? You might have seduced me for secrets. The next thing I know, you'll be sneaking out the door while I'm in the shower."

"There's a huge hole in that theory."

"Oh?"

"I live here. I wouldn't be sneaking out."

Cade makes a face. "Dammit."

I laugh. "But obviously I slept with you purely to determine if this tattoo has some secret meaning."

I trace my fingers over the Asian lettering, dying to know what it means.

Cade picks another piece of dough out of my hair. "I'll translate the first character, but if you want to know the remaining four, you'll need to seduce it out of me."

Ohhhhhhh, I like this plan.

Cade slides his hand up along the back of my neck and gently draws my mouth toward his.

"The first symbol," he says before kissing me, "is Chinese for life. A reminder to live life fully."

Then he gives me a slow, sexy, deep kiss, one that makes heat build in me all over again.

Cade breaks the kiss and stares at me. "Now, you know the first one."

Oh, this man is so *hot.*

"Any chance I could learn the second one tonight?" I suggest.

"Yes," he replies without hesitation.

We both laugh.

"You know what I think?" I ask. "We're both covered in flour and dough. We really should have a shower before dinner."

"We?" Cade asks, clearly intrigued by this idea.

I run my hand over his chest, amazed by how muscular he is, and gaze into his eyes.

"I might need help washing dough out of my hair," I say, playing the seductress.

His jade eyes flicker with desire as he stares at me.

"Yes, you will," he says, drawing my mouth to his.

"I could wash your back," I suggest.

Cade responds by brushing his lips against mine before speaking.

"Yes."

I relish the feel of his warm mouth against mine. I slide my hand down, skimming over his amazing abdominals.

"Your abs," I say against his mouth.

Cade kisses me and then abruptly breaks it.

"I've never wanted to be clean so bad in my life," he says urgently. "Shower. *Now.*"

I giggle as he gets up and scoops me into his arms. I lock my hands around his neck, and he carries me to the bathroom. As I feel his hot skin against mine, his laughter against my cheek, his powerful arms holding me to him, I know this is the place I was meant to be.

And I see myself here forever.

I STIR FROM MY SLEEP AND FEEL CADE'S WARM BODY pressed against mine. A smile spreads across my face as I see his arm is locked protectively around my waist as he sleeps.

Bliss.

I relive the evening in my head. We made love. I learned the tattoo after "life" is "dream," because Cade thinks it's important to have a dream and follow it. Then Cade refused to tell me anymore because he didn't want me to quit seeing him once I had gathered all of the information.

God, if he only knew. I have completely fallen for this man, his soul, his passion, his humor, his heart. After being with him, I can't imagine ever being with anyone else.

Or him with anyone but me.

I bite my lip as Skye's warning rolls around in my head. Love, for most people, is a long road.

Cade has made it clear he's not in any hurry to rush in. I have to keep my focus on each day we're together and hope he gets to where I am.

Because I don't want to think what it would like if Cade never does.

I hear an unfamiliar alarm go off, and I feel Cade

shift next to me in bed. The tone stops, and he rolls back next to me, immediately drawing me back to his body.

"Mmm," I say, loving the delicious warmth of his skin against mine.

"Good morning, my sweet Josephine, it's time to get up," he murmurs in my ear, then places a gentle kiss on my temple.

My sweet Josephine.

He called me *his* Josephine.

I want him to say it again. And again. And again.

I want him to say it forever.

I turn around so I'm facing him. Cade gazes at me with a gentle expression, and I lift my hand to brush his dark hair away from his forehead.

"I don't usually like Monday mornings, but I do today," I say, smiling at him. "I like having you wake me up in person."

Cade reaches for my hand and links my fingers with his, squeezing lightly.

"I can't believe the weekend is over already," he says.

I nod in agreement. For all intents and purposes, Sierra and Cade traded places this weekend. She stayed with Jude, and Cade stayed here. But while we've spent all our time together, and I'm not even close to ready for it to end.

"You're leaving today," I say, an ache forming in my stomach.

"Yeah. Media day is today, and then we go straight to Colorado Springs for training camp."

"You won't be back until Thursday night," I say,

moving my hand to his face and caressing it. "I'm going to miss you."

Cade gazes down at me, a questioning look in his beautiful eyes. Instantly, I regret saying I would miss him. Shit! Panic grips me. Was that too much? Saying I'm going to *miss* him because he's going to be gone for three days? In the normal dating world, three days is a *normal* separation for two people dating in the same city, let alone someone who *travels* for a job.

I shouldn't have said it.

I never should have told him what I was feeli—

"You'll miss me?"

"Yes," I admit, praying my admission isn't too much too fast for him.

"You promise?"

I blink.

"What?"

"Do you," Cade says, taking my hand and placing it over his heart, "promise you'll miss me like I'm going to miss you?"

Relief rushes through me, followed by joy.

"Yes," I nod. "I promise."

"Good," Cade says. "Because I'm going to miss you, my sweet Josephine."

I already miss him.

And I can't wait until he comes back on Thursday.

CHAPTER TWENTY-TWO

I CAN'T CONCENTRATE ON CUPCAKES.

No, that's not an accurate statement.

I can't concentrate on anything.

I'm in the test kitchen on Wednesday morning, and thanks to my non-stop thoughts about Cade, I totally messed up the first batch of batter by adding salt instead of sugar.

I scrape the Funfetti batter out of the bowl and dump it into the trash can. As I do, for the millionth time since he left on Monday, my thoughts drift to Cade.

We've had Connectivity Video Chats every night since he's left. And texted. Snapchatted. Instagramed. You name the social media channel, we've used it to stay in touch.

It's been interesting to see his life as a hockey player. On media day, Jude posted a funny video on Snapchat of Cade getting promotional pictures taken, telling him to show his abs for the ladies.

Of course, I completely understood; his abs are unbelievable.

And they belong to me.

I pause as I re-measure the flour and dump it into a bowl. Okay, they don't *belong* to me. I mean, Cade and I aren't even *technically* boyfriend and girlfriend.

We've only been going out for ten days.

Claiming his abs would be wrong.

Yet knowing it is wrong doesn't mean my heart agrees.

I reach for the sugar—verifying my container is yes, actual *sugar*—and pour some into a measuring cup.

The door to the prep room swings open and Sierra walks in, pushing a cart filled with ingredients.

"Hey!" she says, smiling at me. "What are you working on?"

"Funfetti cupcakes."

"Mmm. Can I taste test for you?"

"Yes, but only if you agree to test the brownie batter one, too," I tease.

Sierra screws up her face as she begins to set up down the counter from me.

"Um, no, that's gross," she says.

"I swear you are the only person I've ever met that doesn't like chocolate," I declare, adding baking soda to the bowl of dry ingredients.

"I know, I'm unique," Sierra says, setting a huge head of romaine lettuce on the countertop. "You know who you should get to test your chocolate cupcake? Maxime. He's a chocolate lover and has stuff shipped over from Belgium because he likes it better."

"Hey, maybe I can use Belgian chocolate in my recipe," I say, my thinking wheels turning.

"Maxime would probably test it for you without you using Belgian chocolate, but hey, let the inspiration take you wherever it may," Sierra jokes.

I put down my measuring spoon. "You know, maybe we can have a little taste testing party when Skye comes in."

"That would be fun," Sierra agrees, arranging things on her cutting board. We both go back to work, and silence falls between us as we concentrate on our tasks.

After I pour the Funfetti batter into the cupcake pan, I grab my iPad to snap a picture to send to Skye. She'll be excited about these, I know it.

I send Skye a quick update of what I've been doing this week. I ask if she wants an elevated brownie batter cupcake with Belgian chocolate, and what is her availability to fly back out for a tasting. I can see Skye is currently online, and as I'm about to send the email, a message from her pops up on my screen.

SkyeReeve: Hi JoJo!!!! How are you?

I can practically hear her bubbly personality in her words.

JoJoR: I'm great! I'm about to send you an email. I have FUNFETTI CUPCAKES going in the oven. Filled with extra Funfetti goodness just for you. ☺

SkyeReeve is typing . . .

SkyeReeve: Funfetti should be served at every meal. Who isn't happy at the sight of FUNFETTI?

I picture Angelique's face if she was being served Funfetti pancakes for breakfast and nearly lose it. Oh! Idea! I quickly type Skye back.

JoJoR: I have an article idea for you-we should do Funfetti for Breakfast. Like Funfetti pancakes!

SkyeReeve is typing . . .

SkyeReeve: PLEASE MAKE THIS HAPPEN. I mean, even if they don't want another article, I can blog it! Oh! Speaking of blogs, thanks for reading that first one I sent you last week. I put it up on Saturday, and you should see the responses! A lot of women emailed me to thank me for speaking the truth about relationships and for sharing how important it is to not be swept away and taking the time to be real about them. I'm so thrilled I could help people!

A knot forms in my stomach. I bite my lip. Skye's words make me wonder if I've made a mistake. She says it's important not get swept away by feelings, but it's too late for me. I've officially fallen. I'm all in, and there's no turning back.

I shove my iPad aside, worry consuming me.

My chest draws tight as a very real fear sweeps over me. I know Cade is not going to fall easily. He's obviously not going to make the same mistake that he did with his ex, Cassidy. He's going to be more than cautious.

He's not going to give his heart until he's completely sure.

I realize I'm gambling all of my heart now. I have no guarantee Cade will ever fall for me in the way I've fallen for him.

And with hockey season starting up, he'll be busy.

On the road.

And away from me.

Will his feelings be able to grow when he's so busy? When he's not here? Will the season take all his focus? Not to mention all the women going after him, presenting him with options at every turn.

Could hockey take him away from me?

Tears fill my eyes. Okay. This is stupid. I can't control the future. I can't control the what ifs. I need to accept that whatever happens will happen. I won't freak him out. I won't go declaring feelings for him. Nor will I demand in two months that Cade tell me where he sees us going.

If we're still together in November, that is.

I angrily pick up the pan of cupcakes and pop them into the preheated oven, resisting the urge to slam the door shut on them.

I put myself here.

How can I be so smart in my career, so strong, determined, and capable of making great decisions, and so stupid with my heart? Especially after what happened with Marco?

I *knew* better, but I did it anyway.

I fell for Cade.

But I know why.

We are meant to be together.

And all I can do is stand back and pray he will realize it, too.

CHAPTER TWENTY-THREE

"MOM," I SAY, SITTING CROSS-LEGGED ON MY BED AND studying her on the phone, "please pull yourself together. It's not the end of the world."

Mom is a mess tonight, crying her eyes out. Not over losing me to a hockey player in Colorado, but because Anthony's girlfriend, Britta, is pregnant. Thank God, Anthony called me to give me the heads up this morning, so I wouldn't be blindsided by Mom's phone call. I texted my other brother, Christopher, to see how bad it was going to be, and he told me to get snacks, I'd be on the phone forever trying to talk her off the ledge. And he wished me better luck than he had had.

With that information at hand, I also made sure to light a lavender serenity candle before connecting the video chat.

"How can you say that?" Mom yells, her eyes flashing. "Did you hear me, JoJo? They aren't getting married! How can they *not* get married? They are playing house. They were too stupid not to use protection, and now they won't get married?"

"Mom," I say firmly, "they aren't getting married *right now.* That doesn't mean never."

"She can't even cook," Mom sobs. "My grandchild will *starve!*"

"You live two doors down. That baby will have more food than I do."

"What? Are you not eating?"

"Mom, does it look like I'm not eating? Of course I am. But—"

"I think I'm going to faint."

"Mom, please don't faint. You are going to be a nonna. This is something to celebrate. Let's be happy about Anthony becoming a father. Anthony is a good man, Mom. He'll be a great father."

"Be happy? Be happy that Anthony is not going to marry the mother of his child? Have you lost your *mind,* JoJo?"

I sigh. There is nothing more I can say because I refuse to be dramatic about this.

"I will not celebrate unless they get married. And they'd better stay married!"

Then she starts sobbing and puts the phone on the kitchen table face side down so my screen goes black.

"Mom. Mom!" I yell. "Mom, get back on the phone!"

I hear Nonna talking to Mom, and then Nonna picks up the phone.

"JoJo, how are you?" Nonna asks.

"What happened to Mom?"

"You don't understand, so she's going to call her mother."

"Oh, God."

My other Nonna-Catherine—is just as melodramatic as my mother. They'll scream and cry and curse Anthony and weep for the baby's future together.

"Eh, they aren't happy unless they can be dramatic about it. The baby is coming, and we will all love the baby, so what is this nonsense?"

I can't help but smile. "I love you, Nonna."

"I love you, my precious JoJo," Nonna says, her eyes twinkling at me. "But now we can talk about the real stuff. How is that nicccceeee boy of yours? If you're still playing board games with him, I'll be mad at you."

"Nonna, can you keep a secret?" I ask.

"I've always kept your secrets, haven't I?"

Yes. She has. We've always had the kind of relationship where we could talk about everything. And right now I want to share with her what is going on with Cade.

"We made love," I admit, heat rising in my cheeks. "And it was *amazing*!"

"Yessss," Nonna says, grinning happily at me. Then she cocks an eyebrow up. "So his cucumber is good?"

Oh, my God. I know my face is on fire. I swear even the roots of my hair feel hot. How do I even respond to that?

"Ahhhhhhhhhh, his cucumber is good," she cries gleefully. "I can tell by the look in your eyes this Cade has a nicccccccceee cucumber. And more importantly, he knows what to do with his produce."

"Nonna, *stop*," I plead, dying.

"This one is The One, JoJo. I know you thought it was Marco, but I never thought it was Marco. This relationship is different."

I freeze. "How could you know that? We just started seeing each other. You haven't even seen us together, you only know what I've told you about him."

"I know."

"But how?"

"Because of what you say about him."

I think back. "Like what?"

"JoJo, do you realize *what* you talk about when his name comes up? How intelligent he is. How amazing his sense of humor is. How he's passionate about history. You are attracted to his brain more than his body. Which I give you credit for because Cade is *nice*."

"Nonna?"

"Yes?"

"What if he never feels the same way?"

"What?" Nonna says loudly. "What are you talking about?"

I bite my lip before baring my deepest fear to her. "He wants to move slowly. He was hurt before, Nonna. And I really like him. I'm just afraid after a few months he won't feel what I'm feeling."

"He will."

"But how do you know?"

"The apron."

"Nonna, that's a legend. That's not proof Cade is going to fall in love with me."

"So you love him."

I hear voices in the living room—male voices. My heart soars when I realize Cade and Jude have returned from Colorado Springs.

"Nonna, Cade is here," I say excitedly.

"I see it in your eyes. You do love this boy."

"I've fallen for him," I admit.

"But you won't say love?"

"I can't say that yet," I say softly.

"You're afraid to say it, that's why."

There's a rap on my door.

"Come in," I call out.

The door opens, and there stands Cade. I melt when I see he's holding a bouquet of gorgeous fall blooms in his hand, a huge arrangement of sunflowers, bright orange Gerber daisies, deep red roses, and touches of greenery.

"Oh, Cade!" I cry, touched by his gesture. "Those are beautiful! Thank you!" Then I turn back to the phone. "Nonna, I have to go. Cade just got back, but tell Mom I'll call her tomorrow."

"Hi, Nonna," Cade says as he enters my room.

"Let me see Cade," Nonna says.

This is always going to be a crapshoot, but I have no choice since they both like each other.

I turn the phone to Cade, and Nonna squeals in delight.

"Oh, you brought my JoJo flowers," she exclaims.

"I did, Nonna," he says, smiling.

"Those are beautiful," Nonna says with approval.

"I wanted something unique. Not just roses. And it

had to be vibrant. Like Josephine," Cade says, lifting his eyes briefly from the phone screen to me.

A tingle radiates down my spine, and I can't wait to jump into his arms as soon as I get Nonna off the phone.

"Oh, very nice," Nonna says. "Now let me say goodbye to JoJo. I need to console Donna-Marie, but I need a glass of wine first. Or maybe two."

Cade grins. "Okay, Nonna. Speak to you soon."

"Ciao," Nonna says.

I turn the phone back around, and Nonna is grinning wickedly at me. I ignore that look and smile at her.

"I'll check on you tomorrow, Nonna. Good luck with Mom."

"Thank you. Goodnight, my love. Ciao."

After she hangs up, I toss the phone aside. Cade places the flowers down on my dresser and opens his arms to me. I stand up, run across the bed, and leap into Cade's waiting arms. We laugh the second I land there, and Cade playfully spins me around the room. Then he lowers his mouth to mine in a sweet kiss before setting me down.

"I like coming home to you," Cade says, cupping my face in his hands and dropping a kiss on my lips.

"I'm so glad you're back," I admit.

He grins at me, linking his hands through mine. "Did you miss me?"

"I did."

"And not just for the sex?" he teases.

I giggle and pull him back toward the bed. We both flop down, and Cade immediately snuggles against me.

"Nope. I missed your sexy brain. And your ability to know any TV channel off the satellite without searching the guide. It was a pain in the ass trying to find channels this week," I tease.

Cade affectionately kisses the top of my head. "So you use me as your human television directory?"

"It's easier to ask you than to search with the remote," I say.

"I feel so used."

I rub my hand across his jawline, relishing the feel of his stubble against my palm.

"How is your mom after the baby news?" Cade asks.

I told Cade via text about the impending family drama earlier today, and he has proven that he truly cares about what is going on with my nutty family. I met his family once on Connectivity Video Connect because they called when we were watching TV one night, and they are so normal and nice. Low-key. No drama. I know my family's antics provide Cade with endless entertainment.

"She couldn't finish a conversation with me because I wasn't justifying her drama," I say.

"Ah, she'll come around. It's not the picture she painted for Anthony's future and, as a mother, that has to be hard to accept."

"You're right," I say. Then I cock an eyebrow at him. "How did you get so smart about relationships?"

The smile evaporates off his face, and I know I've hit a nerve.

"I'm good with family relationships, but I'm an idiot with personal ones."

A chill goes through me. What happened to him to make him think like this?

"I don't see that at all," I say.

I long to tell him he's already the best man I've ever dated, but I hold back. I can't take a chance of my words scaring him.

"I'm trying to learn from my mistakes," Cade says thoughtfully. "Which is why it's so important to go slow. To not jump right in. I'm not going through what I went through last time. I can't with y—"

He abruptly stops speaking. My heart hammers nervously inside my chest. Cade was going to say "you." He can't *what* with me?

"Anyway, we have other things to talk about," Cade says, drawing my hand to his and placing it on his chest. "Like hockey season."

My brain is reeling. Cade is changing the subject. Normally I'd never let a man do that, but Cade is different. I have to protect what we have. It's new, *so new*. I can't go all JoJo on him and demand he tell me what is going on in his head.

And a new fear hits me when I realize he wants to talk about the season. Will he use this as a reason to be more casual? Will he want to cool things down because his schedule will cause him to be gone a lot?

I force myself to speak.

"What about the season?"

"Hey, why do you look scared?" Cade asks quickly. "Josephine, what are you thinking?"

"Nothing," I say, pushing down my feelings. I know moving slowly is important. So I can't let him know how invested I am at this point, that I've fallen, and it terrifies me that he might want to take a step back. "What were you going to say?" I redirect the conversation.

"I need to explain what will happen with hockey starting up. I'm going to be gone a lot. I play at night. I get home late. I'll be on the road. Sometimes up and back, sometimes gone for a week. Things will be different for us, and I want you to understand what you are getting into with me. I'll be at the stadium when you get off work. When I get home, we'll have a bit of time before you have to go to bed so you can get up for work the next morning. But I want you to know that what time I do have, I want to spend with you."

While I'm relieved to hear he wants to continue spending time with me, I can't help but wonder if my fears are justified. It seems like he is setting things up so if it isn't love for him, he has a good excuse to distance himself.

No, I can't think like that. I can't project my own fears onto him. I need to stay the course, give him time, and hope his heart gets to the same place mine is at in the end.

I put a smile on my face, deciding while I can't do anything about the future, I can appreciate the moment I'm in right now. With a man who wants to spend as much time with me as he can.

"I understand that hockey takes up a lot of time," I say, "as it should. Whatever we have to do to spend time together, we'll do. As long as I get to see you when I can, I'm happy."

I see relief flash in his eyes.

"I'm happy, too," he says, drawing my hand to his lips and kissing it.

Swoon.

He clears his throat. "We have a preseason game here next week. I'd love it if you'd go."

Ahhhhhhhhhh! He's asking me to go to one of his hockey games!

I know I'm beaming when I respond.

"I wouldn't miss it." Then I cock an eyebrow at him. "Are you going to spend a lot of time in the penalty box?"

Cade laughs. "Um, I can't promise that I won't. But I won't play a lot, so odds are my time there should be limited."

I grin. "Okay. Will you lift your jersey up to flash women your abs?"

"You saw that stupid Snapchat Jupe put up, didn't you?"

He looks embarrassed, and I'm dying.

"They say on social media you do it because the female fans like it."

"Ha! Wrong. I do it because I need something to wipe my sweat off."

"Right. You're just showing off those amazing abs."

"I only show those off for one woman."

Ohhhhhhhhh!

I reach for the bottom of his Denver Mountain Lions hoodie and snake my hand up underneath it, running my hand over the cut muscles. I feel desire flicker in me the second I do.

"You could show those off now," I suggest.

"Are you trying to get another tattoo symbol out of me?" he teases.

I grin. I already know the first one is life, the second is dream, and the third is passion, as in a way to live your life and pursue your dreams. Passionately. Now I'm trying to get the fourth symbol out of him. But of course, I have to tease him first.

"No. I snapped a picture of them when you were sleeping, and I have already decoded them," I lie playfully. "Like any good agent would."

"This is why I like you, my sweet Josephine. You're so smart," he says, lowering his mouth to mine.

As we kiss, I'm pretty sure I'll be learning the fourth tattoo very soon.

CHAPTER TWENTY-FOUR

"I HAVE A SERIOUS CASE OF OPENING NIGHT butterflies," Sierra says excitedly as we walk into the Denver Mountain Lions arena concourse.

"Me, too," I admit as goose bumps prickle my skin.

It's October 13th.

Opening night for the Denver Mountain Lions.

Eager fans fill the arena, ready for the start of the new season. We walk through a sea of maroon and white jerseys, and I can't even explain the thrill I get when I see someone wearing a "Callahan" jersey with Cade's number on it.

My man's jersey.

Pride surges through me. The past few weeks, I've truly lived in Cade's world, from going to my first ever hockey game and meeting the players' wives and girlfriends in the private room reserved for them, to sitting in the arena and watching Cade play. I've missed Cade when he's traveled for exhibition games. I've woken up to greet him when he's come home at 2AM.

And, despite all the craziness, our relationship has *flourished.*

I smile as I follow Sierra down the steps, adjusting my maroon and plaid blanket scarf around me as I do.

Off the ice, I'm Cade's top priority. Whenever he has free time, we spend it together, from me cooking us dinner to watching *Cupcake Wars* on TV and Cade telling me I'd totally win if I would be brave enough to go on the show. We also got out the calendar and marked off two days in October when he's free for special dates. This Sunday is one of them, and I have a surprise planned just for him. The other day will be spent at a big Halloween party thrown by one of his teammates.

Sierra enters the row where the WAGS—wives and girlfriends—have reserved seats and sits down. I'm still getting to learn everyone's names, and Sierra has given me a heads-up on which ones are nice and well . . . which ones are not. Sierra told me the WAGS are like a sorority—we are all bonded together, but while you will be close to some, others you won't. I'm thankful my best friend is already in the group, which makes my adjustment a lot easier.

We missed warm-ups, thanks to being at work, but at least we are on time for puck drop at center ice.

The fact that I now know what that is makes me laugh out loud.

"What?" Sierra asks, taking a sip of her bottled water.

"I know what puck drop at center ice is," I say, shaking my head. "Before I met Cade, I knew nothing about sports. And now I'm speaking hockey."

"You're a WAG now," she says, grinning.

"Oh, no, Cade and I are dating, but he hasn't asked me to be his girlfriend yet," I say, correcting Sierra.

"You don't think you're his girlfriend?" she asks, her tone incredulous. "Are you kidding? He's *crazy* about you. Trust me, he wouldn't invite you to his game if he weren't. You're the first girl he's invited to a game since I've known him."

"As good as that makes me feel, and it does, Cade hasn't used that word yet," I admit.

"Does he have to? I think you know how he feels. Be confident in his actions. The words will come."

I'm about to respond when the Houston Scorpion players skate onto the ice. The lights go down, and the crowd lets out a cheer. The video board over center ice comes alive with images of the Denver Mountain Lions set to pulsating rock music. My eyes are glued to the screen, which shows dynamic plays from last season.

Including Cade in a huge fight.

I wince. I absolutely *hate* the idea of him being hit. Thinking about it makes me queasy. The angry look on his face when he punches an opponent—it's hard to believe that is the same man who showers me with affection and always has to caress my face when he kisses me.

I know Cade already explained his rough behavior on ice, but I can tell it's going to take a while for me to get used to the hockey side of Cade.

The video montage concludes with the Denver Mountain Lions logo flashing on the screen. Then the PA announcer welcomes the crowd to the season's opening game. Because it's the first game of the year, all of the trainers and assistant coaches are introduced, along with players who are injured or scratched for tonight's game.

Finally, it's time for the players to be announced for tonight's game. I'm so excited I'm sitting on the edge of my seat. I can't wait to see Cade introduced.

They are going in numerical order—except for the alternate captains and the captain, Gavin Tremblay, who will be introduced last.

"Number 21, from Birmingham, England, JUDE PARKER!" the public address announcer roars.

"JUUUUUUUUUUUUUDE!" the crowd roars.

I cheer wildly with Sierra for Jude, who skates out on to the ice and raises his stick to the crowd in greeting. Then he takes his spot on the ice. More players are announced, and it feels like forever before it is number 82's turn.

Cade's number.

But finally, finally, finally, it's his turn.

"From Poughkeepsie, New York, number 82, CADE CALLAHAN!" the announcer says.

A huge cheer goes up, none louder than mine. Cade skates onto the ice and raises his stick to the crowd, just like Jude did. I'm so proud I could burst. Cade's skill and determination led him here, to a professional hockey team, to play the sport he's so passionate about.

And now I get to be a part of this world of his.

"From Brussels, Belgium, number 11, your alternate captain, MAXIME LAURENT!" the announcer says, interrupting my thoughts.

The crowd roars again, and I can't help but smile because I adore Maxime as much as they do.

The other alternate captain skates out after Maxime, and then Gavin is introduced. Everyone rises for the anthem, and I can't wait for the game to get started. To see Cade not in pre-season form, but in the full-on hockey, take no prisoners, aggressive style that he is known for.

As the anthem finishes, I try to calm the manic butterflies dancing in my stomach. The players head to center ice for the puck drop, and I find it hard not to hold my breath.

I'm about to see Cade play in his opening night.

And there are no words to describe the excitement I feel.

BY THE START OF THE SECOND PERIOD, I'M A WRECK. The Mountain Lions are up 1-0, thanks to a goal from Brayden Kelly, so I should be elated.

But gah, watching YouTube did not prepare me for how hard Cade plays his game.

Will I ever get used to this? Cade is a *beast* out there. I'm terrified he's going to kill himself.

In the first period alone, Cade crashed opponents into the boards, upending one and sending a Houston player careening over the bench. He's slammed into opposing players and bounced off the glass, and I keep gripping Sierra's arm in anxiety, wondering how he hasn't injured a hip, dislocated a shoulder, or incurred a horrible concussion.

But every time Cade takes a hit, he bounces right back, determined to continue playing in his aggressive, passionate style.

Which apparently will be every shift.

"Oh, here we go!" a guy a few rows in front of us yells.

I snap out of my thoughts and see Hunter Riley, an enormous defenseman for the Houston Scorpions, drop his stick and put up his fists at Cade.

Shit! Hunter is *huge.* He could kill him! I grip Sierra's arm as Cade drops his stick and *bam!* He punches Hunter right on the jaw. Hunter's head snaps back, and he swings at Cade, landing one on his cheek.

The crowd roars, flying to their feet to see the fight while screaming for Cade to "kick his ass!" The two exchange multiple blows then tumble down to the ice before, mercifully, a referee breaks up the fight.

Cade is yanked off Hunter, and he screams at him as he's dragged back to the penalty box. Hunter yells back. I look up at the video screen and see Cade has a cut on his left cheek that is bleeding. The second he is in the box, he throws a stack of Gatorade bottles on the ground then angrily snaps his stick in half. Cade then slams himself down onto the bench, rips off his helmet, and shakes out his hair. I can see him breathing hard on the screen, trying to catch his breath.

Once I can see he's okay, my fear changes into another emotion.

Cade is freaking hot when he's a bad ass.

I decide I will hold on to that thought whenever he takes the ice. He's tough. He can handle this.

And I can take care of him after the game, I think happily.

With that thought in my head, I relax a bit and look forward to seeing Cade later tonight.

Off the ice.

And in my arms instead.

CHAPTER TWENTY-FIVE

As soon as I get the text from Cade that he's back from the arena, I grab my overnight bag. The Mountain Lions won their home opener, 2-1, with Cade having an assist on a goal scored by Maxime. Sierra and I waited for them after the game so we could see them briefly to congratulate them, but then we left so I could get my things together to spend the night at Cade's place.

"I'll send Jude upstairs for you," I tease, smiling wickedly at Sierra.

Sierra grins at me. She still hasn't changed out of her "PARKER" jersey.

"Are you sending Jude up for my benefit or so you can have Cade to yourself?" she asks, arching an eyebrow.

I laugh. "Both, of course. See you tomorrow."

"Night," Sierra calls out after me.

I shut the door behind me and catch the elevator to go downstairs. It was so exciting to see Cade play tonight, but I realize watching Cade play is always going to be stressful for me. The game has an inherent element of danger, but his continual need to pursue his game with such passion causes him to constantly hard-hit other players, slam them into boards, and the worst part, start all-out fights.

I bite my lip. Whenever he got punched, I felt as though I was receiving the blow myself. I worry about concussions. I worry about how much abuse his body can take. I mean, this was *one game.* He has eighty-one more to go.

Eighty-one.

Ding!

The elevator chimes and I step off, anxiety gripping my heart. I know he won't go through the season unscathed, no athlete does. But it doesn't make it any easier for me to accept.

I ring the door bell and Leia starts barking, but then I hear Jude's voice and she immediately stops. I can hear Cade and Jude talking, then Jude laughing, and finally the lock turns on the door.

Cade pulls it open. Tonight he received a cut across the top of his right cheekbone, compliments of Hunter Riley, and the urge to kiss him all better is so irresistible I can't stop myself.

I slide my hands up around the back of his neck, draw his face down to mine, and kiss him slowly and sweetly on the lips. Cade laughs softly against my mouth and lifts his head.

"Is this how I'm always going to be greeted after I come home from work?" he quips. "I have to say, I like this better than you greeting me with a cocktail at the door."

I brush my fingertips over his battle scar, and a feeling of concern comes over me.

"Are you *sure* you're okay?" I ask.

Cade wraps his hand over mine and leads me into his apartment. "My sweet Josephine, I promise you my answer is the same as when you asked me after the game. I'm *fine.* Sore, but it's hockey. I'm always sore after a game."

I try to feel reassured as Cade brings my hand to his lips and brushes a gentle kiss across my knuckles.

"You're so complex," I say aloud, studying him.

"What do you mean?"

"Here you are, giving me a romantic, sweet, gentlemanly kiss on the hand and an hour and a half ago this same hand was punching another man across the face."

Cade's eyes flicker. "Does that bother you?"

"No, not at all," I say. "I know the man you are, on and off the ice. It's just such a striking difference, that's all."

"I promise you I don't raise my fists outside the rink. The only reason I ever would was if I had to protect you or someone else. I fight as part of my career. I'm passionate about the game. It can piss me off, and I react. But I leave all that on the ice."

"Yeah, the only thing he throws around here is scorched Pot Noodle cups in the bin, not punches," Jude quips, coming into the room with Leia by his side and a duffle bag slung over his shoulder.

"Shut up," Cade says, grinning.

"You could try to burn ramen instead of my imports," Jude says, picking up his phone.

"I'll just eat your ham and pickle chips instead then," Cade says.

"Don't touch my *crisps,*" Jude says, shooting Cade a look.

"What? Did you say ham and pickle potato chips?" I ask.

Jude smiles at me. "Yes. They're *brilliant.*"

"Those are okay, but the prawn flavor is gross."

"Shrimp potato chips?" I ask, wrinkling my nose. "Don't they smell bad? Ewh."

"What is it with you Americans? My crisps are great," Jude declares, putting a leash on Leia. "Go ahead and try some. You can thank me later for changing your life. All right, I'm headed upstairs. See you guys tomorrow."

I watch as they head out, and Cade snakes his arms around my waist, drawing me into his chest.

"See? Jupe reaffirmed that I only throw Pot Noodles," he declares, smiling down at me. "I'm harmless off the ice."

Oh, you are dangerous off the ice, but not in the way you think, I say to myself as I stare into his ruggedly handsome face. *I've fallen for you, and I don't know what I'll do if you never fall for me in the same way.*

Cade bends down and kisses me, and I try to let my fear go and focus on our present.

He breaks the kiss and cups my face in his hands. "Still no hints about what we're doing on Sunday?"

"You're already thinking about Sunday? It's Thursday. And you're flying out to Los Angeles tomorrow. We have a few days before our date."

"I prefer to think about spending time with you."

Ohhhhhhhhhhhhh!

"It's a surprise," I say, resting my hands on his strong chest and feeling the fabric of his dress shirt underneath my fingertips.

"I hate surprises," Cade groans. Then he smiles. "Unless it's a sexy woman in an apron needing my oven. That turned out to be a *great* surprise."

I smile at him. "For me, too."

Cade kisses me again, and I focus on the moment, of being one of the surprises in his life that has made him happy.

And hopefully my plans for him on Sunday will make him just as happy, too.

"I CAN'T BELIEVE YOU PLANNED THIS," CADE SAYS AS WE head up the trail. "My city girl is taking me hiking!"

It's a beautiful, crisp, Sunday morning in Golden, Colorado. The skies are blue with streaks of puffy white clouds. The mountains peek up from behind the towering, golden aspen trees that line both sides of the path. The Horseshoe Trail, which leads to the Frazer Meadow, is littered with rich autumn leaves, and the views this autumn morning are nothing short of spectacular.

"I know how much the outdoors rejuvenate you," I

say as we walk. "I thought this would be perfect after your first road trip, and before you go back on the road at the end of the week."

"It does. And I like sharing it with you," he says.

I'm glad he can't see the swoony smile that lights up my face.

"How did you find the Horseshoe Trail?" he asks.

"I wanted someplace close to Denver. My research said this trail is good for kids, so while it will be a breeze for you, I should be able to handle it. *Should,*" I emphasize.

"If you get tired, I can carry you piggy-back style."

"Don't tempt me. I might get exhausted before we reach the meadow!"

"The views will make it worth it," Cade declares.

I shift my gaze from the pines and the aspens to Cade's backside, taking in the way his gray T-shirt fits his broad back and the way his ass looks so incredibly sculpted from weight work and skating. God, does he look h—

All of the sudden, I tumble over a rock and fly forward, letting out a cry as I hit the ground face-first.

"Josephine!"

Oh shit, I want to die. Mortification fills me as Cade hurries to my side. I push myself into a sitting position.

I wiped out because I was checking out Cade's ass.

"I'm fine," I blurt out. "I tripped on a rock."

I rub my hands, which are now covered in dirt, against my shorts while Cade carefully lifts my chin.

"You scraped your chin," he says gently. "I've got some stuff in my backpack. We can clean it off."

I forget about my stinging chin and scraped knees and wonder what Cade must be thinking. His ex-girlfriend could share adventures with him, from serious hikes to zip-lining. So far I've injured him while fishing and fallen face-first on a trail recommended for *children*.

Cade rips open a packet and removes an antibacterial wipe. He gently lifts my chin and begins to clean me up.

"I'm sorry," I whisper.

"For what? You *fell.* You need bandages for your knees," he says as he cleans them off.

Cade was so nice about the fishing incident. And he's being so sweet now. But will he think my clumsiness is okay when he wants to do a big climb and I can't? Or camp overnight? Just thinking about either totally freaks me out.

I watch as he rifles through his backpack for bandages. "I'm sorry I'm crap at hiking," I admit.

Cade looks up at me. "Josephine, you fell down. That's not crap. It happens. Especially if you get distracted by the beauty out here, it's easy to do."

I can't help it. The idea that I was out here being mesmerized by nature kills me, and I burst out laughing. Cade furrows his brow at me.

"What?"

"I was looking at your ass when I fell."

"What?"

"I was checking out your ass, and I didn't see the rock," I admit, my face burning with embarrassment.

A huge grin spreads across his face, and I melt when I see his dimple pop out.

"My ass is that distracting?"

"Yes."

Cade laughs loudly.

"Good to know you pay attention to the important things," he teases. "Like my great ass."

"You do have a great ass."

Cade smiles as he puts bandages on my knees. Then, to my surprise, he places a gentle kiss over each bandage.

"There. A kiss to make it better," he says, brushing my hair away from my face. "Or two kisses, I should say."

My heart holds still. Here I am, under a glorious canopy of towering aspen trees of gold with an amazing man who is so romantic in the way he cares for me. Cade is kind and loving, yet strong and passionate.

And on this beautiful autumn day, underneath the aspens and pines, I know one thing for sure.

Nonna is right.

I love him.

My heart explodes to life as I gaze into his eyes.

I loved Marco, I'm not denying that.

But it wasn't love like this.

I love Cade for his beautiful soul, his heart, his mind. His sweetness. His fire. All of the complex things that he is, I love him with a depth I've never known.

I need Cade. I'm a better person with him by my side, which is what I didn't have with Marco. I'm not complete without Cade, I'm not.

"Come on, I'll give you a ride for a bit," Cade says, extending his hand to me and pulling me up.

"What?"

He turns around and bends over. "My damsel in distress needs a ride."

"You are going to carry me for the rest of the hike?"

Cade turns over his shoulder, his eyes twinkling. "Nah. But I will for a little bit. Gives me an excuse to hold you."

I grab his backpack off the ground and slip it on. Then I climb up onto his back, and we laugh as he carries me up the trail.

As I have my arms locked around him, and we're laughing and being stupid together with him carrying me piggyback, I know I want this forever.

I want to be in Colorado under the aspen trees, laughing with this man, and sharing our lives.

Always.

Now more than ever, I hope Nonna is right about the legend of the apron.

Cade is The One.

And I hope with all my heart he will realize I'm The One for him, too.

CHAPTER TWENTY-SIX

Today's Purpose and Passion Statement:

Today I will ask Angelique for another development project with the purpose of building off the assignment Tiffany has given me. I will also meet with Tiffany for feedback on my cupcakes, which she tasted last week. I will update her on the scheduled tasting with Skye and explain how we will be ready for photos when she comes in next week. Finally, I will follow up on my cereal cupcake concept to see if she will give me her approval.

I pin my words next to Julia Child's smiling face and re-read them.

"Today's purpose and passion statement?" Cade asks.

I glance over my shoulder. Cade is eating the breakfast I made for him—designed to fuel him for practice on this late October day—of a ham and cheese omelet, homemade whole grain wheat bread with strawberry chia seed jam, fresh fruit, and Italian roast coffee. He has practice before flying out this afternoon for Cleveland. He's on a three-game East Coast swing and won't be back until Friday.

"Yes," I say, nodding. "Big meeting with Tiffany today. And I'm going to go back to Angelique and ask for a more challenging project."

The microwave beeps, signaling my oatmeal is ready. I retrieve it and sit down next to Cade, who is demolishing his meal. I can't believe how much food he packs away.

"Angelique needs to be cross-checked," Cade declares, taking a bite of his toast.

I steal a glance at him. He's wearing a navy and orange plaid flannel shirt and his Denver Broncos baseball cap, which he always wears backward.

"This toast is the best toast I've ever had," he says, interrupting my thoughts. Cade turns to me. "I still can't believe you make bread for me."

I make you bread because baking is a form of love, I think, staring at him.

"I want you to have the best fuel possible," I say, keeping my other reason to myself.

"And this jam," Cade says. "I love it."

"Chia seeds have a great nutritional profile."

Cade puts his hand on the side of my face. "Do you know how grateful I am that you have a shitty oven?"

I grin at him. "Daily."

"Yes. By the way, can you do me a solid and pick up

the Halloween costumes for Saturday?" Cade asks, wiping his lips with a napkin.

Cade asked me to go with him to a party the captain, Gavin Tremblay, is throwing this Saturday night. Apparently, Halloween—and dressing up—is a big deal in the hockey world. We went last week on one of his off nights to get our costumes.

"Yes, of course," I say, nodding. "When will they be ready?"

"Thursday. Make sure there are three. I had another one special ordered."

I furrow my brow. "Okay. A World War II airman costume, a Rosie the Riveter costume, and what's the third?"

A wicked gleam enters his eyes. "I have a surprise for Jupe. Payback for putting Icy Hot in my gloves a few weeks ago at practice, that wanker."

I cock an eyebrow at him. "What kind of surprise?"

"You'll see when you pick it up. And don't tell Sierra. It will ruin my prank."

"Why do I have a feeling his Luke Skywalker costume is going to go missing?"

The door opens, and Cade quickly takes the last bite of his eggs.

"Hey, guys!" Sierra says, walking in the door with Jude following her. Leia bolts in behind them.

"Hey," Cade and I both say at the same time.

"Are you about ready?" Sierra asks, grabbing her lunch out of the fridge.

"Yeah, let me go finish up," I say.

Cade stands and picks up my bowl and his plate

then takes them to the sink. I head back to my room and finish getting ready, quickly adding some light makeup to my face. I hear Sierra talking with the guys, and I'm still curious as to what costume Cade is going to stick poor Jude with for Saturday night.

When I'm ready, I come out and say goodbye to Cade. I hate when he has to leave, which seems to be every few days this month. He said his travel schedule is really bad during November and December, and I'm dreading it because I miss him a lot already and this is a light travel month.

Cade draws me to him, sliding his hands around my waist.

"I already miss you," I whisper, pressing my hand to his cheek.

Cade wraps his hand over mine. "Me, too. But I'll be home all next week." He leans down and gives me a kiss. "Bye, my sweet Josephine."

"Bye," I say, letting him go.

Jude gives Sierra a quick kiss, and our guys head to the door.

"Go kick some ass," Sierra says.

"That's his division, not mine," Jude quips.

I can't help but smile. I swear Cade spends more time in the penalty box than anyone on the Mountain Lions.

"And Josephine?" Cade says as they step out the door. "Go revisit your Purpose and Passion statement. I adjusted it."

Then he shuts the door behind them.

Curious, I hurry over to my vision board, and I see

that Cade has taken a pen and added to my plan for today:

Be purposeful in dealing with Angelique. I find a right hook to the face is effective in driving a point home. And her elitist ass deserves it.

Don't use all your passion in the kitchen. Save some for your boyfriend when he gets home. You've learned my tattoos for Life, Dream, and Passion. You might be able to seduce the fourth symbol out of me this weekend.
Missing you already.

Cade

Oh, my God.

My eyes re-read the word boyfriend over and over as if my brain is playing a trick on me.

But it's not. It's right in front of me, in Cade's distinct handwriting.

He wrote "boyfriend."

Cade called himself my boyfriend.

"JoJo, are you okay?"

I turn toward Sierra, and the biggest smile spreads across my face.

"He called himself my boyfriend," I say.

"I told you it would come soon enough," she says. "I'm so thrilled for you. You guys are such a great couple, and you need to be together!"

"I know! I'm so happy. But I can't freak out about it," I say, trying to reel in my excitement. "Yes, it's a big step, but it's only one step. Cade still says he wants to go slowly, so I can't get ahead of myself and start planning our future."

"JoJo, I know why you're being so careful, I do, but at some point, I'd love to see you be secure in what you have with Cade and live it fully. Like you do at work. You're so fearless in what you say and in asking for what you want. I wish you'd trust your heart enough to follow that with the man you love."

I consider her words for a moment. I long to do what she suggests. To say what I feel and not have to worry about it destroying what I'm building with Cade. To live with passion and let my words follow. To tell Cade what I feel in my heart instead of hiding it.

But I can't. I can't take the chance that my words could overwhelm Cade and ruin what we have.

"We're still really early in our relationship," I say. "Cade's not going all in until he's one hundred percent sure about us."

"Calling you his girlfriend isn't all in?"

"I mean forever all in like Jude is with you. He was forever after the first kiss in the elevator, you told me that. Cade isn't like that. He's protective of his heart."

"Oh, I think he is all in. Maybe he won't let his brain admit it yet."

Oh, how I hope Sierra is right.

I clear my throat. "Anyway, I'm glad to be his girlfriend. If the rest is meant to be, it will happen when Cade's ready."

As we grab our bags and head out the door, I know I'm full of crap.

We *are* meant to be.

I knew it when I met him wearing that apron.

I know it now more than ever.

If we don't have a forever, it will devastate me.

And there will be no recovery from that.

"You're unsatisfied with the assignments I'm giving you," Angelique says, her green eyes flickering with annoyance behind her glasses.

Well, this conversation is already crap after oh, two minutes.

I've come into Angelique's office to ask if I can do a development project for the April issue, as I'm nearing completion on Skye's project.

"Doesn't Tiffany have any more little *teeth-cutting* projects for you?" Angelique asks pointedly, removing the tea bag from her mug and tossing it into the trash. "After all, you're her *protégée* now."

Cade is right. Giving her a right hook is indeed a better way to get my point across.

"I'd appreciate it if you wouldn't speak to me in such a condescending tone."

Your jealousy isn't very becoming, I add in my head.

"Don't be so sensitive," Angelique says, pausing to take a sip of her tea. "I was merely pointing out that Tiffany already lets you do special projects under her guidance. I have a work schedule to complete, and I need you on task."

"I can complete ingredient testing and brand

comparisons while working on another development project. I would love to do something for the April issue."

Angelique purses her lips. "If you insist. I was thinking of adding a challenge feature where unusual ingredients are used in desserts. People love baking challenges on TV."

Alarm bells go off in my head. People do love those shows on TV, but that doesn't mean they want to make a chicken cupcake on the weekend.

"What kind of baking challenge?" I ask warily.

"I'm thinking spring. Time for picnics. And *bugs*," she adds, smiling serenely at me.

"Bugs?"

"I want you to come up with a collection of desserts that use *insects* as an ingredient," Angelique says, pressing her fingertips together and tapping them gleefully. "You have to be able to taste the insects, of course."

Oh, hell no.

"With all due respect, while watching a chef use mealworms on TV is fun, I don't think our readers, for the most part, will want to replicate that at home."

Angelique frowns. "It's too challenging for you, isn't it?"

"No, absolutely not."

"I understand it may be a little tricky for someone at *your level.*"

"Oh, I can do it," I say confidently, hanging on to my calm by a thread. "And I'll present you an array of insect-infused desserts if that is what you would like to see."

She bites her lip. I think she expected more of a fight from me on this.

"Once they are completed, I'll schedule a tasting for you," I add.

Angelique's face falls. "Tasting?"

"Tiffany has tasted all the items in my development project for Skye, and I expect you to do the same, of course. What do you prefer, Angelique? Crickets, mealworms, or ants? Or should I surprise you?"

Angelique begins to turn green. It's all I can do not to laugh.

"I'll go with a surprise," I decide for her. "Now if you'll excuse me, I'll need to order cricket flour because I'm pretty sure we don't have that in the pantry."

I turn and walk out of her office, a huge smile spreading across my face. I find myself rather inspired to work with bugs for my dessert collection.

And I can't wait to tell my *boyfriend* all about it.

With that thought in my head, I head off to my desk to research what wonderful creepy, crawly, crunchy things I can find to stuff into cookies for my dear boss Angelique.

CHAPTER TWENTY-SEVEN

Cade finds a spot a block over from Gavin's house and parallel parks his SUV. It's Saturday night, and we're going to the captain's house for his annual Halloween bash.

"Will you grab Jupe's costume from the back seat?" Cade asks as he unfastens his seatbelt.

"Jupe is going to *kill* you," I say.

I reach behind me and retrieve Jude's Luke Skywalker costume, which Cade stole and locked in his car earlier.

Cade grins wickedly. "Did you hear all the British cuss words flying out of his mouth when he found the Pot Noodle costume I left for him?"

I can't help but giggle. Jude was *pissed.* And Cade told him he couldn't have the Luke Skywalker costume until he showed up at Gavin's in his green Pot Noodle cup outfit, complete with a noodle hat.

"Don't worry, he'll get me back," Cade says, opening his door.

I do the same, and shiver as the brisk October air hits my bare legs. My Rosie the Riveter costume is a denim chambray shirt with the sleeves rolled up, a red bandana tied around my dark locks, and the costume was "Halloweenified" by pairing it with high-waisted chambray shorts. In other words, made sexier.

I move around to the front of the car, and Cade is tugging on his vintage leather bomber jacket. He's so incredibly delicious dressed as a World War II airman, complete with hat and aviator sunglasses.

He comes around to me, putting his hand on the curve of my waist.

"You look so *hot,*" he says, his hand skimming over my backside and to the bottom of my shorts in a teasing way. "You're the sexiest Rosie ever."

My cheeks grow warm from the compliment. "And I think you're dashing as an airman," I say, reaching up and adjusting his tie. "All kinds of sexy."

"Save that thought for later," Cade says.

I grin as he takes my hand in his. Gavin's house is a block over as all the parking on his street was taken already. As we are walking, Cade's phone goes off again, and I know it's Jude without him telling me.

Cade laughs. "I'm still a knob."

I shake my head. "And you two are best friends?"

"Of course. Otherwise I wouldn't go to all the trouble to have that Pot Noodle costume made for him."

I see people in costumes going in and out of a brand new, three-story, contemporary home. I can see a rooftop deck filled with more Halloween revelers.

"Nice house," I say, imagining how fun it would be to have a rooftop deck like Gavin's.

"You think so?"

I glance over at Cade, but can't read his expression due to the sunglasses he's wearing.

"Well, the rooftop deck is cool, but I'm not really a modern house type person. I like a more traditional home."

"I want an old house," Cade says. "It has to have history."

"I know you don't want to buy one now, but have you looked at older properties here?"

"Yeah, I've looked," he admits. "But nothing has spoken to me yet."

He hasn't found his Springwood, I muse.

I watch as a man dressed as a bar of soap and a woman in a big loofah sponge costume head up the sidewalk. I can't help but laugh at their costumes.

"Who is that, can you see?" I ask. After all, it's dark out, and Cade has sunglasses on.

"That's Brayden, one of our rookies. I have no idea who the girl is, though. He's always with a different girl. I can't keep track."

"Ah," I say.

"He doesn't have a Josephine yet," Cade adds, his voice soft.

Swoon.

I smile up at him. "I like being your Josephine."

The dimple pops out of his cheek, and my heart melts in response.

"Right now you're my Rosie," he says, squeezing my hand.

We make our way up the sidewalk, and music is blaring from the house. I assume his neighbors know this event happens every year and let their beloved Mountain Lions party their hearts out on this night.

Cade leads me into the party, and I spot all kinds of incredible costumes. Man, Cade wasn't kidding when he said Halloween was a big deal in the hockey community. I see Maxime dressed as Robin Hood, complete with a sling of arrows across his back and swashbuckling boots. No Maid Marion with him, though, unless she is somewhere else at the moment. If he doesn't have a Maid Marion, he could easily have one by the end of the night dressed like that.

I spot Eric from *The Little Mermaid* with an Ariel in a gorgeous sequined costume. I see three guys together dressed as two ducks and a goose. Two ducks and a goose? Then it hits me. *Duck, duck, goose,* just like the children's game. Very clever.

Gavin walks toward us dressed as the King of the North from *Game of Thrones,* complete with a black curly wig covering his blond locks.

"Hey, Callahan, what's up?" Gavin says easily. Then the handsome captain with the bright blue eyes turns to me. "I see you brought your better half tonight instead of Jupe, eh?"

He's Canadian, I think. *And he knows the Jupe story.*

"Jupe will be here," Cade says. "Gavin, I'd like for you to meet my girlfriend, Josephine Rossi. Josephine, this is Gavin Tremblay."

I shift the Luke costume to my other arm and extend my hand to Gavin. "It's a pleasure to meet you. And you can call me JoJo."

"JoJo it is," Gavin says, shaking my hand.

"Is Veronica here?" Cade asks, glancing around.

Veronica. I remember Sierra telling me about her. Veronica is Gavin's girlfriend and a total bitch, at least according to Cade and Jude. I haven't seen her at the private lounge for wives and girlfriends, which is odd now that I think about it.

"Yeah, somewhere," Gavin says. "You can't miss her. She's dressed as Khaleesi."

Hmmm. From the way Cade and Jude talk about her, it sounds like Cersei—the villainess—would be a more appropriate costume choice.

Gavin's eyes shift to the costume I'm holding. "Are you changing later?"

"Oh, no, this is Jude's," I explain.

"We're holding Jupe's costume hostage," Cade says. "In fact, why don't you hold it up in a threatening pose and we'll send a picture to Jupe?"

Oh, my God, Cade is *killing* me right now with the mischievous smile on his face.

He's absolutely wicked.

And I love it.

"Excellent! Let me get a glass of red wine, and we can act like we're going to spill it on the costume while JoJo takes a picture."

I hand the costume to Cade and retrieve my phone from my mini Kate Spade crossbody bag.

Cade removes his sunglasses, and as sexy as he

looks in them, I prefer to see his beautiful jade-colored eyes.

"Can you hold on to these?"

I nod and take them from him, stashing them carefully inside my purse.

A few more hockey players walk up and talk to us, and I recognize some of the girlfriends from the games. I'm officially Cade's girlfriend and now I'm one of "them." We're definitely moving in the right direction as a couple, and I hope Cade feels it, too.

"I have something even better," Gavin declares, coming back up to us. "Scissors!"

"Brilliant," Cade says, his eyes shining brightly.

Gavin furrows his brow. "Now you sound like Jupe."

I laugh because it's true.

Cade gives me a side-eye glance. "Don't agree with him."

"I'm only here to take the picture," I tease.

I hand the costume to Gavin, who holds it up while Cade puts the pair of scissors next to it.

It's all I can do not to laugh as I take the picture with Cade's phone.

"Got it," I say. I hand the phone back to Cade.

"Now to send it to Jupe," he says gleefully.

I watch as his fingers fly across the phone screen.

"I told him he has ten minutes to get here with his costume on or we start cutting," he says mischievously.

"Awesome," Gavin says.

Buzz!

We all look at Cade's phone, knowing it's probably Jude with a string of British swear words for Cade.

"I should put this upstairs," Gavin says, lifting up the costume.

"Tremblay!" a male voice yells. "We need you on the deck for pictures!"

"Here," I say, taking the costume from Gavin. "Just tell me where I can stash it."

"Thank you, that would be great. You can put it in my room," Gavin says. "Second floor, third door on the right."

"Callahan, come on," a guy dressed like a Teenage Mutant Ninja Turtle shouts. "You, too!"

Cade glances at me as if to see if I'm okay with him leaving my side.

"Go," I say, nodding. "I'll put this upstairs and meet you on the deck."

"Don't be too long," Cade says.

I make my way through the party toward the floating staircase. I head up to the second floor and locate Gavin's room. It's completely modern, like the rest of the house—decorated in shades of gray, white and black with sleek furniture. It's obvious it's the purse dump spot because there are some dropped on the floor next to his bed.

I stop when I see a beautiful woman dressed like Khaleesi from *Game of Thrones.* She must be Veronica. She's talking with Madison, a girl I sat next to at a game who is dating the other alternate captain, Paul Phillips.

"Excuse me, I'm just going to place this here," I say, smiling at them.

Madison smiles. "Hi, JoJo, good to see you tonight!"

I smile back. Madison was pleasant, but I got the

impression she isn't interested in getting to know me beyond superficial conversation.

"You, too," I say.

Veronica smiles at me. "So you're the new Cassidy. I'm Veronica, nice to meet you."

My stomach tightens when I hear the name of Cade's ex pass her lips, but I refuse to let my anxiety filter to my face. I force a smile on my face and lock eyes with Veronica.

"I'm Cade's girlfriend, JoJo Rossi," I say.

Her icy blue eyes flicker with interest when I say "girlfriend."

"Pleasure to meet you," Veronica says. "And surprising at the same time. You're completely different from Cade's usual type."

"Pardon me?" I ask, confused.

"Cade's previous girlfriends have all been blond," Madison clarifies for me. "You're the first brunette."

Girlfriends? I knew Cassidy was the last one, but how many have there been before her? I realize I have no idea.

Am I one of many?

An icy cold feeling fills my chest.

"The last break up hit him hard, according to Gavin," Veronica says knowingly, stroking her cascading locks.

"Paul said that, too," Madison confirms.

I realize if guys in the locker room knew Cade was broken up about the relationship falling apart, he must have been completely in love with her. His pain must have been obvious.

My panic continues to rise. Unlike me, who realized Marco was a mistake and the breakup was a gift from the heavens above, does he secretly wish he could be with Cassidy now if he could have her back?

"Cassidy was everything he wanted," Veronica declares as she continues to play with her hair.

My panic is replaced by anger. I want to cross-check her.

"Sometimes what you want changes over time," I say, challenging her.

"Yes," Madison interjects. "And I'm sure you have so many of the qualities that are important to Cade. Like I bet you are a really adventurous girl, right?"

I'm going to be sick.

"Um, no, I'm not," I admit, as Veronica has somehow hit on my one insecurity.

Veronica's eyes widen in surprise. "Really? Cade is such an outdoorsy guy. I swear that is what he and Cassidy did every free moment. Mountain biking, kayaking, hiking, fishing. Those two *lived* outdoors. They invited Gavin and me camping once but I was like 'hell, no'. I think Cade thought there was something wrong with me.

"He bought her this amazing Christmas present—an adventure at an eco-camp in *Greenland* this past summer," Veronica continues. "Kayaking with whales and hiking on the tundra. He was so excited about it. Too bad she broke up with him right before he could give it to her. I heard he was going to propose to her there."

I feel as though my world is collapsing around me.

These girls were around during the Cassidy period of Cade's life. I know he says he doesn't mind that I'm not outdoorsy, but he never mentioned the elaborate trip he planned for her or the fact that he was going to propose. Is that true?

Nausea rises in my throat.

Cassidy fit him in ways I do not.

In ways I never will.

Maybe that is the real reason why he wants to take things slowly.

Not because he was hurt before.

But because he's unsure if I'm the sort of girl he wants as his forever.

"Um, if you'll excuse me," I say, working with every power I have to keep my voice from breaking, "I'm going to head back."

"Oh, okay, well, nice meeting you," Veronica says, smiling at me.

"I'll catch up with you in a bit," Madison says, not meaning it.

I nod and head out. I go down the hall and find the guest restroom empty. I slip inside and lock the door behind me.

Facing the mirror, I take a good hard look at myself.

But it's hard to see through my tear-filled eyes.

I'm in love with a man who might never love me back.

And with that thought, I burst into tears.

CHAPTER TWENTY-EIGHT

I REACH FOR A WAD OF TOILET PAPER AND BLOT MY EYES. I have to pull myself together. I mean, what am I going to do? Pull Cade aside right now and ask him if he's falling in love with me? Is he going back and forth in his head wondering if he sees a future with a girl who falls on hiking trails and runs fishhooks through his knee? Am I a novelty choice? Maybe he's trying me out as something new. What happens when he wants to explore the side of some mountain in a remote area and I tell him I can't because that kind of vacation sounds like a nightmare to me?

I lift my eyes and examine my swollen, blotchy face in the mirror. If I lived Skye's mantra and waited to fall in love, I wouldn't be crying right now. I'd be drinking a beer by Cade's side on the deck, having fun and not worrying.

But I'm not Skye.

I don't want to wait and see.

I want it all from him.

I want his love.

And there's no guarantee I'll ever get it.

"Dammit!" I yell at myself. I throw the toilet paper in the wastebasket and bite my lip.

How can I be so together at work and such a mess when it comes to my heart? How?

Buzz!

I sniffle and retrieve my cell phone out of my bag. It's Cade.

Did you get lost? Where are you?

I drop my phone back in my purse. I need to act like nothing is wrong, put on a smile, and have fun with my boyfriend. This is not a conversation we should be having while we are still supposedly taking our time and figuring things out. If I want to keep Cade, I'm going to have to swallow my feelings and insecurities, as hard as that will be for me.

But I'll do it for him.

For a chance at us being forever.

I pull open the door and find Maxime on the other side.

"Oh!" I gasp, surprised.

"There you are," Maxime says, smiling at me. "Cade's looking for you."

"Right," I say, my voice thick.

Maxime's expression turns serious. "What's wrong, JoJo? Have you been crying?"

I blink. Oh, God no. Maxime can't know about any of this, nobody except Nonna and Sierra can.

"What? Oh, I'm fine, just allergies," I lie.

Veronica and Madison come down from the third floor, and Veronica stops at my arm.

"So lovely getting to know you," she says, smiling. "I look forward to talking more later."

Then they head to the first floor.

Maxime watches them and turns back to me, his eyes intense. "What did she say to you?"

"What? Nothing," I say quickly.

Maxime takes my elbow and guides me back to Gavin's room. I don't fight him, as his quiet determination tells me blowing him off isn't an option.

He guides me to the edge of the bed, and I sit down. Maxime sits next to me.

"What did she say to upset you?" Maxime asks again.

"Nothing."

"I know you don't really know me, JoJo. You don't have to trust me or tell me anything, but Cade is one of my closest friends, on and off the ice. You're important to him, which makes you important to me. And if I can dispel any crap Veronica said, I'd love to do it."

I study his blue eyes, and I see nothing but sincerity in them. Maxime loves Cade, and he's made me a part of his tight-knit circle because of that bond.

I know I can trust him.

I clear my throat. "You can't tell Cade this."

Maxime nods. "Okay."

"She brought up Cassidy. Pointed out how different I am from her."

Maxime's expression gives nothing away. "And that upset you?"

"I don't know if I can be everything Cassidy was for Cade," I admit. "Adventurous. Athletic. That's not me, Maxime. It never will be."

He is silent for a moment before speaking.

"Don't you think if Cade wanted those things he'd find them?"

"What if he's just looking for the opposite of Cassidy?"

"How is that bad?"

I shake my head. "But what if I'm not enough, Maxime?"

To my surprise, Maxime stands up and walks toward the door before turning toward me and locking his eyes on mine.

"But what if you're *everything?*"

Then he turns and walks out.

My heart stops. His words repeat on a loop in my head.

What if I'm everything?

Could Maxime be right? Could my differences from Cassidy be a positive, rather than a negative? Cade could have an adventurous woman, but maybe that's not everything to him.

If Nonna were here, she would smack me for doubting Cade in the first place.

Has he told me he loves me yet? No. But he does want to be my boyfriend. He chose me, knowing I'll never climb a physical mountain with him.

Maybe that's not the mountain he wants to climb with me.

I spring to my feet and catch up with Maxime, putting my hand on his arm and bringing him to a stop.

"Why don't you have a Maid Marian?" I ask. "Because you're one *amazing* guy."

"I don't need Maid Marian to put a chink in my armor," Maxime teases.

Oh, you so do, I think to myself. I have a feeling Maxime will be tough to crack, but the right woman can do it.

Just like Cade cracked my resolve to not be involved with anyone after Marco.

"There you are!"

We look up and see Cade coming up the stairs. He flashes me a huge smile, and love for my aviator pilot fills my heart.

"I got sidetracked with girl talk," I say, thinking I had better girl talk with Maxime than I did with Veronica and Madison. "Maxime found me."

Cade links my hand with his. "Come on. Jupe's downstairs in his Pot Noodle cup. It's better than I imagined."

I grin at the man I love, trying to push away my fears and focus on what we are building together.

"Is he still calling you a knob?" I ask.

"I'm the knob of the year. A grade A wanker. And a few other choice words that may as well have been French because I have no idea what they mean. But come on, you have to see it!"

Cade leads me down the stairs, and I turn and look over my shoulder at Maxime. He winks at me, and I have nothing but gratitude for him.

I'm in a good place. I have an amazing man. I have a welcoming group of new friends. I have a fantastic job with a boss I can handle. I'm learning new things every day. And I'm doing it all in a city I want to call home for the rest of my life.

It's okay if Cade hasn't told me he loves me yet. He doesn't have to.

I just have to believe he'll get there. And he will, but on his own time, not mine.

And if waiting means I'll get my forever, I'm more than okay with that.

"So are you okay with Skye crashing on our couch tomorrow?" I ask Sierra while finalizing plans for Skye's tasting tomorrow.

It's a rainy Sunday in November, and there's no hockey game on the schedule. We're lounging around our apartment before going out to dinner and a movie with Cade and Jude.

"Of course," Sierra says, flipping through channels on the remote from her seat on the sofa. "She's so nice, and I'm sure she gets sick of hotels."

"I think she wants more time to hang out with us," I say, tucking my legs underneath me as I sit in an oversized chair.

"Jude will taste the brownie batter on my behalf," Sierra declares, pausing on *Say Yes to the Dress.*

"So will Maxime. He's a chocoholic," I say.

"Ugh, I can't imagine anything grosser."

I grin. Sierra's intense hatred of chocolate never ceases to amaze me. Who can hate chocolate?

A knock at the door interrupts my thoughts.

I glance at Sierra, whose brow is furrowed.

"I'm not expecting anyone," she says.

I get up and go to the door. I check the peephole and am surprised to see it's Cade, holding a Pyrex glass dish.

"It's Cade," I say, and I open the door.

"Hi," he says, his eyes sparkling at me.

"Hi, yourself," I say, grinning as I let him in.

"I know I'm seeing you tonight, but I have a surprise for you," Cade says, putting the glass baking dish down on our table. "I just made this myself. For you. It's pumpkin crunch."

"For me?" I ask, moved by his sweet gesture.

"Well, you hiked and fished for me, so I thought I'd try baking for you," Cade explains.

Oh, I love this man.

If only he knew how much.

"Cade, this is so sweet," I say, staring at the cake in disbelief. "I can't believe you went to all this trouble."

"I wanted to show you I could try my hand at your passions, too."

I'm so moved I want to cry.

"Thank you," I say, hugging him tightly. I press my ear to his flannel shirt and hear this heart beating, and wish I could stay like this for the rest of the day. In his arms, hearing the heart of this soulful man beat against my ear.

Cade kisses the top of my head.

"You're welcome. I know it's probably not Josephine quality, but I'm dying for you to try it." Then he looks over at Sierra. "You too, Sierra. There's no chocolate in it."

"You're a good man, Cade Callahan," Sierra declares, rolling off the couch and heading into the kitchen. "I'll grab plates and forks. Is Jude coming up?"

"Yeah, I need to text him that you girls are here," Cade says, taking out his phone.

"It smells amazing," I say, inhaling the sweet scent of warm pumpkin and spices. "What's in it?"

"You won't break up with me if I say cake mix, will you?"

I laugh. "No."

Cade lets out an exaggerated breath. "Whew. Good. I was worried about telling you that part. It's cake mix, pumpkin, evaporated milk—I Googled that ingredient, thank you—sugar, and spices."

I love the image of Cade sitting on a flight somewhere looking up a pumpkin crunch recipe and trying to figure out what the hell evaporated milk is.

"You're cute," I say, leaning over and kissing his cheek.

There's a quick knock on the door, and then we hear a key as Jude lets himself in.

"Is it time for cake?" Jude asks, stepping in through the door.

"It is, and there's no chocolate!" Sierra declares excitedly, handing Cade a spatula.

Jude moves to Sierra's side and wraps his arms

around her waist. "I know that is reason enough for you to celebrate," he teases.

I watch them together and can't help but smile. Jude loves her so much, and I'm so glad they found each other.

And that I found Cade.

"Josephine gets the first piece," Cade says, cutting into the cake and putting a piece on a plate.

I hear pride in his voice, and my heart swells with happiness. I still can't believe he made this cake just for me.

"Here you are," Cade says, handing me a plate.

I grab a fork and take a bite. Oh, no. Oh, no. I nearly choke because it is so dry. Like sawdust! I can barely swallow it, but I somehow manage to force down the powdery, dry cake. I know Cade has forgotten an ingredient, something to bind it and add moisture.

Cade is watching me eagerly, so anxious to please me, and I can't bear to tell him the truth.

A white lie is definitely in order.

I clear my throat, trying not to cough. "It's full of pumpkin flavor! So good, Cade!"

I pray Sierra and Jude will play along.

Sierra takes a bite, and I will her to say it's good. I watch her, and I can see in her eyes she's detecting the same problem I am. I bite my lip as she starts coughing.

"Yum!" she spits out. Then she falls into a coughing fit due to the sawdust texture of the cake.

Shit.

Jude pats her back. "You okay, love?"

"Wrong pipe," Sierra covers.

"I'll get you some water," Jude says, quickly going to the fridge.

I watch as Cade stuffs a bite into his mouth. His expression changes to one of complete distaste. He knows the cake is hideous. He begins coughing and puts down his plate.

"This is awful!" he says, then he turns to me. I'm taken aback when I see a wounded look in his jade eyes. "How could you tell me it was good, Josephine?"

I cringe. He's wounded by my white lie.

"Cade, I'm sorry, I didn't want to hurt your feelings. I know you worked so hard on it," I say.

"So when you don't like something, you're going to lie instead of telling me the truth?" Cade accuses.

What? Where is this coming from?

"Are you?" he snaps, the wounded expression growing into one of anger.

"Um, let's take Leia for a walk," Jude suggests, quickly taking Sierra's hand and leading her out of the apartment.

"Cade, I think you're overreacting," I say, confused by his weird reaction.

"To a lie? No, I'm not. I won't tolerate lying," Cade snaps.

"It was a little white lie," I emphasize. "I didn't do it to be malicious. I said it because you worked so hard on it. You wanted me to enjoy it so much, and I wanted to give that to you. But it's a *cake,* Cade. I lied about a *cake.* I don't understand your reaction."

To my shock, Cade picks his phone and keys up off the kitchen table.

"I won't tolerate you lying about your *feelings,*" he says angrily. "I *won't.* What else have you lied about? What else, Josephine?"

Then he storms out the door before I can answer him.

Now my fuse is lit.

I run out after him, angrily grab him by the arm, and make him stop. My promise to keep my thoughts to myself flies out the window.

"You know what? I won't tolerate this from *you,*" I yell angrily as a look of shock appears on his face. "This isn't about cake, Cade. You obviously have some deep-rooted issue about lying. And you're putting it on me. I've *never* lied to you. A lie about a freaking bite of cake isn't a lie that will damage a relationship unless you're determined to let it. I'm insulted, to be honest. Pissed off. And if you think I'll put up with it, you're *wrong.*"

Then I turn around and storm back into my apartment, slamming the door behind me.

CHAPTER TWENTY-NINE

I'M SO MAD AT HIM.

I angrily rip open a package of yeast and dump it into a bowl of warm water. I just fought with Cade, and he didn't follow me back to the apartment. Now I need to do something constructive. Eating a cheesecake was option number one, a la *The Golden Girls,* but since I don't have one, I'm going to bake bread.

And punch the hell out of the dough.

As I begin to stir the yeast into the water, there's a knock at the door.

I know it's Cade.

I put down the spoon and rub my hands on my apron. I open it, and Cade stands before me, a worried expression etched on his face.

"May I talk to you?" he asks softly.

I don't say anything. I step aside, he enters, and I close the door behind him. Cade turns to face me, and I fold my arms over my chest in a defiant manner. Cade winces in response.

"You have every right to be mad at me," he says. "I was a total asshole to you a few minutes ago."

I don't soften. Cade rakes a hand through his dark hair, and I can tell he's anxious about what he has to say.

"You were right, Josephine. It wasn't about the cake. I didn't even realize it until you called me out on it," he admits. He lifts his eyes to meet mine. "It's because of what happened with Cassidy."

My heart plummets to my stomach, forming a huge knot. My anger gives way to fear, and I drop my arms to my sides. I dig deep and force myself to ask a question I don't know if I want the answer to.

"What happened with Cassidy?"

Cade reaches for my hand, and I give it to him. He leads me over to the sofa and sits down, and I sit next to him. His hand remains wrapped around mine, his thumb moving over the top of my hand.

"She wasn't honest about her feelings," he admits slowly. "Cassidy said things she didn't mean. Little things at first. The little things eventually became bigger. And I was blindsided when she dumped me."

Suddenly, I see it. In his mind, my little white lie could be one of many I'm telling him. The start of the end.

If he only knew I loved him, I think, hesitating. *Maybe I should tell him. Tell him he's my everything, and he doesn't have to worry about me ever dumping him.*

Because I see us as forever.

"Josephine, I'm stupid. I know we're at the

beginning here. We're still getting to know each other. I shouldn't have let my mind get ahead like that."

I bite back the words as a chill rushes over me.

Cade is still hesitant about us. He still wants to go slowly.

I can't share my feelings now, I can't.

Unless I want to lose him.

"But I'm *crazy* about you," he admits, taking my hand and squeezing it and interrupting my tortured thoughts. "All I want is for you to be honest about how you feel."

I lift my hand to his face, and he closes his eyes as if relief is sweeping over him from my touch. Cade opens them and stares intently at me. I try to let go of my doubts when I see the look in his jade eyes. I can *see* how much he cares. He isn't ready to tell me he loves me yet, but I hope with all my heart that someday he will.

"I understand your reaction now," I say softly. "But I promise you, I'm not Cassidy."

Because I want forever with you.

"I know," Cade says, running his hand through my hair. "And I'm grateful for that. I want you. Just you."

He presses his forehead to mine, and I close my eyes, relieved that our fight is over.

"Forgive me?"

"Yes."

Cade lifts his head and drops a sweet kiss on my forehead.

I sit back and look at him.

"Cade?"

"Yeah?"

"Your cake was *awful.*"

He grins at me. "It was *shit.*"

"Did the recipe call for oil or butter?"

I see a light bulb go off in his head.

"Oh, hell, I have melted butter in the microwave," Cade says, groaning. "I forgot to dump it in."

Oh, my sweet, dear, kitchen-impaired boyfriend, I love you so.

"That's why it tasted like sawdust."

Cade's expression turns to one of complete embarrassment. "Oh."

"Oh, indeed," I say, smiling at him. "But I don't care about that. You were sweet to bake a cake for me. I *adore* you for it."

"Yeah?" Cade says, lifting an eyebrow at me.

I slide my hand to the back of his head, running my fingers through his hair.

"Yes," I say.

"So I should try it again?"

"No."

We both laugh.

"Not without my intense supervision, anyway," I add.

"Your kind of supervision is the kind I like," Cade says sexily.

His lips find mine in a slow, sweet kiss, and I know exactly where I am with Cade. He's crazy about me, and the fear of losing what we have caused him to overreact.

Cade still needs time.

And I'm more than willing to give it to him.

CHAPTER THIRTY

Skye watches as I arrange cupcakes on white rectangular plates. It's Monday night, and everyone is gathering at our apartment for a little cupcake tasting party. Skye flew in from Los Angeles this afternoon, and I was given permission to leave work early so I could take her to dinner. After all, she's a client.

But in reality, she's my new friend.

"I can't get over how *beautiful* these are," she declares, her blue eyes dancing in delight. "You're an artist. Baking is your canvas. You're so gifted."

"Thank you," I say happily.

"It's taking all my willpower not to grab one and dip my finger in the pink Funfetti frosting," Skye says. "But I'll refrain until the guests show up."

"I know, the urge is strong with Funfetti," I tease. "But your willpower is holding up nicely."

Skye laughs and I do, too.

"What kind of feedback are you looking for, JoJo?"

"Well, if you were another tester, we'd talk about the

crumb, the moistness, the sweetness of the frostings, if the flavor combinations work, stuff like that. But with you and the boys, the main question is: do you like it?"

Skye winces. "Portraying myself as a cupcake baker was the worst career advice I ever received," she admits quietly, regret clear on her face.

"Okay, so you aren't a baker," I say. "But you *love* cupcakes. And you *will* bake them with my help. What if your angle was that you want to learn more about the baking process? You can show how you change as you learn new things. Then you can share your experiences on your blog as a regular feature. That way you are being honest with your audience, which I know is important to you."

To my surprise, Skye's eyes fill with tears.

"You know what? I never thought I'd say this, but I'm glad I did that show if for no other reason than it gave me you as a friend. That was worth every awful thing I've gone through to have a genuine friend like you in my life."

"Okay, don't make me cry," I say, fighting back happy tears. I give her a quick hug. "And I'm glad I found you, too."

Skye steps back from me and nods. "I feel like I'm starting over. I'm so grateful you will be a part of this new chapter of my life."

The door lock turns, and I know it's Sierra with Jude, Cade, and Maxime. They went out for dinner while I got everything ready with Skye.

"We're ready for cupcakes," Sierra declares, grinning as she steps through the door.

"Good, they're ready to be tasted," I say, smiling at them. Cade grins at me, and I get a tingle of delight in my stomach at the sight of my boyfriend.

Jude and Cade walk in behind Sierra, followed by Maxime. Maxime stops the second he sees Skye, a look of complete shock passing over his face.

Did Jude and Cade not tell him she was on TV? Surely they did. And if Maxime hung out with them, he knows they are both obsessed with *Is It Love?* They even Tweet back and forth about it whenever it's on. I don't know how Maxime could have *avoided* seeing Skye from last season.

"Skye, I'd like for you to meet Maxime," I say, leading her over to him. "Maxime Laurent, this is Skye Reeve."

"I know you," Maxime says, his eyes riveted on Skye's face.

Skye blushes furiously. "I know, from the show, right?"

"No," Maxime says slowly. "You were in a café. In Brussels."

What?

"You were sitting out on the terrace," Maxime says with conviction, as if he is replaying a movie in his head. "A garden terrace. You had a coffee, and your hands were wrapped around it as if you were cold. And you were crying."

Skye gasps in shock. "But . . . how . . ."

"I was sitting at the table next to you."

Oh, my God.

"I was in Brussels after the show aired," Skye admits,

her eyes searching Maxime's face as if trying to place him there. "I took a self-imposed exile in Europe for a month. I did have coffee on a terrace there, I remember. It was a beautiful afternoon."

"You braided and unbraided your hair over and over, like a distraction," Maxime says softly. "And you never drank your coffee. You stayed until they closed."

"How do you even remember all of that?" Skye asks, incredulous.

"Because I couldn't forget."

Ohhhhhhhhh!

Skye's eyes widen in surprise. It's dead quiet in the apartment. We're all too stunned by this strange coincidence to speak.

And shocked by Maxime's obvious interest in Skye from the moment he saw her.

"Let me rephrase that," Maxime says. "You looked very sad. Your eyes were haunted. I'll never forget that."

Oh. So much for my romantic scenario.

Skye winces, and I can tell the embarrassment and pain over *Is It Love?* is flooding her memory again.

"I'm sorry. I'm making this awkward for you," Maxime says, tugging at his leather necklace, and I can tell he's uncomfortable.

"It's okay. It was an awkward time in my life, to say the least," Skye admits, averting her eyes to the floor. But as if she can't resist staring at Maxime, she returns her gaze to his face. "You were there that whole time? Watching me?"

"I couldn't help it," Maxime says softly. "I wish I could have done something for you. To see you smile.

But I didn't want to upset you further. So I stayed in my world. And you stayed in yours. Until now."

Skye's eyes widen in response. Maxime's eyes never leave her face.

I can't believe what is happening in front of me. Two people, strangers in a Brussels café on the other side of the Atlantic ocean, are brought together again by fate in Denver. The fact that Maxime never forgot her, the woman with the broken heart, means something.

I know it does.

"I can't believe this," Skye says, shaking her head. "What are the odds? What are the odds that we'd be sitting next to each other one day in Brussels and meet here, in Denver, months later? Out of all the cafes in the world, we pick the same one. And now we're here. Because of *cupcakes.*"

"You know why? Because *cupcakes* bring people together," Jude declares.

I can't help but laugh. I love Jude.

"I totally should have gone on a cupcake show instead of a reality dating show," Skye quips.

"You were on a TV dating show?" Maxime asks, a surprised expression passing over his face.

"Dude, we told you over a million times to watch it," Jude says. "Now you see why. Skye was one of the finalists."

"That's why I was crying," Skye admits. "I had my heart broken on that show."

"But now she's here, doing a magazine feature, and we're going to make sure these cupcakes are perfect for her," I say, changing the subject.

"Now you're talking," Cade says, following my lead. He wanders over to the kitchen countertop, where I have the tasting plates set up. "And thanks to your baking skills, I'll be at the optional skate tomorrow burning this off."

Maxime and Skye are still staring at each other in shock, but I decide to go ahead and talk cupcakes.

"Okay, if everyone can take a plate," I instruct, passing them out, "I'll tell you what is in front of you."

"I feel like a judge on a baking show," Jude says.

I laugh. "I know, right? Oh, Sierra, your plate is obviously the one without the brownie batter cupcake."

"Bless you," Sierra teases.

After everyone has a plate and a fork, I do my little presentation.

"Today you have three cupcakes to sample," I say. "First, we have the Sugar and Spice and Everything Nice. It's a cinnamon spice cake filled with snickerdoodle cookie dough and topped with brown sugar Italian buttercream. Next, we have Chocolate Brownie Bliss, which is a chocolate cupcake made with Callebaut cacao powder. It has a lush brownie batter filling and is topped with dark chocolate whipped ganache, also made with Callebaut chocolate."

I see Maxime's eyes light up as Callebaut is a famous Belgian chocolate company.

"You know your chocolate," Maxime says.

"I do," I say, smiling at him. "Lastly, we have the Sweetheart Cupcake, which is a vanilla and cherry Funfetti cupcake topped with cherry buttercream and adorned with a conversation heart. I hope you enjoy."

"These look beautiful, sweetheart," Cade says, cutting into the Sugar and Spice cupcake. "She's so talented," he tells Maxime.

Warmth radiates through my cheeks from Cade's compliment.

I hold my breath as everyone begins to eat.

"Please be honest," I implore. "If something isn't working, I need to know. These are the refined recipes, and Tiffany will taste them tomorrow one more time for final approval."

"Mmm," Jude sighs after taking a bite. "This is brilliant."

"Oh," Skye moans, "I'm in *love* with the Funfetti cupcake. It's delicious and so fun. It's perfect. This is me. In a cupcake."

I glance at Maxime, who still hasn't taken his eyes off Skye.

"I agree with Jude," Sierra says after trying the cinnamon spice one and interrupting my thoughts. "The cinnamon one is my favorite. You balanced the spices nicely. And it has a great crumb."

I grin. Sierra and I can speak in the foodie language that the others can't.

"Thank you," I say, nodding.

"I like the cherry confetti one the best," Cade says, polishing it off. "I love anything with cherries in it."

I smile to myself. I've been working on a holiday pound cake recipe for Cade for Christmas, and knowing how much he loves cherries, I'm developing a cherry vanilla one just for him. I'm keeping that a surprise for later, though.

"The chocolate one is my favorite," Maxime says. "The center—how did you get it to stay a batter?"

"Bakers have secrets. That's one of mine."

"Josephine can be very *operative-like* in her work," Cade says, winking at me as he makes a sly reference to our briefcase banter.

We continue to eat and talk, and it turns out to be a fun evening. I notice Skye stealing little glances at Maxime throughout the night, too, and I can't help but hope something will eventually happen between them.

"I should get going," Maxime says finally. "I have to drive back to Boulder."

"Will you be at optional skate tomorrow?" Cade asks.

"Yeah, I'll be there," Maxime says, sliding off his barstool seat. "Jupe, you skating?"

"I have to after all these cupcakes," Jude groans.

"Sorry," I apologize. "I won't ask you to taste my next project."

"Oh, I'm not saying that," Jude says, grinning.

"No, you need to say that," Cade insists. "She's cooking with bugs for the next project. Unless you *fancy* a cupcake with mealworms, then you can have at it, Jupe."

"*What?*" Skye cries. "Cade, you're joking."

"He's not," I say. "I have to find creative ways to put bugs in cupcakes."

"No!" Skye cringes.

"Yes. You can try some tomorrow after your photo shoot," I say, smiling. "Cricket flour is good."

"Ack! No, no, no!" Skye declares, sticking out her hand. "Never!" Then she shivers in disgust.

"We do some odd things for our work," Sierra says. "Like eat bugs. Or offal. I've done that. Eating nose to tail is a big thing right now."

"Okay, this conversation has to stop, or I swear I'm going to be sick," Skye groans.

"Have you had steak and kidney pie, Skye?" Jude teases.

"Stop it," Skye pleads.

"No brains for you?" Cade asks. "Or duck tongue?"

"They have duck tongue?" Jude asks.

"Come on, Skye, walk me out so you can get away from these two," Maxime interrupts. "I'll take care of them at practice for you tomorrow."

Skye's eyes light up at Maxime's invitation. "Okay."

Maxime thanks me and says goodbye, then he walks out the door with Skye. As soon as they're gone, we all stare at each other in shock.

"Shit, can you believe that story?" Cade asks, incredulous.

"How random is that?" Sierra asks. "He remembered her from a café this summer?"

"And Maxime had no clue she's a TV star," Jude adds. "No idea. His recognition was purely from his memory."

"He does have a good memory, though," Cade says thoughtfully. Then he turns to me. "You should see him when we break down film. Max will remember things from like five games ago against a certain team."

"I don't know if that's just memory," I say. "She made an impression on him."

"Well, she's gorgeous," Sierra says, pausing to take a

sip of her bottled water. "And the crying probably made her mysterious, too. Guys like that."

"I don't know," Jude says, shrugging. "Sometimes we like girls who smell like fajitas."

Sierra turns bright red, and I laugh. When they met, Sierra had been testing fajitas all day and smelled like a Mexican restaurant.

"Or girls in aprons," Cade says.

I love my man so much.

We continue talking about how odd the whole situation is, but we immediately shut up when Skye re-enters the room.

"We should go home," Jude says, stretching. "Skye, good to see you again. Sierra, are you ready?"

"Yep, let's go," Sierra says. She turns to Skye. "My room is ready for you. Towels are on the end of the bed."

"I feel so bad," Skye says, wincing. "Like I'm kicking you out of your apartment."

"Please. I practically live with Jude anyway," Sierra says easily.

Jude and Cade get up to leave, and I give Cade a kiss goodnight.

"I'll wake you up in the morning," Cade murmurs against my lips.

"Okay," I say.

The guys leave with Sierra, leaving Skye and me alone.

"Maxime," Skye says aloud, sinking down on the couch. "I can't believe he remembered me. We sat next to each other in Brussels and he remembers. How on earth does that even happen? How do two people end up next to each other in Europe and meet again in America?"

She begins braiding her long, blond hair. "I hate that he saw me at my worst. I was such a mess he couldn't help but remember me that way."

I sit down on the other end of the sofa. "I think it's more than that."

"No, that's what I was, a tragic mess. He even said so, JoJo."

"But Maxime remembered *details* about you. You made more of an impression than being sad," I insist. "Otherwise, you would have been a girl in a café that was crying, The End."

"He was right there, and I had no idea," she says softly. "Maxime sat next to me that whole time, and I was oblivious to him. How could I not see someone who saw everything about me? Under different circumstances, I would have noticed him immediately. Maybe we would have talked. Maybe we would have hit it off . . . " her voice trails off, and I know she's thinking "what if."

I furrow my brow. "It wasn't your time. But you've got a chance now, Skye."

"Oh no, he thinks I'm a mess. Did you see his face when the guys told him I was on reality TV? He disapproved," Skye says, biting her lip. "I could see it on his face. And he didn't ask for my number or anything, he just said he was glad to see me again and know I was okay."

I think on this for a moment. Maxime is very

private. From his inner circle to his secluded home in Boulder, he keeps things quiet. Out of the public eye. His life off the ice is his, and he protects it. He only has secret social media accounts and very few people have access to them. Privacy means everything to him.

Skye is the opposite. She proclaimed love in front of a TV camera. She fell apart in front of a massive TV audience, and she's now sharing her raw feelings on her blog. She wears her heart on her sleeve for the entire world to see.

My head sees the differences between these two.

My heart, however, thinks there is an undeniable connection.

There's a reason they ended up in the same café at the exact same time in a major European city full of people. And there's a reason they met again tonight. I know there is.

However, it's up to them to write that story.

Buzz!

I pick my phone up off the coffee table and see a text from Cade:

I'll miss sleeping with you tonight, my sweet Josephine.

Swoon.

While I might not know if there will be a romance between Skye and Maxime, I do know one thing.

I was destined to fall in love with Cade.

I was fated to meet him, to fall for him, to surrender my heart to this man in a way I never did to Marco.

As we approach the busy holiday season, I'm happier than I ever have been.

All I want for Christmas is for Cade to say he loves me.

And I have a feeling I will be getting that present this year.

CHAPTER THIRTY-ONE

I can't believe it's already Thanksgiving.

I wipe my hands on my apron as I cube bread for the stuffing. I'm back in my mom's kitchen in Chicago. Our house has always been the gathering spot for family and friends, so meal prep is huge. I stayed up last night and baked four maple and vanilla-bean-infused pumpkin pies before the oven was overtaken by a twenty-pound turkey, which is now roasting in the oven.

Mom is working on trimming green beans in between wailing about Anthony and Britta, who are spending the holiday with her parents. What does this mean for the baby? Why won't they get married? Thanksgiving will never be the same, blah blah blah.

My solution is to throw myself into making stuffing while trying my hardest to ignore Mom's tiring dramatics. Nonna's solution, on the other hand, is to have a second mimosa.

I'm beginning to think her solution is better.

I still can't believe I'm back in Chicago. November

flew by after Skye's visit. She completed her photo shoot and much to Angelique's horror, Skye asked me to be in a few pictures. She saw other celebrity cookbooks where the celebrity is photographed with their recipe collaborator and suggested the idea to Tiffany. So not only are my recipes going to appear in the Valentine's Day issue of *Bake It!* magazine, but so am I.

Maxime sent Skye a Connectivity request and followed her on Snapchat and Instagram, and while he hasn't done much except comment on a few of her posts, and her on his, I believe these two might have a romance. I know logistically it would be insane considering she lives in Los Angeles and Maxime is in Denver, but my heart says these two people *belong* together.

That part of November has been great.

But the rest of the month has been hard. Cade has been distracted and quiet lately. He had a week-long road trip up and down the East Coast, and the Mountain Lions dropped three games, including two in overtime. He's with the team in San Diego for the holiday because they play tomorrow.

His mood is understandable. The team is struggling, and he's so passionate about his work it has to weigh on him.

But I can't help but wonder if something else is on his mind.

I swallow hard and dump the bread cubes into a huge mixing bowl. Normally, I'd be happy right now. At home, cooking with my nonna, catching up with the family after being gone for so long.

But I have this anxious feeling gnawing at the pit of my stomach. I can't help but wonder if Cade has reached the doubt stage of our relationship. We've been dating since late September. Isn't it usually by the third month one decides if a relationship is going to be more serious or end? Didn't I read that in a magazine?

And when he's on the road, away from me, does he have a clear head about his heart? Is Cade reevaluating us in that brilliant, logical mind of his?

"What are you thinking, my JoJo?" Nonna asks as she peels a potato.

I blink. "What?"

"You look sad. Do you miss Cade?"

"JoJo, you will never have Thanksgiving with him when he's on the road, do you realize that?" my mom interrupts, momentarily shifting her anguish over Anthony on to me. "Once you marry him, you'll never come home for Thanksgiving. All my children are going to leave me!"

"My poor Donna-Marie, this is breaking her heart," my other nonna, Nonna Catherine, declares. "I need to pray for strength for us."

I watch as Nonna reaches for the champagne bottle and tops off her mimosa.

"Mom," I say firmly, "Cade and I are *dating.* Who knows what the future holds?"

"If he's at home, you'll stay with him," Mom declares. "If he's on the road, you'll come here but that will be never I'm sure!"

"My poor JoJo, her husband will never be home," Nonna Catherine adds.

"And the babies! I'll never see your babies, and Britta will never let me have a holiday with her baby. This is the beginning of the end of our family traditions!"

My brother Christopher steps into the kitchen for a moment, takes one look at my mom, and smartly retreats back to the living room before she can wail at him for not having a girlfriend to love.

"Mom, I have no idea what the future holds, but this family will always be a part of it, okay? Now, if you don't pull yourself together, we'll have no food for Thanksgiving, and that *is* something to cry about," I say firmly.

I turn back to cubing bread, and Mom shifts back to green beans at the table, consoled by Nonna Catherine and a few of my cousins who are obviously more sensitive than I am at the moment.

"You do know what the future holds," Nonna says softly to me. "The apron has already told you."

"Well, Cade hasn't told me," I blurt out.

Nonna stops peeling. "What?"

"I shouldn't have said that," I admit. "It's not fair to him. I can't dictate when Cade will fall in love. I can't make him fall faster just because I did."

"Have you told him how you feel?"

"No," I say, shaking my head. "That would scare him off."

"Do you want a man who is scared off by feelings?"

I think about this for a moment, but Nonna continues before I can answer.

"I believe in Cade," Nonna says. "His eyes speak to me, and they say he loves you."

"Nonna, you've only talked to Cade a few times."

"That's all I need," Nonna says knowingly, pausing to take a sip of her mimosa. "The apron and his eyes confirm everything. He deserves to know how you feel, JoJo."

I consider Nonna's advice. Should I tell him first? It's a huge risk. Huge. And I'm not sure I can handle Cade not feeling the same way, or if he backs off our relationship because my feelings are too intense for him.

I wish I were brave enough to do it.

But I'm not.

"We'll see," I say.

"You aren't going to tell him."

I laugh. "Do you live inside my brain, Nonna?"

Nonna grins. "I know my granddaughter. I also know you should join me for a mimosa if you hope to get through this day with your mother."

I glance over at the kitchen table where Mom is holding court discussing Britta's vegetarian diet and, oh my God, are they going to have to serve Tofurkey if she comes over? Will the baby know what a real turkey is?

"You're right," I say, reaching for a champagne glass. Then I look at Nonna. "Is it wrong I want to drink it straight up and not cut it with orange juice?"

Nonna grins wickedly at me. "That's my girl."

I AM SO FULL.

I lie on the bed in my old room, staring up at the ceiling, and unbutton my jeans. I ate too much. Way too much. Turkey. Stuffing. Mashed potatoes and gravy. Green bean casserole. Rolls. Cranberry sauce. And pie. With extra whipped cream because whipped cream is awesome.

Oh yeah, and multiple glasses of champagne which is making the ceiling spin a little bit. I feel sappy inside, and I'm missing Cade. And his tattoos. I know four of the five now. Number four is for happiness. But he refuses to tell me the last one.

I'll call him.

Because I need to know the final tattoo.

And because I miss him.

Shit. Where's my phone?

I get up and stumble over my boots, hitting the floor and landing with a thud. I'm sprawled out on my stomach like a starfish.

Oh, crap, I'm so drunk.

I wonder if anybody noticed at the table that I'm very buzzed.

No, probably not. Mom's antics receive all the family's attention on holidays.

I spy my purse and reach for the strap, pulling it across the floor toward me in a move of epic laziness. I have trouble correctly lining my thumb on the button to unlock the screen and it keeps saying my thumb isn't on it. But my thumb is on it, dammit!

"Stupid thumb button thingie," I mumble, finally accessing my screen. I hit the Connectivity Video

Connect for Cade, and to my delight, he answers, his face popping up on the screen.

"Heyyyyyyy," I say, grinning at him. "Happy Turkey Day!"

"Sweet Josephine, Happy Thanksgiving. Although we said that to each other this morning. And this afternoon."

"Oh?" I ask, trying to remember.

"Why are you in the dark, sweetheart?"

I pause and look around. "I don't know. I miss you. I wish I could have pumpkin pie on you."

Cade furrows his brow. "Um, you want to eat pie *on* me?"

"What? No," I say. "Not on you. But that would be fun. I could lick your chest."

"Are you drunk?"

"Yesss," I admit, sitting up on the braided rug on the floor of my room.

Cade bursts out laughing. "Okay. Did Nonna do this to you?"

"Of course she did. It's the only way to deal with my mom."

"I'll thank Nonna for taking such good care of you."

"I love my nonna. I love both of them, but you know which nonna I'm talking about, right? The fun one. Not that the other one isn't fun, but the fun one."

"I do, sweetheart."

"Cade?"

"Yeah?"

"I miss you sooooooooo much it makes my stomach hurt. Or is that the pie?"

I absently touch the screen as if I could touch him right now.

"I miss you, too. I'll be home Tuesday night."

"I ate too much pie," I groan. Ugh, I'm starting to feel tired. "Pumpkin pie and champagne. So good. Like ridiculously crazy good, Cade. Did you have any?"

"Any what?"

"Champagne?"

"No."

"I'm sad for you," I say, thinking he should have some. "Did you have pie?"

"Pie, no crust."

"What?"

"Too much fat in the crust, I scraped it."

"As a baker, this hurts me. I need to make you a pie. With a good rust."

"I don't think I want pie with rust."

"What?" I say, trying to focus.

"Josephine, why don't you crawl into bed? We'll talk later."

"Cade, I need to know your last tattoo. Why won't you tell me?"

Cade smiles at me. Or at least I think he does. He's still blurry.

"I told you I will tell you when it's the right time. Until then it's a special secret."

"Ugh. I hate not knowing."

"I know. But the moment has to be right," Cade reassures me. "But you really need to get into bed now. I won't call you until you text me and tell me you're awake, okay?"

"I don't think I can get up," I mumble. "I can sleep here. But I don't want you to go. I want you to stay with me. I miss you, Cade."

"I won't go anywhere until you're asleep. I promise."

"Don't go anywhere ever," I say softly as I lay back down on the floor.

"I promise."

Then I smile and close my eyes as Cade talks to me, letting his voice wrap around me like a comforting blanket, and drift off to sleep.

What the hell am I doing on the floor?

I sit up, and oh, crap, I'm so sore. My back hurts. My neck hurts. I have a huge headache.

I try to remember last night. I remember eating too much and drinking bottomless glasses of champagne—

Oh, no.

I drunk-called Cade. I remember telling him I missed him and the rest is kind of fuzzy, but I think it involved pie.

I reach for my phone, which is next to me on the floor. It's nearly dead, but I have enough battery to retrieve my text messages. One from Sierra, telling me next year we are doing a friends Thanksgiving because her family is driving her nuts. The next three are from Cade:

Stayed on the phone with you until you passed out. I messaged Nonna on

Connectivity to check on you and make sure you were okay. She said you were, but you refused to get into bed. She said I was a peach to check on you. She also gave me her cell so if I need her in the future, she'll be easier to find.

I have the sweetest boyfriend ever. I can't believe he tracked down Nonna to make sure I was okay.

And I'm glad the only produce reference Nonna made was about him being a peach.

I read the next one:

Good morning. Call me when you are up. I loved hearing from you last night, even if you wanted to bake me a rust pie.

What? Heat burns in my cheeks. Good Lord, I'm afraid to hear what I said last night.

I reach the last message:

I'm so thankful for you.

My heart fills with love for him. Maybe Nonna is right. He's not saying the words I want to hear, but his thoughts and gestures do. If he's quiet and distracted, I have to trust that it's not because of me.

Cade is *The One.*

And he'll tell me I'm *The One* when he's good and ready.

CHAPTER THIRTY-TWO

I WALK ALONG THE SIDEWALK WITH JUDE IN CHERRY Creek North, the swanky shopping district in Denver, on a snowy Saturday in December. The windows are filled with holiday displays. People are bustling with shopping bags and juggling coffee cups as they finish up last-minute Christmas shopping.

And I'm helping Jude pick out an engagement ring for Sierra.

I glance at Jude, who has been quiet as we head toward the jeweler. His expression is serious, and I understand why. He's about to change both their lives with his proposal. Jude told me it's important to him that the ring is everything Sierra has ever dreamed of, so he asked me to come along and help him find the perfect one for the love of his life.

What Jude doesn't understand is that no matter what ring he buys, Sierra will love and cherish it because it came from Jude, the only man she has ever loved. The man she wants forever with.

That's how I'd feel if Cade proposed to me.

I bite my lip as snowflakes swirl around us. I thought Cade's mood would pick up after Thanksgiving—when he told me he was thankful for me—but as soon as I got home he resumed his quiet, distracted state. The Mountain Lions are winning again, and Cade's game has been solid. It's not hockey that is causing him to retreat.

My stomach tightens again as I allow my brain to go to the dark place that it has been visiting on a regular basis.

Our relationship must be weighing on him.

Does he miss Cassidy? Is he imagining what it would have been like to spend the holiday with her as his fiancée after proposing in Greenland?

Sickness consumes me. I blink back tears. Is he second-guessing me? While he likes me and cares about me, is he thinking this can't be forever for him? Is that why he's moving through the robotics of tree decorating and lights and holiday baking with me, knowing my idea of adventure is using a different sugar cookie recipe? Because he can't see me as his forever? Is his head fighting his heart?

"Here we are," Jude says, interrupting my tortured thoughts.

I follow Jude into an exquisite jewelry boutique, one with windows filled with gorgeous diamond rings and necklaces and elaborate ornament and ribbon-boxed displays, each beckoning that the perfect holiday gift lies inside this shop, in a magical box with a bow.

And yet all I can think of is my perfect gift wouldn't be anything found in a jewelry store.

It would be for Cade to say he loves me. That's all I want for Christmas.

I sigh. I've officially created my own sappy Hallmark Christmas movie moment in my head.

Hopefully, like all good Hallmark movies, my Christmas wish will have a happy ending.

"Hello, may I help you?" an elegant woman asks. She's tall and thin, and her platinum hair is perfectly coiffed. She strides up to us in an impeccable black pencil skirt suit with the most gorgeous holiday brooch on her jacket lapel.

"Yes," Jude says. "I'd like to see your engagement rings, please."

Her eyes light up as she looks from me to Jude. "Oh, yes, of course," she says, smiling brightly. "My name is Elise."

"Nice to meet you, Elise," Jude says. "I'm Jude, and this is my friend, JoJo. She's going to help me pick out a ring for my fiancée. Er, I mean, future fiancée. If she says yes, that is."

Jude's a bundle of nerves, and it's funny to see because he's always so relaxed and steady. He rolls with everything. Unlike Cade, who explodes when he's pissed off on the ice, Jude is always calm.

But when it comes to buying an engagement ring, he's anxious.

"You know she'll love anything you select, Jude," I say, trying to reassure him.

"No, it has to be perfect," Jude says with determination. "She deserves a ring that she will love forever."

Elise leads us to a counter and slips behind it. Jude leans forward across from her, gazing down at the dazzling array of choices under the glass.

"Anything in particular you'd like to see?" she asks. "A certain cut of diamond?"

"I need something unique, not traditional," Jude says. "But not modern."

Then he turns to me and smiles wryly. "That's not confusing, is it?"

"Don't worry, we'll find one that is perfect for her," Elise says confidently.

She pulls out some trays and puts them on top of the glass. Jude studies a few, but while they are all gorgeous, nothing is uniquely Sierra.

"Can we try a more vintage style?" I ask.

"Of course," Elise says, returning the rings to the case. "If you will follow me down here, I have some vintage rings for you to see."

We move down to the end of the long counter, where Elise pulls out another display for us to view. This selection contains truly unique rings, different from the diamond cuts and platinum bands that are popular right now.

Jude pauses and picks up a ring that has a cluster of diamonds shaped like a snowflake.

"Sierra loves the snow," Jude says softly, studying it.

"That one has been here a while," Elise says. "But it has a fascinating history. It is a Georgian period ring made in 1780 in England."

"It's an English ring?" Jude asks, his eyes lighting up.

Elise nods. "Yes. This ring has a long history, that's

for sure. The diamonds are set to resemble a snowflake in sterling silver, and the band is 15-karat gold."

"Sierra is like a snowflake to me," Jude says softly, continuing to study the ring. "Nobody is like her."

Tears prick my eyes when I hear the love in Jude's voice.

"Nobody else will have a ring like this," Jude continues.

"That is correct," Elise says, smiling at him. "Now the ring is a six, but we can resize it for your intended, of course."

Jude and I stare at each other, knowing that is Sierra's exact ring size.

"This is her ring," Jude says, nodding with certainty. "Just as it is."

"Congratulations," Elise says, smiling brightly at him. "I think she'll love it. Let me ring this up for you and bring you all the paperwork."

I smile at Jude as Elise walks away. "You didn't need me at all," I say. "You picked out the perfect ring all by yourself."

Jude grins at me. "I can't wait to propose to her on Christmas Eve. I already asked her father, and the whole family knows, so after dinner, I'm doing it."

I lean forward and hug Jude. "I'm so happy for you guys."

Jude hugs me back. "Thank you."

I step back from him. "So what made you decide now?"

"We were taking in the Christmas lights a few nights ago," he explains. "It started to snow, and she was laughing and was so excited about Christmas and me spending it in Indianapolis with her family. I always knew I was going to marry her, hell, I pretty much knew it straight away, you know. But in that moment, I realized I wanted it *now.* I want her to be my wife next Christmas. I want to spend every Christmas with her as my wife. *Forever.*"

A tear slips down my face, and Jude blinks in surprise.

"JoJo? Are you okay?" he asks, his voice filled with concern.

I force a smile on my face. "Happy tears."

I'm so happy for Jude and Sierra. My best friend is going to marry a wonderful man, and I'm overjoyed for what the future holds for them.

"All right, Jude, if you want to come have a seat over here, we'll take care of you," Elise says, interrupting my thoughts.

"Perfect, thank you," Jude says, following her to a desk and having a seat.

I linger at the counter, absently staring at the engagement rings in front of me, wondering if the man I love more than anything will ever want to propose to me. I don't want a proposal now, but I deserve to know what is going on in his head. If he can see this being a possibility in our future. I thought I could swallow down my feelings and just wait for him to get there, but the more Cade pulls away, the less patience I have.

I need to talk to him. Tell him what I feel. I have to know if I'm the reason he's been acting weird since November. Is it because he's not sure? Is it because of

Cassidy? Even if I'm overreacting to things, I need his reassurance. And if it's not me, I need to know what's wrong. Real couples communicate. Not bury their feelings like I have been doing. Or remain quiet and withdrawn like Cade.

I'm going to do it.

I'm going to do what Nonna told me to do a few weeks ago. I'm going to have an adult conversation with Cade, express my concerns, and see where we stand when all is said and done.

And I pray with everything I have that my heart isn't left in pieces in the end.

CHAPTER THIRTY-THREE

I'M GOING TO BE SICK.

Cade and I are supposed to go out to eat, get coffee, and then stroll around Denver taking in the Christmas lights for a romantic holiday evening, but I can't do it tonight.

I can't celebrate anything with Cade until I've had an honest conversation with him about how I'm feeling. How confused I am by his behavior. If he's not falling for me, he needs to tell me. I want to know what his doubts are about us, if he has any. After what happened with Marco, I can't be blindsided again.

Tears fill my eyes. I know if Cade tells me he's having doubts and concerns, I'll be devastated. But I can't ignore this anymore. I can't live in this state of trying to guess what the problem is. If it's me, I need to know.

Even though knowing that will destroy my heart.

I rap on the door, anxiety washing over me as I wait

for him to answer. Soon the lock is being turned and the sound turns my stomach into ice.

Cade opens the door, smiling at me. "Hey, come on in."

Cade reaches for his coat off the hook on the wall, but I put my hand on his arm to stop him.

"Cade, we need to talk," I say, my voice thick.

His jade eyes widen in shock. I can tell I've caught him completely off-guard with my request. Cade's hand remains frozen over the coat as if he's unable to move.

"What?" he repeats in a whisper.

I swallow hard to force the words out. "We need to talk. About us. About what I'm feeling."

Cade drops his parka on the floor. He takes a few steps backward, and I see nothing but anguish on his handsome face.

"Don't do this," he says, sticking his hand out. "Please don't do this."

"Don't talk about how I feel?" I ask, incredulous. "You don't want to know how I'm feeling? I'm your girlfriend. You should *want* to know what I'm feeling."

Cade begins pacing. "No. I don't. Not before Christmas. Please don't."

His reaction is not what I was expecting. Cade looks panicked and fear-stricken. Does he think we've reached the end? That it's time to commit to moving forward or split up?

"I don't care that it's before Christmas," I snap, anger surging through me. "I'm not going to schedule my feelings to suit you."

Cade stops dead in his tracks, his eyes flashing. "Is

that what you think? That this is somehow inconvenient for me?"

My emotions are escalating beyond my grasp, but I don't care.

"You know what, Cade? I don't know what to think. I agreed to go slowly with you. And I was fine with that. But now you're being all distant and strange, and I can't read you at all. If you don't see us moving forward, you need to tell me. You asked for honesty from me, remember? And now you don't want it?"

"What?" Cade asks, his own voice rising. "What are you talking about?"

"You have been a different person since November," I say, my voice shaking. "You're quiet and distant. I thought it was hockey. I convinced myself of that. But now the team is playing well, so I know it's not. It has to be me. Are you confused about how you feel for me, Cade?"

"Josephine, you're wrong. You couldn't *be* more wrong," Cade pleads passionately.

"Am I?" I shout at him. "How would I know? You've withdrawn from me. How do you expect me to feel? It's the holidays and my boyfriend acts like he'd rather it be over than celebrate it."

"I do wish they were over!" Cade yells back, catching me off guard. "I hate Christmas!"

"What? Why?"

"Because people say things they don't mean just because of the freaking season!" he spits angrily.

I gasp at his admission.

My instincts were right.

Cade doesn't want to say he loves me.

Because if he did, the season wouldn't matter.

He would simply say it.

"I fell in love with you," I choke out. "And I didn't want to tell you because you were so tentative about love. So, I buried it inside and vowed to wait for you to fall in love with me. But you can't, can you?"

Cade looks as though I've slapped him.

"You *love* me?"

Oh, God. Cade didn't want to hear that from me. He isn't even close to loving me. The shocked expression on his face reveals that painful fact.

I can't take this. I can't look at him for another second or I'll fall apart in front of him.

"I'm leaving."

I turn and open the door, but Cade's hand bears down hard on the wood, slamming it shut with urgency.

"No," Cade commands. "You're not leaving now. Not after saying what you just said."

I whirl around, anger consuming me. And before I can stop myself, I blow up.

"You don't have a choice in what I do! Open the door!" I yell, turning back around and jerking on the door handle.

"I will not. You don't get to drop bombshells and retreat," Cade snaps angrily.

Furious, I turn back around. We're inches apart, nothing but anger filling the small space between us.

"You want more from me? Now you're willing to listen? When two seconds ago, you dictated that I not speak until after the freaking holidays? Fine. I'll give you more. I want someone who can be open and honest with what is in his heart. You're incapable of that. And I think it's because you wish I were more like Cassidy. Are you having doubts because I can't fish or hike or do all the things she did?"

I see pure anger flash in Cade's eyes.

"Now you're pissing me off," Cade says, his voice low. "How can you even *think* I want you to be like Cassidy? If I *wanted* someone like that, I'd *date* someone like that, so don't you throw that on me."

"Throw it on you? Are you serious? You have left me sitting in the dark, grasping at straws, trying to figure out what's wrong because you couldn't tell me your feelings," I rail at him.

"Are you really going there? You accuse me of not being honest when you've had all these doubts, obviously the whole time, and you *never* brought them up with me? So your rules apply to me, but not to you? Talk about convenient, Josephine."

His words strike me. I realize he's right, but I'm so upset and furious, I can't admit it to him.

"I need a man who can tell me how he feels," I say, my voice shaking in anger. "I thought I could live without that, but I realize now I can't. I need a man who can share his worries with me, his doubts, his deepest fears. If you can't open up to me, I know I'm not that woman for you. Because if you did love me, or if you were falling in love with me, you would share it. Now let me out!"

To my surprise, Cade lets go of the door. I storm

past him, but as I head down the hallway to the elevator, he calls out after me.

"You want from me what you couldn't give," Cade says.

I turn back to face him.

"You didn't tell me what you were feeling until you let this build up, and you come in like a bull in a china shop, accusing me of having thoughts I *never* had. How about you being open and honest? Because you're no better at it than I am."

Anger is so strong in me I can't say anything.

Or is it because deep down I know he's right?

I whirl back around, tears streaming down my face, and jab the elevator button. The doors open, and just as I'm about to step inside, Cade has the final word.

"Josephine, *I loved you.*"

I freeze. My heart drops out, and Cade stares at me with nothing but anguish in his eyes.

But before I can reply, he storms back into his apartment and slams the door behind him.

CHAPTER THIRTY-FOUR

I STAND AT THE ELEVATOR, IGNORING THE DOORS THAT have opened for me to step inside.

Josephine, I loved you.

Cade's anguished words ring over and over in my head. I remain rooted to the floor, unable to move. The doors close and the elevator goes up, leaving me alone in the empty hallway.

I loved you.

I feel my knees wobble underneath me. I can't breathe. Heartbreak engulfs me, drowning me whole and leaving me with a pain I have never felt before. I sink to the floor, gasping for breath as panic takes over.

I've lost Cade.

And he loved me.

An anguished sob escapes my throat, and breathing becomes harder the more I cry. I want to take everything back. I want to undo what I've done, to have not charged in there and ambushed him. I want to tell him he's right. I expected all this honesty from him when the truth is, I was too afraid to give it myself.

Maybe if I were calm, he would have felt safe enough to tell me what was really going on inside his head. If I wouldn't have started yelling and acting so out of control, Cade and I could have talked like rational people . . .

If, If, If.

Ding!

I hear the elevator doors open.

"Oh, my God, JoJo!" Sierra's voice cries out. "What's happened?"

Within seconds, Sierra is on one side of me and Jude is on the other. Leia sniffs my nose with hers and then licks the tears off my face.

"Did someone hurt you?" Jude asks urgently.

"No," I gasp, shaking my head.

"Are you sick?" Sierra immediately questions. "What happened?"

"Where's Cade?" Jude says.

At the mention of Cade's name, I begin to hyperventilate.

"Sit up," Jude says, forcing me to sit back. "I'll get him."

"No!" I manage to gasp. "No! No Cade!"

"Okay, okay, no Cade," Sierra says, shooting Jude a look. "Breathe. You need to calm down and breathe."

Sierra begins stroking my hair, my best friend doing all she can to try and soothe me.

"Shhh," she urges softly.

My heart is spiraling in panic. I'm crying and can't

breathe. Sierra continues to mumble soft words, but I can't focus on what she is saying. Leia is right next to her, not leaving my side, and neither does Jude, who has his hand wrapped over mine, trying to help me.

After what seems like an eternity, I calm down. I continue crying, but I can breathe again.

"We broke up," I say, choking the words out. "And he loved me."

I fall apart all over again.

"We're going to take you back to the apartment," Sierra says. "And we'll talk."

I nod. Sierra and Jude lift me to my feet and guide me into the elevator. As soon as we step inside, Leia stands in front of me as if to protect me.

In the middle of the greatest pain I've ever known, I see my family has me. Not my Chicago family, but my Denver family. The family not created by blood but by choice.

"I'm so grateful for you both," I say softly.

"We love you, JoJo. And whatever happened, we'll fix it."

I swallow hard. I love Sierra for wanting to try, but Cade said, "loved." Not "love." He *loved* me, not the bull in a china shop accusing him of not being honest with his feelings when I wasn't honest with my own.

We get back to our apartment, and Sierra and Jude guide me to the couch. Sierra helps me take off my coat, and Jude hands me a box of tissues off the end table before sitting down next to me.

"Thank you," I say softly.

Sierra comes back, reaches for the thick throw

blanket across the back of the sofa, and gently drapes it across my lap before sitting down on the other side of me.

"Can you talk about it?" she asks softly.

A huge lump swells in my throat. It's a few moments before I can speak.

"We had a huge fight," I say, my voice barely above a whisper. "I couldn't understand why he's been acting so quiet and reserved during this whole holiday season. It started before Thanksgiving. All I could think of is that maybe Cade started to realize how different I was from Cassidy. I'm not brave and adventurous and I'll never kayak in Greenland. I wondere—" I stop, as I have to compose myself to finish the sentence, "I wondered if he doubted if I was what he truly wanted."

I feel Jude sit straight up beside me. I glance at him and see something in his blue eyes.

"Did he say anything about Cassidy?" he asks, his eyes searching mine.

"That if he wanted someone like her, he'd date someone like her," I admit.

Jude exhales slowly. "You need to know something."

Fresh tears spill down my cheeks. "That he was going to propose to her in Greenland? I already know that."

"What?" both Jude and Sierra ask at the same time.

"He was going to propose to Cassidy?" Sierra asks, incredulous.

"Where on earth did you get *that* idea?" Jude asks, shock resonating in his voice. "He wasn't going to propose to her."

I stare at Jude in confusion. "What?"

"I mean, of course, he talked about seeing a future with her, but you did that with your ex, too, right?"

Guilt consumes me. Jude's right.

"Yes," I admit, heat burning in my cheeks.

"Cade never got further than that. Greenland was just a trip," Jude says. Then he pauses for a moment and clears his throat. "But there's something you need to know about the breakup with Cassidy."

I sit very still, my heart hammering in my ears as I wait for him to continue.

"Cassidy broke up with him on Christmas Eve in a text," Jude says.

"*What?*" I gasp, stunned. "I knew it was a text, but on *Christmas Eve?*"

"Yes. Cassidy told him she was swept up in the holiday. That she felt compelled to say things she wasn't sure she truly felt. White lies that began to snowball into bigger ones. When Cade told her he loved her, she felt like she *had* to say it back. She tried to convince herself that she should love him. He was perfect on paper, and it was Christmas, what kind of girl tells her boyfriend she's not sure during a holiday? She not only broke his heart, but humiliated him by dumping him on Christmas Eve."

The wind is knocked out of me. The room stands still as realization hits me full force.

Oh, my God.

His remoteness makes sense.

Cade was terrified of history repeating itself.

"They started fighting a lot. He thought it was

growing pains. Cassidy finally told him the truth on Christmas Eve, and it destroyed him," Jude says. "He lost trust in women for a long time after that. He told me if he were to get into another relationship, he'd be really cautious. To make sure it was real. Honesty was going to be a priority for him."

The cake fight flashes in my head. How I couldn't understand why he was getting so upset over a stupid cake.

But now I get it.

He saw my white lie as history coming back around again.

I bite down hard on my lip, tasting the saltiness of my tears. Cade's distance was fear of me not loving him back, and he was too scared to admit his own feelings first because of it.

Just like I was scared of admitting my love to him.

Cade loved me, just as I was.

Loved.

"Excuse me," I say, abruptly standing up.

"Are you okay?" Sierra asks.

"I need to talk to Nonna," I say, moving over to the breakfast bar and picking up my purse. Then I turn to Jude. "Thank you for telling me all of that, Jude. Things make sense now. And even if—" I stop speaking as tears threaten to break loose again. "Even if Cade doesn't want to get back together, at least I'll understand what happened," I manage to get out. "Thank you for that."

I turn and go to my room, shutting the door behind me. I need my Nonna. I need to hear her voice. I need her wisdom. I need to know if she thinks there is any way Cade and I can work this out.

Through my tears, I retrieve my phone and request a Connectivity Video Connect, praying she's home and not off at bingo or something.

Before I know it, Nonna accepts my request.

"JoJo, what a surprise on a Saturday night!" she says in delight. When she sees my face, her expression changes. "What's wrong?"

"Oh, Nonna," I wail, losing it. "Cade and I broke up. Can you talk to me? Alone?"

"You are not broken up for good, my sweet JoJo. The legend of the apron is *never* wrong," she says. "It's just me and Pops here right now, go ahead and talk."

The whole story pours out of me. I tell her about Cassidy and the fight we had and how he said he loved me in the past tense. Nonna listens without flinching, letting me cry my heart out until I'm finished.

"Are you done?" Nonna finally asks.

I nod. "Yes."

"JoJo, do you know why you are fearless at work? How you stand up to your troll of a boss and say what you believe? How you aren't afraid to speak from your heart? Because you are *confident* in your work. You *know* you are an amazing baker. You believe in your gift, and you passionately defend it. But love? With love, you don't believe in yourself. You didn't share your feelings because fear of losing Cade crippled you."

Nonna is right.

When I'm confident, I live passionately and freely and will fight for what I want.

With Cade, I held myself back. For fear of chasing him off. For not being a forever choice for him.

"Nonna, you're right."

"Of course I am."

"But Cade doesn't love me anymore. I killed that."

"Don't be your mother and overdramatize," Nonna says. "Cade still loves you, deeply and with all his heart. I know it. The apron is never wrong."

"Nonna, I don't believe the apron has anything to do with this."

"Oh, yes, it does. That man fell for you when you were wearing an old *apron* and that says volumes about him. He saw the apron and the woman underneath it, and he liked what he saw that night. He saw the real you, JoJo. He fell in love with you, the baker in the vintage apron. You, just the way you are."

A flicker of hope is lit in my heart.

"Do you think he can forgive me?" I ask.

"Do you forgive him?"

I nod. "I do."

"He'll forgive you. You just have to be brave enough to go after love. To fight for it like you fight for everything else in your life. You have to leap before you can fly, my love. You might fall. Or you might soar. But you'll never know until you are brave enough to try."

I stop crying. Nonna is right. *Cade does love me.* Me. Not some girl who can kayak. He's not pining for Cassidy. He's in love with me, the Chicago girl with a crazy family and a passion for baking.

Just as I love him. The hockey player who is hated all over the league but sweet and gentle off the ice. The man who is passionate about history and the outdoors and wants to write novels when his career is done.

This is the man I love.

If I want to fly, I have to take a leap of faith first.

And I'm willing to take that leap for Cade.

"Only one question remains," Nonna says.

"What's that?"

"Why are you talking to me when you should be with Cade? Go to him, JoJo. Don't let another moment pass. Go to the man you love, and tell him everything that is in your heart. *Now.*"

CHAPTER THIRTY-FIVE

The second I hang up with Nonna, the door to my bedroom flies open. I gasp as the doorknob smashes into the wall, leaving a hole, and find a furious Cade standing in my doorway. He reaches behind him, yanks the door out of the wall, and slams it shut behind him.

I spring off the bed, shocked by his appearance. His jaw is set, and his chest rises and falls at a rapid pace. Cade's hands are balled at his sides. I've only seen this look when he's pissed off on the ice, about to fight an opponent.

Despair and panic consume me.

Oh, God, Cade *hates* me. He's going to—

Wait.

My eyes meet his. I see something unexpected.

His jade-eyes are rimmed with red, and they are desperately searching mine.

Not in anger.

But in anguish.

"Cade," I whisper, my voice breaking. "Cade, I—"

The second I say his name, Cade strides toward me, closing the gap between us. Then his mouth is on mine, kissing me hard and fast. His kiss is desperate as if he fears he will never be able to kiss me again. I feel his hands in my hair as his mouth sears against mine, pulling me closer.

As if he can't bear to let me go.

Tears spill from my eyes as I touch his face, feeling the familiar stubble against my fingertips, inhaling the familiar scent of the sage and citrus soap lingering on his skin.

Cade breaks the kiss and frames my face in his strong hands. He stares down at me, his eyes filled with unshed tears.

"Josephine, *I love you,*" he says, his voice thick. "I waited forever to find you. I can't lose you now. I can't. Please, please forgive me. Don't let go of us. Please."

My gaze never wavers from his. "I love you with all my heart, Cade. I love you, and you have to promise to forgive me. Because what you said was the truth. I'm so sorry I didn't tell you everything going on in my head."

I watch as Cade swallows hard as if he's struggling to keep it together.

"I'm sorry, too. I put the past on you, Josephine. And it wasn't yours to bear. I know you don't understand what I'm saying. I'll explain everythi—"

"Jude explained everything," I say softly, pressing my palm against his cheek. "Including the Christmas Eve text."

Cade winces. "I should have told you that part, but I didn't want you to feel sorry for me."

"But now I understand why the holidays were weighing on you."

"I'm so sorry, Josephine. It's not fair. Or even rational. But I was so afraid you might get swept up in the romance of the season, and I was sick to death over the thought of losing you when it ended."

"I was swept up in you long before Christmas. Or Thanksgiving, even," I admit. "Cade, I fell in love with you right away. I kept questioning if I could really have these feelings so fast, but my heart knew. It knew you were for me all along."

"I fell half in love with you that night you showed up at my door wearing that apron. You've had my heart ever since," Cade says gently as he runs his hand through my hair and cradles the back of my head. "You have my heart in a way no woman ever has. Or ever will. I fell hard and fast, and I tried to slow it down, but I couldn't. My heart knew you were The One. *It knew.*"

He pauses for a moment. "Josephine, I was terrified of losing you. Now it sounds so freaking stupid, but I kept reliving last Christmas in my head. But this time it was different. Because you were *The One.* I knew I wouldn't survive if you decided I wasn't the man for you."

"You are," I say, letting the tears fall freely. "I knew that same night in your apartment, Cade. And I believe now more than ever there's no timetable for love. When it's right, you *know.* I love you for the man you are. How you live your life with passion. Your intelligence, your humor, your soulful heart. I was terrified I'd lose you, too. We both feared that because of our previous relationships. And I was worried that I couldn't compare to Cassidy. I'm never going to be the girl who wants to ride river rapids with you. I'm so different from her, and I wondered if I could be enough for you long-term."

"Sweetheart, don't you see? You don't compare to Cassidy because you're *you.* You're the woman I love. I love how driven you are at work. How you are so passionate about baking and building your career. Your kind heart. I love your super-taster ability, your insane knowledge of *The Golden Girls,* and how you treasure the family history in your apron. I don't need for you to be an outdoors girl. I need for you to be you. And for you to love me."

"I do love you," I murmur. "So much."

Cade drops a gentle kiss on my lips, and I have nothing but joy in my heart.

"I was going to tell you after the holidays that I loved you," he admits. "God, I'm such an asshole. I should have told you as soon as I knew it."

"No," I say firmly. "You were *scared.* I was, too. But we had to get over our fears of taking that leap so we could fly. We just did that, Cade. We did it together. We didn't crash. We have love instead."

Cade smiles at me. "Those are very wise words."

I grin up at him. "Nonna gets the credit."

Cade locks his arms around my waist. "Do you know why I've refused to tell you the last tattoo on my ribcage?"

"You said there would be a time to tell me because it's the most special one."

"It is. You know my tattoos are all things that are

important to me. About how I want to live my life. Life. Dream. Passion. Happiness."

I nod.

"The last one," Cade says, his eyes going soft, "is *love.* I've found it with you. I got this tattoo after I broke up with Cassidy and vowed that someday I'd find real love. And I would only share that meaning with The One when it was time. It's time now. My love belongs to you, Josephine. Always."

Tears fill my eyes. "You mean . . . the last tattoo is for me?"

"Yes. You're my love, my life, my dream, my passion, my happiness. You complete the list for me."

"I love you so much," I say, drawing his face to mine for a kiss.

We kiss slowly and sweetly, and I'm so happy I could burst. I break the kiss and look up at him.

"Nonna told me our love was worth fighting for," I say. "I was about to go find you when you burst through the door."

"I'm impatient," Cade jokes.

We both laugh.

"I can't wait to meet your family in person," Cade says, grinning at me. "And be a part of it."

"You'll regret saying that. We're dramatic. Loud. Crazy."

"But they gave me you," Cade says. "I love them for that alone. The rest is just fun."

Oh, I love this man so much.

"You won't regret having to go hiking by yourself?" I ask.

Cade shakes his head. "No. You can do the easy walks with me, and as long as you can refrain from staring at my ass, you'll be fine."

My cheeks grow hot, and Cade laughs.

"But my sweet Josephine, even if you didn't want to hike, that's fine. I can have my outdoor interests be mine. Just like baking is yours. Because you don't want me burning up our kitchen someday, do you?"

Our kitchen. I have a future with this man, this gorgeous man with a beautiful heart, and I feel so incredibly grateful to call Cade mine.

"If you burn down my dream kitchen, I'll go postal on your ass," I tease.

Cade's expression goes serious. "I'm going to give you that, Josephine. I'm going to marry you, and I'm going to build you a chef's kitchen."

"What else do you see in our future?" I ask.

Cade smiles. "I see a full house. Filled with our friends and family and children."

"How many children?" I ask, lifting an eyebrow.

"Three?"

"I'm one of three. I like three. Two dogs?"

"Two dogs, for sure."

"I see you at the big kitchen island with our kids baking Christmas cookies. You're in your apron. Holiday music is blaring—the old classic kind—and our dogs are roaming around near your feet. You have a beautiful smile on your face as you juggle it all."

"And you come home from practice," I say, picking up our story, "and kiss my cheek in greeting. The kids will cry 'Daddy!' the second you're in the room. You'll chase them around the living room, and I'll warn you all to make sure the tree doesn't get pulled down."

Cade's eyes dance.

"Then after I read them a bedtime story and they're tucked in, we'll open a bottle of wine and enjoy the fireplace and our Christmas tree before I take you upstairs and make love to you."

"I thought you hated Christmas," I tease.

"Not anymore," Cade says, wrapping his hand over mine. "Because I'll always think of Christmas as the time I first told my future wife I loved her. I do love you, Josephine. And I always will."

As his lips close over mine, I know I have forever with this man.

I break the kiss and smile up at him.

"I love you so much," I say, brushing my fingers through his dark hair. "But you're still going to have to fix the hole in my wall, Cade Callahan."

Cade glances at the wall, spots the hole, and groans.

"Shit, I'm sorry. I'll pay to have that fixed."

"Don't worry. I know how to patch it. My dad makes his living as a repairman, so I can handle some drywall."

"Oh, can you now?" he asks. Cade eases me back on to the bed, and I giggle in delight. "That's *hot.*"

"I can. And I can handle you, too," I say playfully.

"We'll see about that," Cade murmurs sexily as he closes his mouth over mine.

As I kiss the man I love, nothing feels as right as this. He is The One, and there is no greater gift I could ever receive this Christmas than the love of this man.

Merry Christmas indeed, I think happily.

EPILOGUE

January 28th
FDR National Historic Site
Hyde Park, New York

"THIS IS SO BEAUTIFUL," I SAY AS WE WALK ALONG THE snow-lined Hudson Valley trail. I stare up at the bare trees in awe, as we hike through the magnificent winter woods. Snow is softly cascading down from the sky, painting nature's canvas once again in a blanket of pure white.

"You don't wish you were in Cabo with Sierra and Jupe?" Cade asks, his breath escaping in a frozen puff of air.

"Not for one second," I say happily. "This is *us.*"

I take in the beauty around me as we walk through Franklin Delano Roosevelt's estate. Cade asked if I wanted to come back home to New York with him for a few days while his best friend is off relaxing on a beach in Mexico during their All-Star break. Not only to spend time with his family but so he could take me to Springwood and the presidential library, two places dear to his passionate history heart.

I glance up at him as we hike, snow crunching underneath our boots. His dark hair peeks out from the edges of a gray knit cap. I squeeze his gloved hand in mine, love for him overflowing in my heart. We're the only people on the trail this cold morning, and it's easy to get lost in my thoughts.

I just celebrated the best Christmas ever with Cade last month. He rearranged his holiday break and flew with me to Chicago to celebrate Christmas Eve, where he experienced his very first Feast of the Seven Fishes. Cade said he'd never seen so much food in his life. My brothers hounded him to share hockey stories, my dad chided him to lay off Landy Holder of the Chicago Buffaloes, and my mom cried because I'll live in Denver forever now. He brought autographed Mountain Lions stuff for my cousins' kids and promised my family tickets for when the Mountain Lions come to play the Buffaloes. Needless to say, he's the most popular member of the family now.

Oh, and Nonna. Nonna *adores* Cade. He cornered her while she was in the kitchen and asked her all about the Rossi family history. She told him the legend of the apron, and Cade told her she was right, which made her beam with happiness. Nonna was over the moon when Cade asked if he could record their conversations and write them into a book for the family. She was so touched she got teary-eyed.

He left the next day to spend Christmas back in

Poughkeepsie, but said he wanted to bring me home during his January break to meet his family if I was okay with skipping a glamorous tropical resort in favor of cold New York.

I remember I laughed and told him the only choice I wanted was the one closest to his heart. There was no way we weren't going to New York for our break.

So here we are. Cade had his last game before break in New York City, so I took time off work to fly up to meet him. He picked me up in New York City with his whole family, and we had an amazing family-style dinner at Mission Chinese Food. I felt like I already knew his parents, Brett and Cecily, from video chats, but I got to know his brother, Shane, and Shane's girlfriend, Liza. It was a fantastic night, and I felt right at home with them.

Ah, work. Angelique is still my boss and still miserable, but sometimes you have to work with people who aren't helpful or good at their jobs. I challenge her and drive her crazy, but I continue getting assignments from Tiffany and being mentored by her is all I care about. The Valentine's spread turned out so beautifully that *Bake It!* magazine asked if Skye wanted to have a monthly feature about exploring things in the kitchen. She agreed, but only if I was part of it. We just finished our April project—the cheesecakes I first pitched to Anqelique. I couldn't be prouder of what we have accomplished together. They are kicking around the idea of a cookbook if the features go well, and Skye has already requested I develop all the recipes. I'm keeping my fingers crossed that it will all work out.

Speaking of Skye, she has been approached to write a book about her experiences on the show and the aftermath, and I think she's going to take it. I'm trying to convince her to move to Denver, and the book advance would allow her to do so. We'll see. I'm still trying to play Cupid for her and Maxime, but my arrows have a better shot of landing if she's in Denver.

Sierra and Jude got engaged on Christmas Eve. It was perfect. Jude had "Will you marry me?" engraved on an ornament. Sierra's brother shot a video of the proposal showing her shaking and crying. She didn't answer right away, but when she did, you could see nothing but love burst from her as she screamed "Yes!" They plan to get married in July in Indianapolis, and I'm going to be the maid of honor. I'm so excited! I'm making the wedding cake as well as a groom's *Star Wars* cake for Jude.

We come to a point on the trail where FDR's house is straight ahead. Cade stops walking to study it for a moment, and I gaze up at him, wondering what is going through that bright mind of his.

"What are you thinking?" I ask.

"I'm remembering," Cade says slowly, staring out at Springwood, "when I told you what Springwood meant to FDR. It was solace for him. This home had his heart."

"I remember," I say, squeezing his hand in mine.

The snow drifts down on us, picking up a bit, and Cade clears his throat.

"I hadn't found my Springwood," Cade says softly, "until I met you."

I turn toward him. Cade cups my face in his hands.

"Josephine," he says, staring down at me, "you are the one who brings me peace and solace. You're the one who rejuvenates my soul when I need it. Once I found you, I realized my Springwood wasn't going to be a home, it's *you.*"

To my absolute shock, Cade drops down on one knee in front of the historical site that means so much to him.

"Josephine Camilla Rossi," he says, gazing up at me through the falling snow, "I love you. I love your passion, your strength, the way you accept me as I am. You make me braver. Stronger. I can do anything knowing you're with me. I love you, and I want forever with you."

I begin crying as he yanks off his glove and reaches into his pocket. Cade retrieves a velvet box and opens it up to me, revealing a sparkling diamond ring set in a platinum band of diamonds.

"Oh, my God," I gasp through my tears.

"Josephine," Cade says, his voice growing thick, "will you marry me?"

Elation bursts through me. "Yes!" I cry, nodding frantically. "I will marry you!"

Cade reaches for my shaking hand, removes my glove, and slips the diamond on my finger. He stands up and kisses me, our first kiss as an engaged couple.

He breaks the kiss, and I gaze up at him through my tears.

"I love you," I say, my voice thick. "I love you, and I can't wait to marry you."

"You make me so happy," Cade says. "I love you. I

can't say it enough, so I'll keep saying it. I love you, my sweet Josephine."

"I love you, too. So much. That was the best proposal ever," I declare, putting my hands over his heart. "We'll find our own Springwood in Denver."

"Wherever you are is my Springwood, Josephine," Cade says, his eyes growing watery.

As we kiss again, I know he's right. We have solace and strength together. Our love is passionate and strong and will carry us through the good times and bad.

Our combination of sugar and ice works, I think happily.

And the legend of the Rossi apron proves once again to be true.

THE END

If you enjoyed *Sugar and Ice,* the next book in the series is *Reality Blurred.* You can grab your copy here: https://www.amazon.com/gp/product/B079C58Z4K

To keep up with all my news and releases, you can sign up for my newsletter here: http://eepurl.com/dvajmT